Praise for Lesley Kelly

The Health of Strangers

'An intriguing tale of crime in a post viral Edinburgh, told with panache.'   **Lin Anderson**

'It's well paced with strong storylines, a frighteningly plausible plot and entertaining banter between its main characters throughout.'   *Portobello Book Blog*

'The characters are brilliant. Their dialogue is spot on and the relationship between Bernard and Mona is great. A truly fantastic read!'   *The Crime Warp*

'Lesley Kelly has a knack of leaving you wanting more...'
                                                Love Books Group

'A crime thriller in a dystopian and ravaged Edinburgh with a great cast and the pages which virtually turned themselves. I bloody loved it.'   *Grab This Book*

'*The Health of Strangers* moves along at a cracking pace and the unsettling sense you get of an all-too-believable Edinburgh of the near future, or perhaps an alternative Edinburgh of today, helps draw you into what, at its heart, is a really well constructed and extremely entertaining thriller.'   *Undiscovered Scotland*

'*The Health of Strangers* is as humorous and quirky as it is insightful and observant.'   *Lothian Life*

A Fine House in Trinity

'Written with brio, *A Fine House in Trinity* is fast, edgy and funny, a sure-fire hit with the tartan noir set. A standout debut, if there is justice in the world this book will find its audience.' **Michael J. Malone**

'The storyline is strong, the characters believable and the tempo fast-moving.' *Scots Magazine*

'This is a romp of a novel which is both entertaining and amusing … the funniest crime novel I've read since Fidelis Morgan's *The Murder Quadrille* and a first class debut.' *Crime Fiction Lover*

'Razor sharp Scottish wit is suffused throughout and this makes *A Fine House in Trinity* a very sweet shot of noir crime fiction. This cleverly constructed romp around Leith will have readers grinning from ear to ear and some of the turns of phrase deserve a standing ovation in themselves.' *The Reading Corner*

'A welcome addition to the Tartan Noir scene, providing as it does a more light-hearted approach to solving a crime. Lesley Kelly is a fine writer, entertaining us throughout. The near-300 pages are deceptive, as this is a book perfect for romping through in one sitting.' *Crime Worm*

Lesley Kelly has worked in the public and voluntary sectors for the past twenty years, dabbling in poetry and stand-up comedy along the way. She has won several writing competitions, including the Scotsman's Short Story award in 2008. Her debut novel, *A Fine House in Trinity*, was long-listed for the William Mclvanney award in 2016. She can be followed on Twitter (@lkauthor) where she tweets about writing, Edinburgh and whatever else takes her fancy.

The Health of Strangers Thrillers

The Health of Strangers
The Art of Not Being Dead
Songs by Dead Girls

Also by Lesley Kelly

A Fine House in Trinity

DEATH AT THE PLAGUE MUSEUM

A HEALTH OF STRANGERS THRILLER

LESLEY KELLY

SANDSTONE PRESS

First published in Great Britain by
Sandstone Press Ltd
Dochcarty Road
Dingwall
Ross-shire
IV15 9UG
Scotland

www.sandstonepress.com

The publisher acknowledges subsidy from Creative Scotland
towards publication of this volume.

CREATIVE SCOTLAND

ISBN: 978-1-912240-52-4
ISBNe: 978-1-912240-53-1

Cover design by David Wardle
Typeset by Iolaire Typography Ltd, Newtonmore
Printed and bound by CPI Group (UK) Ltd, Croydon, CR0 4YY

To Dave, Fiona, Martin,
Pam, Robbie and Sophie

CONTENTS

MONDAY

CAGED BIRDS

I

The man fell, his hands clutching wildly at the air, grabbing at imaginary handholds like a desperate climber
reverse mountaineering his way to the earth. The jacket
of his suit flapped as he fell, an ineffective parachute that
did nothing to slow his inexorable journey toward the
ground.

As he passed the second-floor balcony the screen
went hazy for a second, before another shot of the body
appeared.

Cameron Stuttle, Chief Executive of the Scottish
Health Enforcement Partnership, paused the recording.
'The boys from IT edited the whole thing together. The
museum's got CCTV on each floor, apart from the very
top one. We thought it would be useful if the four of
you from the Health Enforcement Team saw his entire
downward journey.'

From this angle, the camera was pointing at the man's
face. Mona winced at his horrified expression, both fear
and confusion writ large. She'd be replaying that image
in her head, she knew, probably just as she was falling
asleep tonight. At least she'd be able to put tonight's
insomnia down to work, rather than her usual concerns
about her love life, or her mother's health.

The screen went fuzzy again, and a third camera angle
kicked in. This time, the screen was empty apart from a

plastic model of something large and scientific. A foot appeared in the corner of the picture, rapidly followed by the rest of the body, which crashed at speed into the sculpture.

'Ooh,' said Maitland. 'That's got to hurt. What was the thing that he landed on?'

'It's a 3-D model of the H1N1 virus,' said Bernard, his eyes tightly closed. 'It's part of their standing exhibition.'

'How come you know so much about it?'

'I'm a member.' Still without fully opening his eyes, he dug into his wallet and produced a small card. Mona took it from him and she and Maitland examined it. It proclaimed the bearer of the card to be a full member of the Edinburgh Museum of Plagues and Pandemics. The flip side highlighted the benefits of this, which included free access to all the exhibitions, and a 10% discount in the café and shop.

'Can we see it again?' John Paterson, the HET Team Leader, was staring thoughtfully at the blank TV screen.

'OK,' Stuttle pressed a button and the recording started again, 'once more with feeling. You might want to look away now, Bernard.'

Mona watched again as the man fell fearfully to his death through the central internal stairwell of the museum. Something about the whole recording unsettled her. 'Is it just me, or does he look mighty panicked for a man that's opted to end it all?'

Paterson nodded. 'Yeah, he's flailing about a lot for a suicide. Don't jumpers just let themselves fall?' He frowned. 'What makes you so sure this was intentional, Cameron? How do you know someone didn't tip him over the top?'

'A couple of things. First of all, as far as we can make out he was completely alone in the building. There's no

4

evidence on any of the CCTV cameras of any movement other than his, and, like everywhere else these days this building has secure Green Card technology. Nobody gets into the building without entering their Green Card in the machine.' He paused, as if waiting for someone to challenge him. Satisfied that they were all in agreement on this, he carried on. 'And secondly, he left a note, of sorts.'

'Of sorts?' Maitland looked intrigued.

'It's a little bit ambiguous. Could be a suicide note, or it could be a resignation letter.'

'From what? What was his job?'

'I'll come back to that in a minute. Bernard, did you have a question?'

Bernard was sitting patiently with his hand raised. Maitland nudged her in the ribs. 'Probably wants to know what was going on while he was too scared to look.'

'Shut up.' She tried not to smile.

Bernard looked put out but kept going. 'It's more of a comment really. I think it's a strange place to choose to commit suicide.'

'Jumpers often choose somewhere that is significant to them . . .' said Mona.

'Yeah, maybe he was also a member.' Maitland smirked. 'Probably wanted one last 10% off at the shop. Check his bag for souvenirs.'

Bernard's cheeks were scarlet. 'That wasn't what I meant. I was trying to say that it was an odd place to choose to jump, because there is no guarantee that you would actually die. You'd end up horribly injured but depending on where you landed, you might survive.'

'A very valid point, Bernard,' said Stuttle.

If possible, it appeared that Bernard's cheeks turned even redder.

'Particularly as in this case, the fall didn't immediately kill him,' Stuttle explained. 'He'd probably have splattered if he'd landed on the marble floor at reception, but the plastic model thingy cushioned his fall.'

'So what did kill him?'

'We're not sure yet,' said Stuttle. 'The pathologists are running some tests even as we speak, but the initial indications are that there was something in his bloodstream that shouldn't have been.'

'Like poison?'

Cameron shrugged. 'Possibly.'

There was a small ripple of interest, which Paterson raised his hand to quell. 'Fascinating as this is, I don't see what it has to do with the HET. We search for people who have missed their monthly Health Check. If this guy is overdue for a Health Check he's got a really, really good excuse for missing it.'

'I'm aware of all that.'

Paterson still looked suspicious. 'This isn't one of those scenarios when you need some dirty work doing, and you're intent on press-ganging us into helping you?'

Mona's mind went back to her recent trip to London with Paterson to search for a missing professor. The words 'press-gang' and 'dirty work' had all been entirely applicable to it.

'I'm hurt that you would think that of me, John,' said Cameron, smiling. 'Let me explain . . .'

He was interrupted by a knock on the office door. Their heads all swivelled round to see Ian Jacobsen from Police Scotland appear. Mona felt a wave of fury rising up from her feet. She tutted loudly, and turned to glare at Stuttle, who was busy not catching her eye.

'Ian, perfect timing. I was just explaining to our

HET colleagues about the unfortunate incident at the pandemics museum.'

'Morning, all.' Ian smiled round at the company. Only Bernard smiled back, then looked slightly panicked when he realised none of his colleagues was extending similar pleasantries. 'I'm hoping that the HET and Police Scotland can work jointly on this.'

'No way.' Mona couldn't believe what she was hearing.

'Mona—'

'No, I'm sorry, Mr Stuttle, but I'd rather resign than work with Ian and his colleagues.'

A look passed between Stuttle and Paterson.

'Seriously, Guv, last time we worked together I nearly got shot.'

It was Ian's turn to tut. 'Last time we worked together I was under the impression I saved your life . . .'

Mona's jaw fell open at this flagrant rewriting of history.

'Mona,' Stuttle's tone was at its most conciliatory, 'just listen to what Ian has to say. I'm sure we can accommodate everyone.'

She was torn between continuing to make her point, and having her curiosity satisfied about the body. She ended up not saying anything, which Ian took as a signal to start talking.

'I have to stress to you all that everything from today's meeting is confidential . . .'

'Of course.' Paterson responded for all of them.

'The gentleman that you just watched take a tumble was called Nathan McVie.'

'I recognise that name,' said Bernard.

'You should. He is – was – Head of Pandemic Policy for the Scottish Government. Which made him probably

7

the second most important civil servant with regards to the Virus. Not, it has to be said, a particular fan of the HETs. He regarded them as largely window-dressing, with limited actual impact on the Virus.'

'Always nice to meet a fan,' said Paterson. 'But I still fail to see what this has to do with us. He's dead, not missing.'

'True. And if that is all there was to this I wouldn't be imposing on your time. But let me tell you about Mr McVie's last day. At 10am last Friday, he turned up here for a meeting—'

'With the museum staff?'

'No, they'd no involvement in the meeting at all. The museum rents out conference spaces on the top floor, and McVie had booked one late on Thursday. Although we are wondering why Mr McVie couldn't find a meeting room anywhere in Victoria Quay, St Andrews House or any of the other Edinburgh buildings owned by the Government. Anyway, four people attended the meeting: Mr McVie, Carlotta Carmichael MSP—' He broke off in response to the low growl of dismay that was coming collectively from the HET staff.

'The same Ms Carmichael who was recently spotted at the North Edinburgh HET office, complaining about the standards of housekeeping and threatening to establish an Inspector of HETs post, if my sources are correct?' Ian grinned.

'Shut up and get on with it,' said Paterson.'

'OK, so McVie, Ms Carmichael, and two other civil servants were at the meeting: Jasper Connington, Director of Health for the Scottish Government, and Helen Sopel, Head of the Virus Operational Response Team.'

'Still not seeing what it has to do with us.'

8

'At 8.30 this morning, Helen Sopel failed to turn up for her monthly scheduled Health Check. As you can imagine for someone in her position, missing a Health Check is unthinkable. She didn't turn up for work this morning, and her colleagues couldn't get any answer from her mobile. While her staff were wondering what they should do about her unexpected absence, her sister phoned looking for her. Apparently she was worried as Helen stood her up for a cinema trip on Sunday night.'

'That's not good.'

'Quite so,' Stuttle concurred. 'The four most important people in Virus policy in Scotland had a meeting here on Friday morning. At 11.30pm on Friday night, one of them kills themselves, and at some point over the weekend, another one goes missing.'

'Carlotta Car—'

'Carlotta Carmichael was absolutely alive and well as of an hour ago, so don't get your hopes up, John.'

'Do we know what the meeting was about?' asked Bernard.

'No, we don't. But we need to get Helen Sopel found and into a Health Check before anyone notices she's gone. Because these are the people at the very top of Virus policy, these are the people who are continually popping up on TV telling us that everything is under control, these are the people who are supposed to be making everything all right. If word gets out that they are going crazy, there's going to be panic on the streets.' He looked round at them all. 'There's going to be bloodshed.'

2

Bernard pressed the on switch of his computer and wondered what to do next. The morning's video show had been horrific, and he was in full agreement with Stuttle that if so much as a sniff of the disarray at the head of the civil service was made public, there would be panic on the streets. He'd fully anticipated that the team would rush back to their offices for a debrief, with an immediate doling out of tasks by their Team Leader.

But Paterson and Stuttle had excused themselves at the end of the meeting, with a muttered statement about a team leaders' meeting over at the Parliament. In a slightly louder tone he'd made it clear that Mona was to take a lead on activity in his absence. Mona had risen to this challenge by heading off to the cafeteria in pursuit of coffee. *Seriously, Bernard, I'm worse than useless until I get some caffeine into me – you want one?*

He'd declined the offer. He was trying to limit his consumption of coffee, ditto his intake of alcohol, takeaways, sugary snacks and any other item that his subconscious might be driving him to regard as comfort food. He was definitely at risk of taking refuge in eating, because there certainly wasn't any refuge in bricks and mortar. Since he had split – just about amicably – from his wife, he'd had a range of increasingly unfortunate living arrangements. A flat-share with a beautician had started promisingly, but had lasted only a matter of weeks, brought to an abrupt end when a HET investigation resulted in his landlady getting her window put in, and a visit from a large and threatening thug.

This had been followed by five nights sleeping on a very short sofa in his mother's sheltered housing flat, until one of the neighbours had complained about her harbouring a flatmate who clearly didn't meet the age restrictions. That had led, desperately, to his current living conditions. The best thing he could say about them was that at least they were ending. In fact, they were concluding that very evening when he picked up the keys to his new one-person flat. Until he was properly settled in his new home and back on an even keel, he was sticking to mineral water and eating his greens, in a slightly doomed attempt to protect his mental health.

Also, he was slightly ashamed to admit, to stop him getting fat. For the first time in his life, he was experiencing unwanted weight gain, noticing an increasing amount of flesh that could be termed 'love handles' appearing. In his life before the HET he had been a professional badminton player, training three hours a day, six days a week. He'd followed a strict, protein-rich diet, which he'd continued to keep to while he'd retrained in health promotion. But with every passing month at the HET he'd fallen further into the world of fast food, snacks from the canteen and chocolate bars from the corner shop. His slow, sauntering journey toward obesity had to stop. He couldn't get fat. Especially not now that he was single.

There was an outburst of expletives from the direction of Maitland's desk. His ire seemed to be directed at the contents of his email Inbox. Bernard chose to ignore the ranting. In his experience of the other HET members, there did tend to be a great deal of swearing, much of which was directed at him. He'd been horrified when he'd first heard Mr Paterson refer to a colleague from SHEP as a bit of a 'c-word'. He was largely able to screen it out now, although, like the junk food, he was doing his best to avoid developing a cursing habit himself. It was a slippery slope from an occasional oath in the office to accidentally telling your mother to F Off.

He returned to his musings about singledom. He and his wife had split by mutual agreement (it wasn't like she'd kicked him out or anything, no matter what Maitland seemed to think) after ten years of marriage. They'd lost their baby son to the Virus, and the marriage had never really recovered, floundering on the difference of opinion about whether to have another child or not. And now he was torn between making the best of things, moving on, maybe even signing up for one of the dating sites that his friends Marcus and Bryce had been talking about. The other half of his brain was thinking desperately of a way to reconcile with his wife, a difficult reconciliation given his reluctance to bring a child into a world filled with the Virus and her insistence on . . .

A stapler crashed onto his keyboard. Startled, he swivelled round on his chair to confront the aggressor. 'What are you playing at, Maitland? You could have hit me!'

'I was aiming for you! You haven't listened to a word I've said.'

'Yes, and . . .'

'Check your emails – I've got one from HR that I don't understand. I must be reading it wrong.'

'If it's got the phrase "P45" in it, I think you are reading it just right.'

Maitland stood up and headed in his direction. Bernard

spun hastily back toward his computer. 'All right. I'll look.'

Maitland shoved him out of the way and double-clicked on one of his emails. 'There – that one. It's been sent to every member of staff.' He began to read aloud. '*Due to the continuing challenges presented by the Virus, we are invoking Clause 74 of your contract of employment. Please note that this may affect your annual leave, retirement, and severance plans.* What does that mean? It's not going to be good, is it? I mean, they're not going to email us all to say they've improved our terms and conditions?'

'Have you looked at what Clause 74 actually says?'

'Of course not! It's not like I carry a copy of my contract around with me in case I need to cross-reference it against my incoming emails.'

'Do you even know where your contract is?'

'At home! Probably. Or maybe I left it at Emma's flat when I moved out. Or it could be in a pile of stuff I left at my mum's. We'll need to get HR to send us new copies out.'

'No, we won't.' Bernard opened the bottom drawer of his filing cabinet and pulled out a ring binder. He flicked past his timesheets and expenses claims for the past six months, then found what he was looking for, neatly stored in a plastic pocket. 'My contract. The same as yours and, I assume, everyone else's.'

Maitland made a grab for it, but he managed to get it out of the way just in time. With his back to his colleague, he found the correct page. 'Oh, this is bad.'

'What?' Maitland made a second, and this time successful, grab for the contract. '*Clause 74: In the event of exceptional circumstances the Scottish Health Enforcement Partnership has the right to insist that all*

13

staff are retained within the HETs in order to meet the requirements of the service. This could include cancellation of annual leave, delaying of retirement and revoking the right of staff members to resign.' He lowered the paper. 'Can they do that?'

'I don't know.'

'What do you mean "you don't know"? The one, solitary contribution that you make to this team is that you understand shit like this.'

'That's not true! I . . .'

'I mean, there must be some regulation or other that protects our rights.'

Bernard retrieved his, now crumpled, contract from his colleague, smoothed it out and re-read the offending clause.

'Did you have provisions like this in your Police contract?'

'I don't think so. I mean, there was something about the right to cancel annual leave, but nothing about having to work for the Police for the rest of my life.'

'It won't be for the rest of your life, just until the Virus is under control.'

Maitland snorted, and turned back to his seat. 'No time soon then.'

Bernard read and re-read the clause, his heart racing a little faster each time. The one thing that had made life at the HET tolerable was the thought that after one too many taunts from Maitland, or Mr Paterson, he could tell them where to go. In fact, he fantasised about it on a fairly regular basis. The cutting jibe he would make about Paterson's leadership style. The pleasure he would take in telling Maitland that the only good thing about him was his girlfriend. And now – now – he was trapped here. Hell is other people, particularly those with the letters H.E.T. in their job title.

'Look who I found.' Mona, and her coffee cup, appeared in the doorway, her arm round a middle-aged woman, with an untidy mop of long brown hair.

'Carole!' Maitland rushed over to embrace his HET partner. 'We've missed you.'

'I've missed you too.' She smiled, but Bernard thought it looked a little forced.

He gave her a discreet once-over. Pale, he thought, her rosy-cheeked good health no longer shining through. There were stress lines around her eyes, and more grey in her hair than he remembered. Something in her stance conveyed a weariness with life that was a complete contrast to her former optimistic self. She seemed to have aged in the six weeks since he'd last seen her, not surprising given the events that had led up to her extended compassionate leave.

'How's the jaw?' *The jaw* had received a booting from a suspected health defaulter, leaving Carole barely able to eat or talk.

She made a show of chomping her teeth together. 'Full working order.'

'And the boy?' *The boy*, Carole's teenage son, had been an unwitting pawn in an attempt by a local drug dealer to get some traction over the HET. A pretty girl, drugs, and teenage bravado had combined to put young Michael in a compromised position. After a bit of nudging Stuttle had agreed to six weeks' leave for Carole to get on top of the situation.

'He's . . .well, he's OK. He's still down living with my cousin in Alnwick. We're thinking about trying to get him into school there, actually. Which brings me to my

15

visit today.' She reached into her bag and produced an envelope. 'I'm afraid I'm not coming back. This is my resignation letter. Is Mr Paterson in?'

'Oh, Carole, are you sure about this?' Mona reached out to her.

Maitland took several large steps backwards and poked Bernard's shoulder. He looked up, and Maitland made a nodding gesture in Carole's direction. Bernard interpreted this to mean that whoever was going to break the bad news to their colleague, it wasn't going to be Maitland.

'Ehm, Carole, I don't think you can resign.'

Her face crumpled a little, and he thought for a moment she was going to cry. 'I know you don't want me to go, Bernard, and I'll miss all of you too, but I really have to put my family first.'

Mona put a comforting arm round Carole's shoulder. 'Of course you do. We understand.'

Bernard looked up at Maitland for help, who repeated his nodding gesture more vigorously than before. He sighed, and prepared to try again.

'No, I mean you really can't resign. We got an email this morning telling us that SHEP's invoking a clause in our contract that means we can't leave.'

Carole's face contorted through a number of emotions. The denial and bargaining stages quickly rushed past before her features landed heavily on anger.

'Are you sure about this?' asked Mona.

'Check your emails if you don't believe me – or have a read of mine.' Maitland rolled his chair out of the way and the two of them pushed in to the computer.

'Where's Paterson?' Carole's voice had the low measured tone of someone who was trying very hard not to completely lose it.

'Him and Stuttle disappeared off to some meeting,' said Maitland. 'I'm pretty sure the "meeting" will be full of HET Team Leaders from across Scotland hiding out until their staff have calmed down.'

'This,' Carole's voice was losing its controlled edge, 'this is WRONG! HOW CAN THEY DO THIS?'

'Carole—' began Bernard.

'Please say you are not about to tell me to calm down?'

'Ehm . . .' He gave up. If unhelpful suggestions weren't to be allowed, he really had no other weapons in his armoury.

'Because I do not feel calm. I feel furious. I've lost two teeth because of the HET. I had to relocate my son to England because of the HET. And now you are telling me I'm trapped here, like a bird in a bloody cage? You're telling me I have to work for them for the rest of my life?'

'It won't be for the rest of your life, just until . . .' Maitland trod heavily on his foot, which he took as a sign to shut up.

Carole glared at them all and turned on her heel.

'Where are you going?'

She snatched up her bag. 'To get a lawyer.'

The three of them sat in silence until her footsteps disappeared.

'When do you think the Guv will show his face?' asked Maitland. 'I'm betting we don't see him before Wednesday.'

There was the sound of footsteps in the corridor.

'Or he might be about to front it out?'

They watched the empty door frame, until Ian Jacobsen loomed into view. 'Your colleague shot past me with a face like fury. What did I miss?'

3

'Are you going to crack a smile at any point today, Mona?'

They were in Ian's car, en route to the Scottish Government's offices in Leith.

'Probably not.'

'I still think this is a pretty poor way to treat someone who saved your life.'

She kept silent, refusing to rise to the bait.

'It could have turned out very badly for you and Bircham-Fowler if Bob and I hadn't ridden to the rescue.'

She leaned forward and turned the radio on. Ian tutted, but at least he stopped talking.

A year ago the name Professor Alexander Bircham-Fowler would have meant very little to her. She'd probably have known that he was Scotland's leading virologist, with a long and distinguished career at one of Scotland's top universities. But as he led a largely private life, aside from popping up occasionally on the Scottish evening news to discuss Ebola, or swine flu, or one of the many pandemics that never quite arrived, he'd have remained one of these half-familiar faces that you could never quite put a name to. But then the Virus had struck, and as the go-to person for commenting on viral issues, he had been catapulted into something approaching celebrity.

Maybe notoriety would be a better word, as the

Professor's approach to the Virus had not won him many friends within the Scottish establishment. He was often at odds with official government policy, and had gained a reputation for speaking truth to power. Not surprisingly, this had given him a large cult following amongst health professionals, trade unions and young people. As a keen supporter of the Health Check regime, he was popular with the HET staff, but his open criticism of other aspects of Virus policy had bought him some serious enemies.

Mona's knowledge of the Professor and his work had deepened significantly some weeks previously. Bircham-Fowler had inexplicably disappeared dangerously close to both his scheduled Health Check, and an important speech he'd been due to give at the Scottish Parliament. Stuttle – a signed-up member of the Bircham-Fowler Fan Club – had ordered Paterson to find him, and in turn Paterson had ordered her to help. With the assistance of Theresa, the Professor's extremely bossy secretary, they'd tracked him down to London, where he had been looking for his estranged daughter.

It transpired that tracking him down was the easy bit. Whatever the Professor had been planning to discuss in his speech, it had alarmed someone so much that they'd spent most of their journey back to Scotland being tailed by a car on the M1. When they'd stopped at a service station, things had taken a turn for the murderous, as one of their unknown assailants had stalked them through the dark and attempted to shoot the Professor. And the thing that had alarmed Mona most about the whole event was that the man who had taken the potshot knew her by name, a turn of events that no one at SHEP had ever explained to her satisfaction.

Annoyingly, there was some truth to Ian's claims to

have saved their lives. Ian, and his colleague Bob Ellis from the Police Scotland Virus Liaison section, had driven down from Scotland to find them, and had arrived in just the nick of time to help.

At least, she'd thought they were being helpful. She'd become increasing suspicious of their motives and had reluctantly left the Professor in their care. Her suspicions had been vindicated when the Professor had a heart attack on the steps of the Parliament. Whether this was down to stress or something more sinister she didn't know, but she did know that every fibre in her body distrusted Ian Jacobsen.

The car turned into the Scottish Government offices.

'Hello there, gorgeous.'

The car bonnet nudged the barrier to the car park. Ian passed both their Green Cards to the woman in the security booth, and blew her a kiss.

Mona rolled her eyes, but the Scottish Government woman didn't seem so bothered. 'Oh, you.' She smiled and handed him his card back. 'You'll be the death of me.'

The barrier to the car park lifted, and Ian drove off.

'Really?' Mona stared at him, arms folded.

'What?'

'"Hello there, gorgeous"? Is that how you talk to Scottish Government staff?'

'What's wrong with that? I've known Margaret for years.'

'And that makes it OK?'

'Yes! It's not like I walked into a meeting and groped the Permanent Secretary's arse, or felt up an intern. Margaret's an old pal and she doesn't mind. In fact, judging by the smile she shot me, I think I made her day.'

'Well, I think it's a really unprofessional way to talk to women at work.'

He swung the car into a space so abruptly that she slid to the side, bumping her shoulder on the door. 'Really, Mona?' He turned off the engine and twisted toward her, a hint of a smirk around his lips. 'You of all people want to talk about behaving unprofessionally with women at work?'

Her stomach lurched, and she turned to look out of the window.

'Sudden silence, Mona? Aren't you going to say, "Why, Ian, whatever do you mean?"'

He knew.

How could he know? How had he found out about the single, stupidest thing that she'd ever done at work? *Oh God, he'd seen the video.* She'd been set up, of course. Amanda Harris, a tiny, beautiful, and as it turned out psychopathic flatmate of a health defaulter, had turned to her for comfort. A reassuring hug had turned into something more, captured for posterity by a camera hidden in Amanda's hallway. Amanda had sent her a copy, a prelude to blackmail she'd assumed at the time, although it hadn't turned into that. She'd always wondered if Amanda had made good on her threat to pass it on to Mona's colleagues, and she supposed that she knew the answer to that now. Stuttle and Ian had probably had a good laugh at it. Why was she even surprised that he knew? People like Ian Jacobsen and Cameron Stuttle made it their business to know about people's indiscretions.

'I mean, it's out of character for you to sit there quietly, not asking any questions.' Ian grinned at her, obviously enjoying the moment. 'Hmm, could it be that you are sitting there thinking, "Oh God, surely he doesn't know

21

about me throwing myself at Amanda Harris. Oh God, don't let him have seen the footage.'" He elbowed her, less than gently, in the ribs. 'And in case that is something you are wondering about, I can confirm that I have seen it. Several times, in fact. Watching the two of you snogging like that, I have to tell you, gave me a definite tingly feeling. Have you told your colleagues about your feelings for the ladies?'

She didn't give him the satisfaction of turning round. She hadn't, in fact, had any kind of discussions with her colleagues about her sexuality, considering it none of their business. 'You're a pig, Ian.'

'And you're a dyke with such poor judgement that she lets herself be filmed kissing a witness in a health defaulter case. Has Amanda been in touch recently?'

'No.' She hesitated. 'Has she been in touch with Stuttle?'

He smiled. 'Not for me to say. Shall we get on with our investigation?'

'You fucker.'

His smile vanished. 'I'm giving you one last chance to play nice, Mona. You were a pain in the arse last time I had to work with you, and I'm not putting up with that again. I know a lot more about you now, and this time you're going to do as you are told.'

The rational part of Mona's brain knew that this would be a good time to shut up, keep her head down and get Ian out of her life as quickly as possible without antagonising him further. Unfortunately her rational brain was a lot less assertive than her emotional one. She turned toward Ian so fast that her seat belt held her back. 'You know a lot about me, do you?' she snapped. 'Then you'll have learned enough to realise that I'm not going

22

to let myself be bullied, especially not by one of Cameron Stuttle's lackeys.'

'Cameron Stuttle's lackey? That's a good one.' He shook his head, still smirking. 'Anyway, let's get in there. And Mona?' He opened his car door. 'Try not to stick your tongue down the throat of any good-looking civil servants we come across in the course of this investigation.'

When Mona closed her door the slam could be heard across the whole of Leith.

Mona was aware of every eye in the Virus Operational Response Team watching them as they walked through the department. She wondered how much they knew about their visit. It might have been more discreet to meet off-site, rather than have everyone in the team speculate as to why Helen Sopel was off work. Did civil servants all sign confidentiality agreements? She certainly hoped so, because explaining to Stuttle why their top-secret investigation was a headline in the *Edinburgh Evening News* would not be fun.

The secretary who collected them from reception was a youthful twenty-something, smartly dressed and immaculately made-up. She showed them into a small meeting room where, by way of contrast, a middle-aged man in a slightly crumpled suit was sitting. To Mona's surprise the secretary sat down at the table and gestured to them to do likewise.

'I'm Anneka Tomas, Deputy Head of VORT.'

Mona reassessed the woman opposite her. Not a secretary, not by a long chalk. She looked impossibly young to be in such an important role, and her perfect hair and presentation made Mona wish she'd at least taken the time to drag a brush through her mop before she left the office.

'And this is Simon, from our team. I thought you might like to speak to him because he took the call from Helen's sister.'

Simon raised a hand in their direction. His slight air of dishevelment and slumped posture combined to give the impression that he was less than happy about being in this meeting.

'Great, thanks for making the time to meet us. I'm Mona Whyte, HET Officer at North Edinburgh, and this is...'

'Ian Jacobsen.' He pulled a notebook out of his pocket, and sat, his pen poised.

Mona noted that he hadn't mentioned he was from CID. Was this discretion, a little sin of omission, so that the VORT didn't start wondering what interest Police Scotland had in all this? Or did it suit the police to keep their distance from this investigation?

'Do you have some particular questions for us?' Anneka asked. Mona detected a slight accent in her voice, indicating that English, flawless though it was, probably wasn't her first language.

'Perhaps you could start by telling us a little bit about Ms Sopel? What is she like?'

'Highly effective.' Anneka's eyes sparkled. 'She is demonstrating great leadership on Virus issues. I regard Helen as a role model, particularly for women in the civil service. She's been very active in work to promote the role of women in public life, and has done a lot of work on international cooperation on Virus issues. And, of course, she is very supportive of her team.'

'So, a joy to work for?'

'Yes, definitely.' She reinforced the point with a curt little nod.

Mona saw a look flit across Simon's face which appeared to contradict this. 'Do you have anything to add, Simon?'

He considered the question, his head on one side as if he was thinking about a number of different angles and potential responses. 'No.' He returned to staring at the desk.

She'd have to finagle five minutes alone with Simon. The expressions on his less than poker face led her to suspect that his experiences of working with Helen Sopel might be quite different from Anneka's, but she wasn't going to get the real story out of him with his boss sitting in the room.

'What is Ms Sopel like outside of work? Did she socialise with colleagues? Did she have any hobbies?'

'Helen doesn't have a lot of time for socialising.' Anneka looked slightly scandalised at the thought. 'She's extremely dedicated to her work. To succeed at her level you have to make a lot of sacrifices.'

'She came to the Christmas party,' said Simon. 'And left early.'

Anneka glared at him, and he shifted uncomfortably on his seat. If this interview was anything to go by, the VORT did not seem to be a particularly happy place to work. She could relate to that. Simon's eyes flicked in the direction of the door, and she saw him pat his suit pocket. *A smoker*. Under pressure and desperate for a fag.

'So, Simon,' said Ian, 'her sister phoned. Is that unusual?'

'Well, yeah. I don't know how often she speaks to her sister but I assume they'd use each other's mobile number. We don't get many personal calls coming through on the office phones.'

'And what did she say?'

'She asked if Helen was there, and I said no, could I take a message etc. etc. She asked if Helen was out at a meeting and when she would be back, and I said that she hadn't come into work this morning, and we'd had to cancel her 9.30 meeting, and we were actually wondering where she was. Then she started to get pretty panicky, and that's when I called Anneka over.'

Anneka picked up the story. 'Her sister – Joanne – was quite upset, saying that she'd arranged to meet Helen at Ocean Terminal last night to see a film, but she hadn't turned up and wasn't answering her phone. I said I would speak to someone senior and get back to her.'

'And that someone senior, what did he say?'

'Well, nothing, yet.' She frowned. 'I tried to speak to the Director of Health, but he's off sick today, which only left the Permanent Secretary who hasn't got back to me. I assume she contacted you?'

Before Mona could open her mouth to lie, Ian leapt in.

'Can I have a word with you in private, Anneka?' Ian slid his notebook toward Mona. The word SIMON was written in capitals, with an arrow pointing in the direction of the door. She didn't like Ian, but she had to admit their minds did operate in the same way. *Divide and conquer*.

'I might step out and go to the Ladies, if that's OK. Simon, could you point me in the right direction?'

He looked mildly relieved that his part in the meeting was over. As the door closed behind them she said quietly, 'Are you a smoker?'

He looked uncomfortable again. 'Yeah, I mean, I'm trying to give up, but—'

She cut him short. 'This would be a good time to nip out for a smoke. I see there's a shelter out the front.'

26

He nodded, a little confused. 'The Ladies are back at the lifts.'

'So, Helen Sopel, a joy to work for?'

Simon snorted and took a long drag on his cigarette. 'Yeah, if you are a fast-track high-flyer who's fluent in seven European languages, and doesn't mind working until 9pm every night. She loves *them*. Anneka and her pals all think Helen is like, I don't know,' he flung his hands up, 'the perfect woman or something.'

'And if you're not a high-flyer?'

'Like me, you mean?' He smiled. 'Only thing she ever speaks to me about is my, and I quote, disgusting smoking habit. The woman's a bully. You don't want to get on the wrong side of her.'

She nodded in what she hoped was a sympathetic manner. 'Not a good way to behave toward junior staff.'

'Not just junior! She bullies everyone into getting her own way. I reckon even the Perm Sec is scared of her.'

'I'm getting the picture. Any thoughts on where Ms Sopel might be?'

He stood up, and took a long time stubbing out his cigarette. Mona sensed there were some thought processes at work.

'Is this all confidential? I mean, if I tell you something it wouldn't come from me?'

'That kind of depends on what you are about to tell me.'

'A piece of office gossip?'

'That I can do. Spill.'

'OK, but remember that this is just gossip. So, all the time I've worked for Helen, which is about three years, she's been single. At least as far as we all know.'

27

'From what both you and Anneka have said, I'm not surprised. She seems to be a workaholic.'

'She is. But the past couple of months there's been a rumour floating around that she's having an affair.'

Mona leaned forward, intrigued. 'What makes you think that?'

'Well, secretive mobile conversations. She's got a voice like a foghorn usually, but she's been sneaking out to take calls on her phone. It's all open-plan here, so it's difficult to hide, and people have definitely noticed her disappearing off.'

She sat back, mildly disappointed. 'It's a bit of a leap to deduce an affair from a few phone calls. She could be ill.' Her own situation popped into her mind. 'Or have a sick relation. She could be dealing with hospital appointments.'

'True. But there's something else. There's a young girl in the team, Taylor, who deals with our admin. She's not even twenty yet, still lives with her parents. And one night, maybe about a month ago now, Taylor saw Helen sitting in a BMW, about eleven o'clock at night, in the car park at Holyrood House.'

'The one that's actually in Holyrood Park?'

'Yes.'.

She pulled a face. 'Isn't it kind of dark there at 11pm?'

'The darkness is the attraction for teenagers. Taylor and her boyfriend had bowled up there for a bit of a kiss and cuddle, out of the way of prying eyes.' He laughed. 'Must be great to be young and in love.'

'Paradise by the dashboard lights, and all that.'

'Yeah, except the boyfriend's no sooner got the car out of gear, when Taylor notices the woman in the big BMW next to them is Helen.'

'Having a kiss and cuddle?'

'No, having a raging argument.'

'And did Taylor see what the man looked like?'

'No, she was so freaked out that she got her boyfriend to reverse right out of there before Helen clocked her. Taylor probably thought Helen would be discussing her car parking behaviour at her next appraisal if she caught her. No doubt the boyfriend was cursing Taylor's boss all the way back to his mum and dad's.'

She laughed. 'That's really helpful. Thanks for your time.'

'No problem.'

They walked back toward the building. 'Well, at least there won't be any bullying going on today.'

'Ha, don't bet on it. Anneka is shaping up to be Helen Mark 2. And she loves it when Helen's off – it gives her a chance to throw her weight around.' He paused with his hand on the revolving door. 'You might want to check Anneka's flat in case she's got Helen tied up in a cupboard.' He chuckled to himself as he went back into the building.

Ian was already in the car by the time she got back to it. He gave her a little wave as she approached, which she took to be a placatory gesture after their earlier fight. She chose to ignore it.

'So, I take it you managed to get Simon on his own?' he asked.

'Yup.'

'Anything of interest?'

'Possibly.' She summarised their conversation, with an emphasis on the fact it was all hearsay and relied heavily on the eyewitness testimony of a couple of horny teenagers.

At the end of her tale, Ian threw his head back and laughed. 'So, we're busting a gut looking for her, and she's probably off on a dirty weekend somewhere?'

'Unlikely. The affair story is just the spin that Simon and his colleagues have put on all this. And despite what Anneka said earlier, I'm getting the impression that Helen Sopel wasn't too popular with her staff, so it probably amuses them all to think that their annoying boss is off doing the dirty.'

'Any idea who the bloke was in the car with Helen?'

'No, the girl didn't get a proper look at him. And whoever he was, I'm not convinced by the whole affair thing. Sitting in a car park at night having a full-blown argument with a man could have a lot of explanations, none of which relate to romance, but could still be relevant to her disappearance. If she was meeting someone in a car park in Holyrood Park it was obviously someone that she didn't want to be seen in public with, and an argument definitely suggests that there was something bad going on.'

'True.'

'Did you find out anything else from Anneka?'

'Nothing useful. I had a very long explanation about the procedure that is triggered when a senior civil servant is unexpectedly absent, because, apparently, if very important people are missing it's vital that we check they haven't been kidnapped or defected to North Korea. Because I wouldn't know that, would I?'

'Aw, did the nasty woman patronise you?' Mona grinned, and felt a momentary disappointment that she hadn't been there to witness it. 'You should have told her she was gorgeous and blown her a kiss.'

'Actually she was pretty gorgeous. That's why I took her phone number.'

Mona's jaw dropped. 'You did what?'

'Ah, the look on your face!' He laughed. 'You are so gullible, Mona. You believe any old guff.' There was a slight, almost imperceptible pause. 'I bet you believed all the nonsense that your friend Professor Bircham-Fowler spouted.'

She felt a tiny thrill of adrenaline shoot through her. So, Ian was still interested in the professor, for no reason that she could immediately see. Until now she'd considered that the professor had been silenced, at least temporarily, and was no longer of interest to Ian and his colleagues. And yet, here was Ian still digging around. 'And exactly what nonsense would that be?'

'You know, the stuff he was going on about when you were down in London . . .' He waited for her to fill in the gap.

'Oh, right.' She lowered her voice. 'You mean the top-secret conversation when he confided in me that he thought that you and your mate Bob were arseholes?'

'Oh, for God's sake, Mona!'

'I'm not talking about the Professor to you! For all I know, you were responsible for his heart attack.'

'Seriously? You think Police Scotland now goes around attempting to murder elderly academics?'

'No, Ian. But then I don't think that you actually work for Police Scotland, even if you do carry a warrant card.'

He shook his head, feigning disbelief. 'So, who do I work for?'

As she didn't know the answer to that – yet – she kept quiet.

Ian sighed and slid the car into gear. He put his arm round the back of her chair as he reversed out. 'He's in his 60s and was under an incredible amount of stress. Why can't you just believe he had a heart attack?'

'He was fine when I left him with you to go to a "safe house". Not very safe, was it? But you mark my words, as soon as he's back at work I'll find out what really happened to him.'

'He's not coming back. He's requested retirement, citing ill health.'

She stared at him.

'Seriously. He's taken his pension and gone.'

'But . . .'

'Leave the man in peace, Mona. See sense. He's well past his prime. Everyone knows he's been talking rubbish for the past few months. We should sit down and have a proper non-confrontational conversation about what he said to you. I could put your mind at rest about a few things.'

'I very much doubt that.'

He sighed again, a long and exaggerated outpouring of frustration. 'Have it your way. Anyway, can we focus on the investigation for a moment? We need to talk to the people at the Museum.'

Mona looked at her watch. 'It's after five now.'

'I'll call you tomorrow morning and we'll sort something out.'

'Can't wait.'

She gazed out of the window, wondering what it was that Ian thought she knew, and why he was so worried about it.

4

Joanne Sopel's flat was extremely pale. A cream carpet extended out to magnolia walls. The sofa and armchair were both beige, with a selection of white woollen cushions fastened with wooden buttons. It was also incredibly neat. Every surface was free of belongings, with the exception of a set of fanned out magazines on the coffee table. Being of that persuasion himself, Bernard wondered how she had managed to create quite such a minimalist space. His eyes wandered round the room, looking for innovative storage solutions he could implement in his new one-person flat.

Maitland seemed considerably less aware of his surroundings, if the clump of mud that had detached itself from his shoe and was now resting on the cream carpet was anything to go by. It hadn't escaped Joanne Sopel's notice, though, and her head inclined toward it in what Bernard felt was quite a pointed manner. After a minute she snapped and stood up. 'Excuse me. I'll just get that.'

Maitland leaned toward him and whispered, 'Fiver says Helen Sopel's off somewhere with a boyfriend.'

Bernard frowned, one eye on the door in case Joanne Sopel came back. 'There's nothing to suggest that.'

'Oh, come on. These high-flying types always have a secret boyfriend. Probably some handsome young tearaway that she's just using for . . .'

Joanne reappeared with a dust-buster and hoovered up the dirt from around Maitland's feet.

'Oh, sorry.' Surprised at the intervention, he contemplated the soles of both shoes. Joanne left the dust-buster prominently displayed by her feet.

Bernard decided to crack on with the interview before Maitland caused further havoc. 'So, Ms Sopel, when was the last time you spoke to your sister?'

'She texted me on Thursday, I think, about arrangements for our cinema trip on Sunday evening.'

'But you didn't actually speak to her?'

She shook her head. 'To be honest I haven't actually spoken to her for weeks. All our communication has been by text. We've arranged to meet up a couple of times and she's had to cancel at the last minute due to something coming up at work.'

'So it wasn't unusual for her not to make your arrangements?'

'No, obviously she was very busy with her job, and the Virus and everything. But she would always, always, let me know that she wasn't coming. It isn't like her to just not turn up. And I've never known her to not answer her phone.'

'Does your sister have a partner, Ms Sopel?'

She shook her head again. 'No, she's single.'

Maitland leaned forward. 'And you would definitely know if she was seeing someone? It's absolutely something she would confide in you?'

She looked irritated. Between the dirt and the intrusive questioning, Maitland wasn't endearing himself to her. 'We're sisters, Mr, ehm—' she peered at his lanyard, 'Stevenson. She would tell me if she was seeing someone.'

'Are you sure? I mean, what if it was someone you

34

wouldn't approve of? Would she still tell you then?'

There was a flicker of doubt on her face. '*Is* she seeing someone? Do you know about a boyfriend?'

Bernard cursed inwardly. There was just enough concern on her face to make him think that Maitland might be right about the boyfriend. He decided to pursue another avenue in the hope of avoiding a smug Maitland for the rest of the day. 'No, we don't. We're just trying to get as full a picture of your sister's life as possible. As you pointed out, your sister has a very busy and probably quite stressful job. Is there any chance that it's all got a bit on top of her and she's taking some time out?'

Joanne sighed. 'Yes, I wondered that. My sister has always worked hard, in fact I'd say she's a bit of a stress junkie, but there must come a point in everyone's life where they just can't go on, mustn't there?'

'Has she said anything to you that would indicate she's struggling to cope?'

'No, not in so many words, but as I said she's been a bit hard to contact the past few weeks. Maybe she's been avoiding me in case I started asking her difficult questions.' She covered her face with her hands. 'If anything has happened to her I'll never forgive myself for not making more of an effort.'

'Please try not to worry, Ms Sopel. There's absolutely nothing to suggest she's come to any harm.' Bernard hoped he sounded sufficiently reassuring. 'But your sister did miss her Health Check yesterday.'

'Missed her Health Check?' Joanne slowly moved her fingers away from eyes, and looked up. 'But Helen would never miss a Health Check. Her whole job was about dealing with the Virus. She was part of the team that set up the system. She used to rant about how irresponsible people were who didn't turn up for the checks. The only reason Helen would miss a Health Check is if something terrible has happened to her.'

Her hands went back to her face again, and her shoulders shook as she started to cry.

Bernard looked at Maitland, who, as usual in a difficult situation, shrugged.

'Can we get you a glass of water, or something, Ms Sopel?'

'No.' She sniffed. 'I'm sorry.'

'Please don't apologise, we totally understand why you are upset. But for what it's worth, I still think that the most likely explanation is that your sister has taken an unscheduled time out. If she was stressed, can you think of anywhere she would go to get away from it all?'

She thought for a moment. 'No, I'm sorry. Nothing comes to mind.'

'OK, well, I'll leave you a card if you think of anything.'

As she showed them out to the door, she spoke again. 'Helen would never, ever, miss a Health Check. Please let me know as soon as you find out anything.'

'We will.'

'You owe me a fiver.'

'No, I don't. There was nothing in that interview that even suggested, never mind proved, that she has a boyfriend. Even if she does have a boyfriend her sister is unaware of, there's nothing to say it's anything to do with her disappearance. People like Helen Sopel do not blow off work to spend time with a boyfriend.'

'Yeah, right.' Maitland flung open the door to the office and marched through. It bounced back and Bernard had to throw his hands up to avoid being hit in the face by it.

'OK, you *will* owe me a fiver in about twenty-four hours' time when we track them down to her secret love nest. Another fiver says lover boy is under twenty-five.'

'Shut up, Maitland.'

His colleague grabbed his arm and pointed at Paterson's office. The 'office' was one corner of the main room, which had been cordoned off, floor to ceiling, using a no-frills selection of inadequately soundproofed materials to give the impression that their Team Leader actually had a private space befitting his status.

'Door's shut. Do you think the Guv's actually shown his face?'

'What do we say to him?'

'You don't say anything!' Paterson's voice thundered through the layer of MDF. 'Because I'm as pissed off as you are.'

They looked at each other. Bernard wondered if it would be a good time to make a tactical retreat to the canteen, although he was pretty sure that in this particular discussion the HET officers actually had the high moral ground.

'Well, come in then, you pair of clowns!'

Paterson's face looked every bit as pissed off as his voice had sounded. 'So, you've seen the memo?'

'Yup,' said Maitland. 'And we noticed that you made yourself scarce while we read it.'

'Not my idea. Stuttle organised a meeting of all the HET Team Leaders from across Scotland . . .'

'I was right!' said Maitland, elbowing Bernard triumphantly.

' . . .so that we could all be briefed on dealing with irate staff and difficult questions. They even had us role playing, for Christ's sake.' He shook his head, as if he

37

still couldn't believe the indignities he had suffered. 'So if you've got something to say, I'm prepared.'

Maitland poked Bernard's shoulder, which Bernard took to mean that if anyone was telling Paterson about Carole's visit, it wasn't going to be Maitland.

'Ehm, Mr Paterson?'

Paterson sighed. 'OK, hit me. "This is an outrage, civil liberties, must be illegal etc. etc."'

'No, it's not that. Well, it is all of that but we . . .' He pointed to Maitland and back to himself. If he was going down, he was taking Maitland with him. 'We thought that you should know that Carole came in today . . .'

'Oh God, really? Today? She has to pick today of all days to come back to work?'

'With a resignation letter.'

He put his head in his hands.

'Did they not cover that in your briefing, Guv?' said Maitland, cheerfully.

'It's a bit of a niche situation, Maitland. How did she take it?' He looked up hopefully, as if there remained an outside chance that Carole might have seen the funny side of her servitude.

'She yelled a bit, then stormed out saying she was going to get a lawyer.'

'Hmm. I suppose if she makes it a legal issue, Stuttle or SHEP's lawyers will have to take over dealing with it.'

'Good one, Guv. Buck neatly passed.'

Paterson glared at Maitland. 'Anyway, how did you get on with finding the civil servant lassie?'

'Her sister wasn't much help, to be honest, Mr Paterson. She doesn't seem to have seen her recently. Maitland's theory is that she's got a secret boyfriend but the sister couldn't confirm or deny it.'

'Ha, you're probably right there, Maitland. You know how it is with these high-flying types. Tenner says the boyfriend's under twenty-five.'

'Good one, Guv.'

Bernard sighed, reflecting that he could be putting up with this sexism for a very long time.

'Well, seeing as the sister was a bit of a bust, we'll have to keep digging around.' A thought occurred to Paterson. 'Unless Mona has a new lead. What's she been doing?'

'She's still out with that Ian bloke from CID, Guv. They were interviewing Sopel's work colleagues. What's Mona's beef with him, anyway? We sensed there was a bit of history there.'

'Oh, I don't know,' said Paterson. He picked up some papers and started leafing through them. 'You know what Mona's like. It's probably the lesbian thing.'

There was a silence of such utter quietness that the proverbial pin would have echoed like a grenade going off.

Bernard wasn't quite sure he'd heard his boss correctly. 'The lesbian thing?'

Paterson's head snapped back up, a look of horror on his face. 'No, I, ehm . . .'

'She's a dyke.' Maitland laughed. 'I knew it!'

'Mona's gay,' Bernard muttered, mulling this revelation over. 'That makes a lot of sense.'

'No, she's not, I mean, who knows, and obviously there's nothing wrong with that if she is, but I definitely didn't say that she was.'

'Think you did, actually, Guv.' Maitland clapped his hands together, grinning broadly.

Paterson sighed and gave up the pretence. 'If either of you breathe a hint of this to Mona, I will make your life so miserable you'll wish you'd never been born. And you could be working for me for a very long time.' He sighed again. 'I can't cope with both Carole and Mona wanting to kill me at the same time.'

'The secret's safe with us, Guv,' said Maitland. 'Come on, Bernie.' He shuffled Bernard back out of Paterson's office and closed the door behind him. 'This is going to be fun.'

'A lesbian,' Bernard repeated. 'Makes a lot of sense.'

5

The Professor's work telephone rang twelve times then switched to voicemail. Mona shifted impatiently on her bed, debating yet again whether she should leave a message. She desperately wanted to know that the Professor was safe and well, and had been ringing him on a regular basis in the hope of him picking up her call and putting her mind at rest. So far, she'd resisted the temptation to leave a message, uncertain exactly who would be monitoring his phone while he was on sick leave. And now, if Ian was to be believed, he wasn't coming back.

Oh, Professor, she thought. *What's happened to you?* Ian seemed to think that Bircham-Fowler had told her something of significance. *Nonsense*, he'd called it. *The nonsense that your friend the Professor spouted.* If the Professor really had been spinning her a line, why was Ian so interested in it? And to her enduring frustration, why couldn't she think of what 'the nonsense' could be?

She lay on her bed and closed her eyes, trying to think of the conversations that they had had. They'd discussed his daughter, obviously, and London. They'd discussed the role of curfews in tackling the Virus, which although controversial, she doubted would be enough to get the Professor nearly killed. They'd discussed his affection for Theresa. They'd talked about bacon rolls and coffee, for Christ's sake! None of this seemed significant, yet there was a dull throb in her temple that wouldn't go away, a pulse, pulse, pulse that spelled out that she had failed him. He'd suspected that he was in danger, he'd given her some vital information that could help to keep him safe, and she'd ignored it.

She sat up and redialled the university switchboard. 'Can I speak to Theresa Kilsyth, please?' If anyone knew the truth about whether the Professor really was intending to retire, it would be his long-standing (and long-suffering) personal assistant.

To her disappointment the phone rang and rang. She counted twelve rings, and was surprised to hear a thirteenth. No voicemail. She let it ring another dozen times, and was on the point of hanging up, when a slightly breathless female voice answered. 'Theresa Kilsyth's phone.'

'Oh right, hi, is Theresa there? Have I missed her for today?'

'She's not working here any more, I'm afraid. She handed in her notice a couple of weeks ago, and she had so much leave to take I don't think she'll be back.'

'Oh, I see.' This wasn't entirely surprising. Theresa and the Professor had worked so closely together that she had rather assumed that if one went, both would go. She tried a bit of digging. 'The Professor will miss her. He'll need to get a new assistant.'

There was a brief silence. 'Professor B's not coming back either. Didn't you know he had a heart attack? It was on the news.'

'Oh, yes, of course. I thought he might be recovered by now though.'

'Is there anyone else who could help you?' The voice was beginning to sound a little curt, and Mona couldn't say she blamed her. Given the Professor's profile, she suspected they would have had a journalist or two fishing for information from his staff.

She declined any further assistance and hung up. It looked as if the Professor had been permanently silenced, chased from his high-profile role at the university, with all the protection of a tenured position. From her experience of him, she thought he would keep working until he dropped. Maybe he really was ill, maybe Ian was right and she should leave the man in peace. Or maybe, just maybe, he was in need of all the help he could get.

If she knew where he lived, she could turn up on his doorstep and assess his health for herself. He was ex-directory, of course, but she could get his address, she was sure, by pulling in a few favours from her former Police Scotland colleagues, but she couldn't guarantee that Jacobsen wouldn't hear about her asking around, and the last thing she wanted was him on her back. She'd already tried phoning the Professor on his mobile, but the number he'd given her had returned a 'this number is no longer in use' message.

The number he'd given her. She jumped to her feet. When they'd parted he'd given her his card, with a vague commitment to meeting for coffee. Except he hadn't just given her *one* card, he'd given her a little bundle of cards, held together with an elastic band. She'd assumed that he'd just absent-mindedly handed over the entire set of business cards he was carrying by mistake. But what if it was deliberate? What if he'd communicated something to her that he hadn't wanted Ian or Bob to see? And, most pressingly, where the hell had she put the cards?

After some digging around she found it in a bowl of bits and pieces on her mantelpiece. She tugged impatiently at the elastic band, which snapped and scattered the cards

43

across the floor. As they fell, she noticed that there was something written on the back of one of them.

She peered at it, trying to decipher the Professor's spindly handwriting. After a second or two of squinting, the letters formed themselves into a sentence.

FOLLOW THE ORDERS OF MRS HILDA MILWOOD.

She frowned at the card. Was this an instruction for her, or just a note to himself? The Professor had gone out of his way to give her the cards, but in the rush to hand it over discreetly he could have given her the whole bundle by mistake. If it was an instruction, it was a pretty poor one. She'd no idea of who Hilda Milwood was, least of all how to contact her. The only thing that she could be totally confident about was that whatever it did actually mean, it was in no way, shape or form, nonsense.

Reaching under her bed she pulled out her laptop, fired it up and opened a search engine eager to see if a simple search would give her a lead.

Hilda Milwood, she typed.

The search returned six results, all of them from sites that specialised in tracing family trees. She sighed, disappointed but not entirely surprised. As far as she was aware, people had stopped naming their girl children 'Hilda' somewhere around 1940. If Hilda was still alive, it was likely that she didn't have an active social media presence.

She caught sight of the clock on her bedside table and realised with a start that it was later than she'd thought. Her dealings with the Professor would have to wait. First thing in the morning she would pull out all the stops to find out who Hilda Milwood was, why she was so significant and where she lived. She'd waste no time tracking her down and doorstopping her. But that would have to be tomorrow's problem, not today's. Tonight she was busy. Tonight she had a prior engagement.

Tonight, she had a date.

6

It turned out that there were three things which were very important to Bernard in a home. He had not been aware of this until recently, but over the weeks that he had been staying at his colleague Marcus's flat he'd thought about the nature of home a great deal. In fact, he'd lain awake hypothesising what his ideal accommodation would be, a model that was based largely on taking his existing living arrangements and choosing the exact opposite.

His first requirement was a bed, a proper resting place with legs, a mattress, sheets and a duvet. Ideally, the bed would be situated in a bedroom, with a door, lockable if at all possible. He'd never realised how important a quality place to lay his head was to him. A bit like the old saying about health, he hadn't missed it until it was gone. Six weeks in a sleeping bag on a blow-up mattress on Marcus's living room floor, tossing and turning in the breeze that blew under the door had rammed home to him the importance of suitable slumber arrangements.

His second prerequisite was silence, or at least the option to have peace and quiet occasionally. Marcus was an excellent IT technician, and good friend, who had opened his home to Bernard in his hour of need. But good friend or not, Bernard had to admit that he was also quite annoying in some ways, and extremely annoying in others. His chief grievance was that Marcus

46

was absolutely the world's worst at taking a hint. Many evenings, as the clock nudged eleven, Bernard would yawn and make noises about going to bed. Marcus would nod enthusiastically urging him to 'go for it' then continue to watch TV and give a running commentary on what was happening on the science fiction channel to Bernard's inert figure lying tense and frustrated on his damn blow-up bed.

His final necessity in a home, although he would rather have died than admit it, was a woman to share his space with. He'd been married to Carrie for a very long time. While nobody could describe their last few years together as happy, the break-up of his marriage had left him with a deep, deep loneliness that no amount of nerdy companionship from Marcus and Bryce could overcome. Although he'd tried to keep this particular feeling to himself, his unhappiness must have been obvious as it had been noted by his companions, who were quick to suggest a solution.

'We know what you need to do,' Bryce had said.

Bernard was still dealing with the novelty of hearing Bryce actually speak. In nine months of working with him, he hadn't heard Bryce utter a single syllable. He was renowned for his taciturn manner, which Bernard now knew to be a manifestation of extreme shyness, a shyness he appeared to have overcome as he'd got to know Bernard better. 'You do?'

'Online dating.' Marcus had grinned. 'Bryce and I are big fans.'

'*Really?*'

He'd dug a little deeper into how two IT nerds, one of whom barely spoke, had managed to negotiate the choppy waters of Internet dating, and had found that their enthusiasm was of a theoretical nature. In spite of their obvious willingness to embrace the world of virtual romance, neither of them had got as far as going on an actual face-to-face date.

He'd allowed them to talk him through the process of signing up, creating a profile, and alienating women through inappropriate use of 'jokes' in emails, but he remained unsure of the whole online dating option. He'd decided to seek more sensible counsel and had canvassed Mona on the subject. She'd reacted with a surprising degree of suspicion to his question about her position on the subject, and had asked him if he was 'having a go' at her, which was a strange response, even for her. He put it down to her usual reticence about talking about her private life. Given what he knew now it could, of course, have been down to her thinking he was prying into what Paterson had tactlessly called 'the lesbian thing'.

But, all in all, he was glad to be moving out. He felt suddenly guilty at his train of thought. Marcus, for all his faults, had offered him a home when he needed it. His hints to Mona and Maitland had elicited no such offers. Mona had directed him to the Gumtree Rooms to Let category. Maitland had told him there was no way he was moving in with him, as he wasn't having Bernard *hanging around the flat with a big hard-on for Kate*. This had made him particularly angry due to the element of truth in it. Kate, the curly-haired goddess, was to Bernard's mind way too good for Maitland.

So, credit where it was due, he had a lot to be grateful for when it came to Marcus. When he stopped to think about it, he had a lot to be grateful to Bryce for too. He'd got to know him much better over the weeks he'd stayed at Marcus's place. Bryce had been sympathetic to his plight, supportive of his attempts to get his life back on track. A tentative friendship had developed between them, which he hoped would outlast his move to his own place.

There was the honk of a horn from outside, indicating that Marcus was here with the car. He picked up his bag and took a last look at the patch of carpet where he'd lain for the past few weeks.

Onwards and upwards.

Marcus's flat was high-ceilinged and airy, reflecting the grandeur and lofty ambitions of Edinburgh house-builders from the era when the nineteenth century had slipped into the twentieth. Bernard's new flat was from the era when the twentieth century was giving way to the twenty-first, and reflected the more modest ambitions of Edinburgh house-builders to maximise every penny of profit from a piece of land. His flat was tiny.

He'd felt claustrophobic even when the letting agent had been showing him around, keeping up a chirpy monologue about the accommodation's many space-saving features. He'd balked when she quoted a rent that was not far off the mortgage on his marital home, but he'd signed it on the spot. What choice did he have? He was still paying the mortgage on the flat that Carrie was now occupying solo. He supposed he could go back and negotiate with her, but as she wasn't working it was unlikely that she'd be able to stump up.

'So, where do you want these?' Marcus held aloft the two large plastic bags he was carrying.

Bernard surveyed the furniture that wasn't his. 'Drop them on the sofa.'

Bryce appeared with the hard drive from his computer.

'We really need to talk to you, Bernard, about these modern inventions called tablets – or even laptops?'

'Sorry.' He smiled. 'I like my PC.'

'Stone age mentality.' Marcus shook his head. 'I'll get the rest of your prehistoric gear.' He turned on his heel, and they could hear him singing the theme tune to *The Flintstones* as he jogged down the stairs.

'I think that's it now,' said Bryce.

'Great. I'll stick the kettle on. Assuming I can find some mugs.' He looked round the kitchen/living room area, trying to work out which box or bag contained his limited selection of crockery. As he did so he caught sight of Bryce, leaning against a worktop with an expression on his face that hinted at worry.

'You're looking very pensive. What's up?'

His frown deepened. 'Bernard, can I ask you something? Something about Marcus?'

He nodded, puzzled.

'Have you noticed any change in him recently?'

Bernard thought for a minute. 'I don't think so. What kind of change?'

'I'm worried about him, Bernard. I'm worried about . . .'

The man in question came bouncing back into the room, armed with a monitor which he dumped on the floor.

'And we nearly forgot.' He reached into his rucksack and pulled out a plastic bag. 'A house-warming present.'

Bernard delved into the bag. 'A pencil holder?'

'Bryce's idea.' Marcus gave one of his distinctive giggles, high-pitched and nasal. 'We thought if you are the kind of luddite that still has a PC, you're probably the kind of freak who still uses pen and paper.'

They had him pegged. He held the ceramic pot aloft. 'That's really thoughtful. Thanks for everything, guys.'

Marcus shot him a cheery grin, but behind his back he could see that Bryce still looked worried. He gave Bernard a sad wave, and with that they were gone. The door closed on Marcus's chattering, and suddenly the flat was very, very quiet.

Bliss.

7

The Delphin was small and cosy, with rough-hewn stone walls and stripped wooden floors. Situated in the basement of a Georgian building on one of the quieter New Town streets, its cellar setting meant that the building was full of nooks and crannies, with tables set at a discreet distance from the neighbouring diners. There really couldn't be a better place in Edinburgh for a first date.

Unfortunately, Mona hadn't yet made it into the restaurant. She stood in a doorway on the opposite side of the road, trying desperately not to give in to a full-scale panic attack. She counted slowly to ten in an effort to get her breathing properly under control, and told herself she was being ridiculous. She'd been shot at, and had picked herself up and kept going without a second thought. She dealt day-to-day with the pressure and politics of the HET without her heart rate rising so much as a beat. The nearest she came to getting stressed was dealing with her mother. Yet here she was, embarking on her first date in years, and turning into a complete basket case. On top of everything else, she was late.

There was a very real possibility that she just wasn't cut out for online dating. Her love life until this point, such as it had been, had been conducted face-to-face and generally in a state of inebriation. It hadn't been planned, there had been no slow build-up, no getting to know someone, picturing what they might be like, wondering if they would like you too or if you were staring rejection in the face. Now here she was, stone cold sober and about to meet up with a woman called Elaine, with whom her only contact had been a series of email messages.

Good emails, though. Warm. Witty. Indicative of someone who did more than slump in front of the TV every night. Emails from someone fantastic, who might turn out to be the kind of person she could spend the rest of her life with. Although it was equally likely her date might take one look at her and reject her good and proper. But she'd never find out if she didn't get her feet to start moving in the direction of *The Delphin*.

The door behind her opened, revealing a New Town matron holding a bag of rubbish. She tutted as she walked past. 'This isn't public property, you know.'

Mona muttered an apology and moved swiftly in the direction of the restaurant. *Here goes nothing.*

The restaurant smelled of garlic and herbs. Her stomach growled; she'd been so busy worrying about the date she'd forgotten that she was actually hungry.

'Do you have a reservation?' The woman at the reception smiled at her.

'Eh, yes, it's in the name of Whyte?'

She looked at her list, and picked up a menu. 'Ah, yes, the other member of your party is already here.'

She walked on, her high heels clicking on the stone floor. Mona followed her, her heart bouncing around like an army truck on a potholed road.

There was a lone woman sitting at a table, her back to them. She had thick auburn hair, cut short. It stuck out at an angle that Mona found endearing. The woman swivelled round as she heard them approach. 'Mona?'

She nodded, her throat suddenly dry.

The waitress stood in polite silence while she lowered herself rather clumsily in to the seat. 'Can I offer you a drink?'

Elaine held her glass up, which was now only half-full. 'I recommend the rioja.'

Mona smiled mutely at the waitress, hoping that she recovered her voice before she looked like a complete idiot.

Her date took a large swig of her wine, then reached for one of the breadsticks that were in a little tub in the centre of the table. She slowly chewed her way through one, all the time staring at Mona in a manner that suggested she was slightly amused by the situation. Eventually she spoke. 'So, Mona, are you a regular Internet dater?'

'No, I'm really not.' She was relieved to find that she could still actually speak. 'In fact, I'm pretty nervous about the whole thing.'

'Me, too.'

Mona was surprised by this. She really wasn't getting an anxious kind of vibe from her date. 'You don't look nervous.'

Elaine leaned in, conspiratorially. 'Promise you won't judge me, but this isn't my first glass of wine this evening.' She laughed, then gently put her hand on top of Mona's. 'So, tell me everything about you.'

Mona was very aware of the pressure of Elaine's touch. She resisted the temptation to pull her hand away. 'Everything? I'm not sure there's much to tell.' Her wine arrived, and with her free hand she lifted the glass and took a very large gulp indeed.

'Oh, I'm sure that's not true, and by the end of the evening I intend to get it all out of you.'

There was something very reassuring about Elaine's voice. She had an overwhelming desire to confide in her, restrained only by a suspicion that there wasn't anything in her life that would be of interest to a stranger. She took another large swig of rioja. 'There's really nothing to tell.'

Elaine gave a mock sigh of frustration. 'OK, let's start with the easy questions. Brothers and sisters?'

She shook her head. 'Only one, I'm afraid.'

'And what did your parents do?'

'Dad, now dead, was a cop, Mum taught nursery school . . .'

And with that, she was off. Over the starter, they continued with her childhood. The main course covered her university years (Napier Uni, Business Studies, hadn't much enjoyed the whole student experience). Two crème brûlées arrived for pudding.

'And the HET, Mona?' Elaine gently hit the top of her pudding with a spoon. 'That must be fascinating?'

'Not really. CID was more interesting.' She peered at the debris on the table. Were they really onto their second bottle of red? 'And I'm fed up of the lack of resources we have at our disposal.'

'Oh yeah? What does it stop you doing?'

'Well, like at the moment we're looking for a missing civil servant, and it's really important that we find her as soon as possible, but there's only three of us actually looking for her . . .'

'I dare say a missing civil servant isn't a big crisis.'

'Yeah, but she's important in terms of Virus stuff, and her colleague has just committed suicide, so we need to find her. Anyway, I don't want to bore you with work.'

'It doesn't sound boring. I'm picturing you chasing bad

guys and wrestling them to the ground.' Her eyes flicked over Mona, as if she was imagining Mona doing just that. 'You look like you'd be very good at that kind of thing.'

'Do I?'

'Oh yes. I can imagine you spend a lot of time getting toned at the gym.'

Again her eyes flicked over her, and Mona felt a surge of lust, followed immediately by a dampener of fear. If Elaine wanted to see her gym-toned body she wasn't going to disappoint. But not tonight. She wasn't quite ready yet. Even if she had been ready, she was now so seriously drunk that she wasn't sure that she could deliver much in the way of bedroom gymnastics tonight. She wasn't entirely confident she could walk, never mind anything more energetic.

'You know what, Elaine? I've just realised I've rabbited on about me all night, but asked you next to nothing about you. Tell me about your life. I don't even know what you do for a living.' She grinned a little blearily. She felt bad for going on about herself, but there was something about Elaine that was so soothing, so familiar that she couldn't help but talk to her. It was like she'd been listening to her voice all her life. Maybe this was the way love felt, being so comfortable with someone that it felt like you already knew them.

'Mm.' Elaine picked up their bottle of wine and poured the last dregs of it into Mona's glass. 'Amongst other things, I write.'

'Would I have read any of your work?'

'Possibly.' She played with her empty glass. 'I mainly work on the radio these days.'

That voice. Somewhere in Mona's booze-befuddled brain the cogs started turning. *That ability to reassure, to get you to talk about yourself.* Elaine's voice sounded familiar because she'd heard it before. She'd heard her on the radio, but she didn't think she was the kind of presenter who played records, no, she was more . . . *Oh God.* The realisation of where she'd heard the voice before hit her. 'You're that DJ that hates everyone! What's your name again?' She snapped her fingers until it came to her. 'You're Cassandra Doom!'

'Guilty as charged.' She gave a little salute with the wine glass. 'Obviously not my real name. Sounds rather better than Elaine McGillvary though, I'm sure you'll agree.'

'Oh God.' Mona rested her head on her hands. 'What did I tell you about the HET?' She couldn't remember exactly what she'd said. Damn the alcohol.

'Relax, I'm off duty.'

Mona looked up at her. Was this true? Were right-wing shock jocks ever off duty?

'My boss would have a fit if he knew I was here. He hates you with a passion.'

'I get that a lot.'

She didn't look particularly upset. Which was more than could be said for Paterson if he ever found out about Mona's evening out. Cassandra Doom had devoted an entire programme to the HET and its infringement on citizens' inalienable rights to go around infecting their neighbours. She followed this up with a regular segment on the absurdities of HET activities across the country, supplementing her radio activity with a weekly column in the *Citizen*. Outraged as Paterson was by the HET comments, Mona suspected that there was a lot of common ground between the two of them on benefits claimants, policing, and the interference of the government in parenting.

'You didn't invite me on a date specifically because I work for the HET, did you?'

'Of course not! I invited you because you were by far the best-looking woman on the site.'

Mona eyed her suspiciously.

'If I'd invited you here just to get information about the HET, I wouldn't have admitted to who I am. This is full disclosure, Mona.' She reached across the table for her hand. 'Because I've really enjoyed tonight, and I'd very much like to see you again.'

'I'll think about it,' she lied. She reached into her purse, and threw some money on the table. She was sobering up fast. 'Work in the morning.'

She scuttled out of the restaurant, hoping to God that there was no way that Paterson, or even worse, Stuttle, could find out about her dining companion.

TUESDAY

POCKET FULL
OF POSIES

I

Bernard was back at his desk, after a very comfortable night's sleep. He'd enjoyed the luxury of sleeping in an actual bed, with clean sheets and a proper duvet. He'd retired to his room at a bedtime of his own choosing, after a peaceful evening which had involved no discussion whatsoever of *Star Trek*, *The Walking Dead*, or *Buffy the Vampire Slayer*.

If he was entirely honest with himself, the evening had dragged a little. Well, quite a lot actually. By eleven o'clock he'd found himself quite missing Marcus's prattling. The key to living alone, he speculated, was to keep yourself busy. Probably the best thing to do with a one-person flat was to spend as little time as possible actually alone in it.

He clicked on his first email, which came from a Police Scotland address. The message drew his attention to its attachment, a photograph of the suicide note left by Nathan McVie.

'Ooh.' He clicked eagerly on the icon, and was disappointed to find himself looking at a very brief scrawled note.

I'm not prepared to go on like this.
I quit.
Nathan McVie

Was it a suicide note? His money would be on a resignation letter, albeit not one that followed conventional best practice. The handwriting was appalling. He'd like to see a sample of McVie's normal writing, to establish if he was naturally messy, or whether this note had been written under duress. Or, of course, the last desperate scribblings of a man about to kill himself.

He checked the email again, and Police Scotland had definitely referred to it as a suicide note. He looked at the note again and shook his head. *I quit.* That was resignation talk, he was sure. But either way, whether McVie had been driven to self-murder or self-preservation, what had he been unwilling to continue to do?

'Morning, loser.' Maitland swept in with a grin. 'Look what I've got!' He held up a little floral book.

'A sudden fondness for Cath Kidson stationery?'

'Very funny. This is Helen Sopel's address book. Her sister was hanging around reception when I came in. She thought it might assist in our enquiries.' He flicked through it. 'Somewhere in here is the phone number of whatever young hunk it is that she's having it off with.'

'I still think that idea's nonsense. And even if she did have a boyfriend's number in her phone, I doubt she's got his address in there with little hearts drawn round his name.'

'The book's a good start.'

'I suppose. Can I help?'

'Your performance over the last nine months suggests that's unlikely.' Maitland smirked and threw himself onto his seat, picking up his phone as he went. 'You just carry on daydreaming.'

Bernard opened his mouth, then realised he didn't actually have a retort. He swivelled back to his computer and fumed. He'd tell Mona how annoying Maitland was being as soon as she got in.

'Hello, my name is Maitland Stevenson and I'm phoning from the Health Enforcement Team . . .'

Mona. He'd almost forgotten the discussion yesterday. The important thing was not to treat her any differently now that he knew that she was gay. Her sexuality was her own business, and nobody had the right to comment on it. He should probably remind Maitland of that fact before she arrived.

' . . .and I have to remind you that under the terms of the Defaulters Act (Scotland) you are not allowed to tell anyone that we are looking for Ms Sopel . . .'

Maitland caught his eye and made a dismissive gesture suggesting that he might want to turn round and mind his own business.

'Morning, Bernard. What's he up to?' Paterson lingered by his desk.

'Helen Sopel's sister dropped her address book off this morning. Maitland's ringing round the numbers in it.'

'Good stuff. Any sign of Mona yet?'

He shook his head.

'Mum's the word on that one, OK?'

'I'm not the one you have to worry about.' He jerked a thumb in the direction of Maitland.

'Fair point. And Carole?'

'Do you really think she'll be back?'

He grunted and walked into his office.

'Mr Paterson, I have a couple of questions.'

'Oh good.'

Bernard assumed this was sarcasm, but decided to press on regardless. 'Helen Sopel's sister is actively looking for her. Doesn't that make her a Missing Person rather than a Health Defaulter? Shouldn't this investigation be the remit of Police Scotland?'

Paterson raised an eyebrow in response.

Bernard was unsure if he got the point that he was trying to make. 'The HET is only supposed to investigate people who haven't been reported missing, as they are much more likely to be suffering from the Virus . . .you know, chaotic lifestyles and—'

'Stop.' Paterson raised a hand. 'I work for the HET, Bernard, I do know that.'

'You looked confused.'

'I was slightly confused by your naivety, that's all. OK, just so you are clear on all this, as of yesterday Helen Sopel is officially both a Missing Person and a Health Defaulter. It's a joint operation between the HET and the Police.'

'But . . .'

'Just let it go, eh, Bernard?'

Letting things go was not Bernard's strong point. 'But our terms of reference clearly say that we only investigate if the person hasn't been reported missing.'

'And Helen Sopel wasn't reported missing at 8.35am yesterday morning when I assume SHEP leapt into action and declared her a Health Defaulter.'

'Why did they . . .?'

'Bernard, close the door.'

He hesitated for a minute, trying to establish which side of the door he was supposed to be on as it closed. He gambled on inside, which, judging by the lack of shouting, appeared to be the correct choice.

'Bernard, I am now going to give you a crash course on how the world works. People of Helen Sopel's importance aren't left to their own devices about these things.

It's not like you or me defaulting. Someone like Ms Sopel misses a Health Check and the emergency telephone in Stuttle's office starts glowing bright red.'

'Really?'

'Not literally, no. But he'd get an early warning of it and make it HET business rather than Police Scotland.'

'But why . . .?'

'Why us and not Police Scotland? Easy. What was Maitland saying to all those people on the phone?'

He considered the question. 'That Helen Sopel was missing?'

'Not that. The Fourteen-Day Rule. Under the terms of the Defaulters Act (Scotland) you are not allowed to tell anyone that we are looking for blah blah blah. Soon as someone goes missing if the press gets a whiff of it they can start asking Police Scotland difficult questions. But if the fourth estate so much as hints that someone has missed a Health Check they're up in court. I wonder if the civil liberties types realised what a powerful tool they were giving to the likes of Stuttle when they pushed for a fourteen-day window of silence.'

'Why is it a powerful tool?'

'Oh, for God's sake, Bernard, don't you get it?' He sighed so heavily a sheet of paper blew gently off his desk. Bernard retrieved it.

'As soon as someone misses a Health Check it gives Stuttle and his cronies carte blanche to poke around in their life for two whole weeks without the general public getting to know about it. Let's them to do whatever . . .oh crap.'

Paterson was staring over Bernard's shoulder, looking out through the small glass window in his office door.

'Was that Carole just arriving, Mr Paterson?'

He sighed, and the sheet of paper was airborne once more. Bernard retrieved it again, and this time weighed it down with a coffee mug.

'Looks like it. Oh well, better get this over with.'

Carole looked up as the door opened, and the conversation she had been having with Maitland ground to an abrupt halt. Maitland grinned and slid back into his own seat. He caught Bernard's eye and winked, obviously delighted to be watching the showdown that was about to take place. Bernard felt rather less happy at the prospect.

'Carole,' said Paterson, with a somewhat forced joviality. 'I'd heard you were back. Feeling better, I hope?'

The look on her face would have driven lesser men to retreat to their office, lock the door firmly behind them and dig deep into their bottom drawer for the bottle of spirits they kept there for just such occasions. Paterson settled for folding his arms.

'Let's get one thing clear, Mr Paterson. I want to resign from the HET . . .'

'That's not actually possible . . .'

'I know. I want to resign, and I will resign. Right now I've got a lawyer talking to SHEP about it.'

'So, why are you here?' asked Bernard.

Carole turned her glare in his direction. 'Because, Bernard, my lawyer thought it would be a good idea if I carried on as normal, until he works out exactly how we can sue SHEP.'

'Well, obviously we're delighted that you're back.'

Paterson gave Carole a rictus smile, which appeared to infuriate her further. She threw her bag in the direction of her desk and followed it.

Undaunted, Paterson continued. 'Yes, it's good that we've got all hands on deck. We need to get this civil servant found pronto. Maitland – any joy from your ring round?'

'Not much. There were only six contacts in the address book, and only one person has seen her this year.'

'OK – you checking that out?'

'Yes.'

'Take Carole with you.'

She didn't turn round. 'I don't think so.'

Maitland and Bernard looked at each other, then at their boss.

After a minute he nodded. 'Probably best to ease yourself in. Bernard – you go with Maitland and...' He stopped as his phone buzzed. 'A text from Mona.'

Maitland burst into a chorus of 'I Am What I Am'.

Paterson looked up from his phone in annoyance. Bernard caught his eye. 'I told you it was him that you needed to worry about.'

Paterson retreated to his office, its walls wobbling as he slammed the door behind him.

2

Mona's whole body was aching. Her head was pounding, and she had a horrible queasiness in her stomach. Two bottles of wine on a school night were bad. She might have got away with it if she'd had a good night's sleep, but her slumbers had been dogged by anxiety dreams. In every one of them she was trying to keep a secret from someone. Sometimes it was her mother, or she was back at school and trying to pull the wool over a teacher's eyes. But mostly the dreams involved Paterson. Her subconscious was not overly subtle.

She must have been crazy to think that Internet dating was for her. You had no idea who anyone really was; people knocked years off their age, or forgot to mention they were married, or, as had happened last night, they completely lied about their motivation. And she had sat there, without taking the slightest time to find out who the woman really was, and had ended up spilling her heart out about the difficulties of working for the HET to a woman who made a career out of slagging them off. She hoped to God she hadn't handed her any ammunition, particularly any juicy snippets that could only have come from the North Edinburgh HET.

And now she was running half an hour late for work, and if the bathroom mirror was to be believed, she looked like a reanimated corpse. She leaned her head against the mirror and groaned. She needed to be well. She needed to get into the office and arrange a meeting with Jasper Connington, the other civil servant who had been at the Museum meeting. And she needed Connington not to act like civil servants usually did, but actually give her a straight answer to what their meeting had been about.

She washed her face, brushed her teeth and stared at her reflection in the hope it had improved. It hadn't. If anything, she looked even more obviously hungover than before. She twisted the lid off a bottle of mouthwash, and swigged it as enthusiastically as she had the rioja the previous night. It had just hit her tonsils when her landline started to ring. She considered just letting it ring; 90% of the calls on it were telemarketers, people enquiring if she'd recently had an accident and wanted to sue someone, fake IT engineers or other assorted scammers and crooks. Unfortunately the other 10% of calls came from her mother. She spat the bright blue liquid into the sink and raced to the phone.

'Mona.' Her mother sounded even frailer than usual. 'I don't want you to worry, but I'm at the hospital.'

'Oh my God, what happened?'

'I fell getting out of bed this morning. Got my foot caught in the blankets.'

'I'll come right over.'

'Don't be silly. You have your work to go to. I'll be fine.'

For a second Mona hesitated, then realised what was expected of her. 'I'll be right over.'

Forty-five minutes later she was sitting outside her mother's ward at the Royal Infirmary. Paterson had been fine about her taking an unexpected morning off. In fact, he sounded completely distracted when she'd spoken to him, leading her to wonder if Carole had turned up for work today. For all her boss's bluster and fury he tended to be flummoxed by female anger directed at him, although given his ability to piss women off, by his mid-fifties he really ought to be used to it. His main response when challenged by a female member of staff was to retire to his office and sulk. She had, in her time, been on the receiving end of many a Paterson huff.

'Ms Whyte?' A female doctor approached her, hand outstretched, and sat beside her on the plastic seats. 'I'm Dr Lewis. Your mother's had a bit of a fall, I'm afraid.'

Mona pictured the worst. 'Is she badly hurt?'

'No broken bones, but I think she's had a bit of a fright. Her ankle is rather swollen, so she's struggling to walk. She needs a good rest.'

'So you'll be keeping her in overnight?'

A look passed across the doctor's face which Mona tried to place. Embarrassment, mixed with something else. Determination? Defiance? 'Actually we were hoping that you could take your mother home now.'

So that was it. The chronic lack of beds meant that a cancer-stricken sixty-year-old was being turfed back out to fend for herself.

'Is she fit to go back home?'

'Not on her own. Could she stay with you?'

'I live in a second-floor flat. She struggles with my stairs even when she hasn't just fallen.'

'Could you stay at hers?'

Mona struggled to find a reason why this wouldn't be possible. She hesitated a moment too long and Dr Lewis stood up.

'Right,' she said. 'I'll get your mother discharged.

70

Would you like to borrow a wheelchair to get her to the car?'

'I suppose I'll need one,' snapped Mona, 'seeing as she can't actually walk.'

But Dr Lewis had already turned away, the look of embarrassment, determination, defiance or whatever, all replaced by one of relief. Another patient out the door.

'I know I shouldn't say this, Mona, now that you work for the Health Service . . .'

'I work for the Health Enforcement Team, Mum, not the NHS.'

' . . . but the NHS isn't what it was. That doctor back there took one look at my notes then thought, well, this one's going to die soon anyway, so we might as well kick her out and give the bed to someone with a fighting chance.'

'Don't say that, Mum.' Mona felt a pang of fear inside her as always when she thought about her mother's impending death. 'They just need the beds.'

'Well, I suppose you feel compelled to defend them, now that you're working for them.'

The fear she had felt a moment ago was edged out of the way by her usual feeling of irritation with her mother. 'I don't work . . .oh, you know what? Never mind.' She snapped the radio on.

'Your father, God rest his soul, would be horrified at the state of the NHS . . .'

She concentrated on the radio, trying to block her mother out. The last thing she wanted to think about under the circumstances was her father's death. She tuned her ear to Radio Scotland, which was broadcasting its hourly news bulletin. The headline was unusually

71

positive. Economic growth had risen for the first time in two years, albeit by a teeny tiny amount.

'The nurses on the night he died were superlative . . .'

Not listening not listening not listening. A new wind-farm was being built on the West Coast of Scotland.

'I was in pieces, with his heart attack being so sudden . . .'

The utility companies were defending their latest round of price hikes.

'Nobody was kicking us out the door back then . . .'

A senior civil servant working on Virus policy had been found dead in an apparent suicide.

Mona swerved the car over to the side of the road.

'What was . . .?'

'Ssh.' She pointed at the radio, but the newsreader had moved on to a jovial 'and finally' item. 'Did you hear that last item, Mum? Did they mention a name?'

'I wasn't listening, Mona, I was talking.'

'Mum, I'm really sorry about your accident, and please don't take this the wrong way, but I'm going to have to just get you settled in and go straight back to work.'

Her mother tutted. 'Of course, Mona. It's always about your work, isn't it? Just like your father.' She turned, pointedly, to look out the window. 'And look what happened to him.'

3

Silence reigned in the HET office. Paterson, Maitland and Bernard were huddled round one computer, while Carole was sat some distance away from them, scrolling through something on her mobile.

'Guv,' Mona panted, slightly out of breath after racing up from the car park. 'I heard on the radio that a senior Virus civil servant had committed suicide.'

Three heads snapped toward her.

'Did they give a name?' asked Paterson.

'No, Guv.'

'Then you know what we know. Brains here,' he tapped Bernard on the head, 'spotted it on the BBC website.'

'I get notifications,' said Bernard, 'whenever there's a story about the Virus.'

'So, he gets a notification thingy, and before I've even had time to look at the story, Stuttle's on the phone saying he's coming over, and bringing that lanky geek from IT with him.'

'Marcus? Why's he coming over?'

'How's your mother, Mona?' Carole looked up from her phone.

'Just a twisted ankle. Thanks for asking.'

'Well, I thought that someone should show an interest, seeing as it was clear that senior management had no interest whatsoever in your family crisis.' She gave a theatrical sigh. 'In my experience HET management have no interest at all in the pressures their staff are under.'

Paterson face turned puce. 'Of course I'm concerned about her mother, Carole.' He turned to her. 'She is OK, isn't she, Mona?'

'Fine, Guv. Do we know if . . .?'

'And I want to make it clear to everyone that I am *very* concerned about the personal well-being of all my staff.'

'Good stuff, Guv.' Maitland grinned. 'Maybe we should all share how we are feeling at the moment. Why don't you start by asking Mona about her love life? Is there some great big manly hunk that you are currently seeing?' He made a to and fro gesture with his arms that clarified what he meant by 'seeing'.

'I said I was interested in my staff's well-being, not their love life, Maitland. Mona's love life is entirely her own business.'

'Well said, Mr Paterson.' Bernard patted her on the shoulder. 'Totally private business.'

Her colleagues were being particularly idiotic this morning. 'Thanks for clarifying that, everyone, but can we focus on this?' She pointed at the BBC website. 'Do we know if someone has leaked the information about Nathan McVie's death?'

'That's the best-case scenario. Worst case, someone's found Helen Sopel's body.'

Footsteps could be heard in the hall, approaching at some speed. When Stuttle appeared in the doorway he was framed on one side by the tall, bespectacled Marcus and on the other side by Ian Jacobsen. Mona was used to seeing Stuttle looking stressed – you couldn't be head of an organisation fighting a Virus that had already killed 100,000 people in Scotland without having a few sleepless nights – but today he looked as if his head was close to exploding.

'Close the door behind us.'

Ian slammed it shut with his foot. Stuttle scowled at them, his eyes moving over each of them in turn. 'What are you fuckers playing at?'

Mona immediately flicked through the Filofax in her brain to see if she could have done anything to cause Stuttle's outburst. He wouldn't be happy if he knew about her dining companion from last night, and she'd definitely be under suspicion if someone had leaked information about Nathan McVie's death. Her memory of the night was hazy, but she couldn't remember referring to him. But then she couldn't remember much about the evening at all. Anyway, if it was specifically her he was annoyed with he'd come out and say it. He seemed to be blaming them collectively for something.

She cast an eye over her colleagues. Bernard was looking mildly panic-stricken, which could mean that he'd done something, but then that was his natural expression when there was work-related shouting going on. Maitland looked confused rather than guilty, but he could have done something and just be too wrapped up in himself to notice. Carole was smiling to herself, but it was unlikely that she'd had time to implement some devilish masterplan since yesterday. Which left the Guv . . .

'Well, one of you say something.'

Paterson sighed. 'Could you lose the attitude for a second, Cameron, and explain to us what it is that we're supposed to have done?'

'That!' Stuttle pointed at the computer, where the death of a civil servant webpage was still showing. 'And the Internet.'

75

'The Internet? We're responsible for that now, are we?' Paterson rolled his eyes. Mona winced. This really wasn't the time to wind Stuttle up.

'If I can interject?' Marcus pushed his little round glasses up to the bridge of his nose and smiled at them all. 'Mr Stuttle is talking specifically about the "What do they know" hashtag, which I'm sure you are all familiar with.'

Bernard nodded vigorously, and the rest of them looked at him in confused silence.

Marcus reassessed his audience. 'OK, let's start with hashtag. Does everyone know what a hashtag is and how they're used on Twitter?'

Four muted yeses were drowned out by a very loud no from Paterson.

Marcus walked over to the whiteboard, picked up a pen and drew a # sign.

'A hashtag. Usually found in front of a word or phrase.' He wrote #football and #community on the board. 'It helps you to search for posts on a particular theme on social media. If you search, for example, for the hashtag football one, it will bring up everyone who has used that,' he pointed to #football, 'in their tweet.'

'OK,' said Paterson, with a hint of uncertainty in his tone. Mona wondered if Paterson had ever actually strayed onto Twitter or Facebook. She suspected he would have some follow-up questions once they got shot of Stuttle.

Marcus wrote #WhatDoTheyKnow on the whiteboard. 'Now, hashtags are often used for political discussions, particularly on Twitter, and this one is used a lot with reference to the Virus.'

'What do they know?' Maitland frowned at the board. 'What do who know? About what?'

'A good question,' said Ian. 'I usually find that nobody knows anything.'

Marcus beamed. 'It's a kind of catch-all, if you like, for all kinds of conspiracy theories. Sometimes there will be a flurry of tweets suggesting that the Scottish Government already has a cure for the Virus which it is refusing to share, sometimes there are tweets suggesting that the Government knows that there is no cure for the Virus and is refusing to tell people. Sometimes it's SHEP and the HETs in the firing line, sometimes the NHS, sometimes Police Scotland. But the general thrust of it is that the public is not being kept informed. So, for obvious reasons we keep an eye on it and today it's been going crazy. So, I phoned Mr Stuttle to draw his attention to it, and he wanted to know . . .'

'Why bloody Twitter is full of information that I thought was confidential to this investigation? How did Twitter know about the civil servants' meeting at the Museum of Plagues and Pandemics? Answer me!'

'Wherever the leak came from, it won't be from here,' said Paterson, firmly. 'But before we get any further into this nonsense, can you at least tell us who they are talking about? Have they leaked the fact that Nathan McVie killed himself, or has Helen Sopel turned up dead?'

Stuttle glared at him as if he was crazy. 'It's neither of them. Jasper Connington was found dead in his bed this morning, with an empty bottle of pills on his bedside table.' He sank into a chair. 'Will somebody please tell me what the fuck is going on?'

4

'Do you ever think, Bernie, that we get the least interesting leads to follow up?'

They were in a pool car, heading to the Royal Bank of Scotland complex on the northern outskirts of Edinburgh. Maitland had insisted on driving, which suited Bernard just fine as it let him surf the Internet, while paying a minimal amount of attention to his colleague's chat.

'I mean, Mona's off with that Ian bloke following up the Connington suicide, and we're schlepping across town to chat to some woman from Sopel's address book who probably won't have anything useful to say to us, on account of not having seen her for months.'

'Is that so bad?' He looked up from his phone.

'Yes! Yet again we're doing the boring drudge work while Mona is off with the exciting leads!'

'I'm not sure how exciting going to see a recently bereaved man is going to be. He's probably still in shock after finding the body. I'm far happier going to see this friend of Ms Sopel's.' His eyes returned to his phone.

'What are you tapping away at?'

'I'm following the #WhatDoTheyKnow hashtag on Twitter. It's no wonder Mr Stuttle's annoyed.'

'Give me a flavour of it, then.'

'OK. Try this one. "What was purpose of Civil Service meeting? No minutes, agenda? #WhatDoTheyKnow".'

'That is actually a fair point. We don't know that either. But how does Twitter even know that there was a meeting?'

'Either someone found out about the meeting and tweeted about it, or they told someone else who did. And given the top-secret nature of our briefing with Mr Stuttle it would have to be someone either from the HET, which I'm assuming it isn't . . .'

'Of course not.'

'Or one of the participants, or someone who was close to them . . .'

'Not Helen Sopel, then, who doesn't seem to be close to anyone.'

'True. Or it could have been a member of the Museum staff?'

'Well, that can be one of our questions for them when we see them later. Hit me with another tweet.'

Bernard scrolled down until he found a good one. '"The Virus is man-made civil service caused this rot in hell #WhatDoTheyKnow." There are a lot of tweets on that particular theme. And we're coming in for a lot of stick too. "HET = Nazis going to kill us all #WhatDoTheyKnow".'

Maitland tutted. 'Why do people persist in thinking that the HET is trying to kill them?'

'I don't know. But they are very persistent in that view, and very vocal about it on Twitter. And then there are the crazies who want to get their retaliation in first. Listen to this one: "time that we killed these HET fuckers whos with me? #WhatDoTheyKnow". Honestly, the grammar and spelling in some of these tweets is appalling.'

'*What*? Did someone seriously write that – a death threat? Do you think we should tell Stuttle?'

Bernard wondered how much time Maitland had spent on Twitter. 'If we're going to tell him about that one, there's about another million he needs to consider as well.'

'Seriously?' Maitland swerved and came dangerously close to the wrong side of the road. A car on the other side beeped at him.

'For goodness' sake, Maitland, don't do the Internet's work for it and kill us both! And slow down – the turning we want is coming up.'

Muttering under his breath, Maitland turned the car on to the slip road with seconds to spare.

'Seriously, Bern, there are people on the Internet who want to kill us?'

Bernard was quite enjoying his colleague's distress. As soon as Maitland had got out of the car, he'd pulled his mobile out to check that Bernard wasn't winding him up about the tweets. Scrolling through them, he had sworn furiously under his breath as he took in the full range of hatred expressed for the HETs.

'Well, it would appear so, wouldn't it?' Bernard turned to the receptionist. 'We've got a meeting arranged with Martine Galloway.'

The receptionist directed them to the seating area to wait.

Maitland threw himself into the chair next to Bernard. 'Why aren't you more upset about this? What's happened to your usual nancy boy tendencies?'

'I'm cautious, I do not have "nancy boy tendencies".'

Maitland snorted.

'Anyway,' said Bernard, 'this is all just Internet noise. Twitter is full of fifteen-year-old boys pretending to be tough. And everyone's upset about the Virus so they're just mouthing off.'

'But there's so many of them! All it would take is one of them to actually follow through on the threat.'

'Maitland, you need to . . .'

'Excuse me, are you the people from the HET?' A woman was standing in front of them. She was in her mid-forties, with long hair with blonde highlights, and was wearing the uniform of female office workers across the world – a black trouser suit. 'I'm Martine Galloway – I believe you're looking for me?'

'Hi, I'm Bernard.' He stuck out a hand.

'Maitland, we spoke on the phone.'

She pointed to the entrance. 'Do you mind if we discuss this outside? I'd rather get away from work before we start.'

They followed Martine out of the building into the weak autumn sunshine. She led them through the green space that surrounded the buildings, following a narrow path alongside an artificial lake. They passed a number of empty benches, but she kept going until she was some distance from her office before sitting down.

'So,' said Bernard, 'when you spoke to my colleague on the phone you said you met up with Ms Sopel quite recently?'

'Well, not really *recently*. We met up a couple of days after my birthday, so it must be, God, over a month ago now.'

'You're good friends then?'

She gave a gentle laugh. 'I don't know – do good friends see each other more often than every couple of months? We're *old* friends; we've known each other since we were at primary school. So we do try to keep in touch – birthdays and Christmas – but I've got two little ones now, and Helen works all the hours God sends, so it's not easy.'

Maitland leaned across Bernard. 'Did Helen have a boyfriend?'

She looked away, staring out across the square expanse of water. 'Can you tell me again why you are asking all these questions about her?'

Maitland rested his pointy elbow on Bernard's leg while he explained that Ms Sopel had missed a Health Check, and gave her the necessary disclaimers. Bernard wondered if it would be considered unprofessional to push Maitland off the bench and into a flower bed. He settled for a gentle shove of Maitland's arm, which led Maitland to lean down harder.

'Are you absolutely sure that Helen missed a Health Check?' Martine was looking increasingly upset. 'I can't believe she would have. That would be her career over.'

She put her hand over her eyes, and Bernard grasped the opportunity to shove Maitland and his pointy elbow off him. 'We're really, really sure. And I know it is upsetting, Ms Galloway, but there is absolutely nothing to say that your friend has come to harm . . .'

'She must have done.' Her tone was flat and resigned. 'That's the only way she'd have missed her Check.'

'So,' said Maitland, 'did she have a boyfriend?'

'Oh, God.' She stood up. For a minute, Bernard thought she was going to run back to her office, but she just paced back and forth.

'It's an offence to withhold information that might be relevant to the retrieval of a Health Check Defaulter,' said Maitland.

'I know that! Stop trying to bully me, I'm trying to think.'

Bernard looked over at Maitland, who winked at him.

This woman knew something significant. And judging by her reaction to his question about Helen Sopel's love life, the horrible prospect loomed that Maitland might have been right all along.

'We could discuss this further at our offices – do you need to make some childcare arrangements because it might take a while?' Maitland stood up as well.

'I don't want to get into trouble.' She looked at Bernard. 'But I don't want to get anyone else into trouble either.'

'Was Helen having an affair?'

After a moment's pause, she spoke softly. 'I think so.'

'Can you give us her boyfriend's name?'

She didn't answer, staring again in the direction of her office.

'Right,' Maitland took her by the arm. 'You're going to have to come with us.'

'No,' she shook her arm free, 'I can't help you because I don't know his name.' She sat down next to Bernard, focusing solely on him. 'This is very difficult.'

'Take your time.'

'OK, right.' She took a deep breath. 'When I met up with Helen, she was really down about something. I thought she was seeing someone, so I asked her about him, and how it was going. And she kind of got really angry, you know? At first I thought she was angry with me for asking, I mean, it was none of my business but she's my oldest friend and I was worried about her.'

'Obviously. Anyone would be in that situation.'

'Yeah. After a minute or two she calmed down and said she wasn't angry with me, but she was really fed up with someone she was involved with, said she hated him, in fact, but that he was someone very well connected and she was afraid what might happen if she told him to get lost.'

'"Well connected"? What does that mean?'

'I don't know really, I didn't push it at the time. I mean, she works with politicians all the time, so I assumed it was someone from that kind of world.'

'But she didn't tell you who it was?'

'No.' She shook her head. 'I did ask, but she totally clammed up.'

'Well, thank you for sharing that with us. We'll look into it and be back in touch.' He stood up. 'We'd better let you get back to work.'

To Bernard's surprise, she didn't move. Given her reluctance to speak to them, he thought she'd be back to her desk like a bullet from a gun.

'There's something else.'

'OK.' He lowered himself back down.

'Helen phoned me the next day, apologising for being so grumpy. Of course, I told her to forget it, what are old friends for and all that. Then she said she needed a favour. She said she wanted to give me a box of things to look after. She said it was her insurance policy, and if she ever got into trouble she'd phone me and tell me what to do with it.'

'But she's not been in touch?'

'No, but she was obviously worried that something was going to happen to her. And I think,' she started to cry, 'maybe something has.'

She buried her head in her hands, and wept. Bernard put a comforting arm round her shoulders, and she leaned her head against him. Over the top of it, he could see Maitland shimmying from side to side in a victory dance. Maitland smiled at him and punched the air.

For the first time in his life, Bernard found himself sharing an emotion with an Internet troll. He could kill Maitland.

84

5

There was a young police officer standing guard at the entrance to Jasper Connington's block of flats.

'Stop here!' Ian tapped the dashboard. 'I'll see what the plod's got to say about things, while you find somewhere to dump the motor.'

Mona waited until the second the car door was shut then drove off at speed, hoping that Ian would take the hint. She was nobody's chauffeur, nobody's dogsbody, just there to park the car and get the bacon rolls in. She was starting to pine for her investigations with Bernard. When she worked with him she got to boss him around, and he was grateful for the direction. This supposed 'joint' investigation by CID and the HET didn't feel like a partnership. It felt more like CID investigating and the HET providing transport, office space, and the occasional cup of coffee.

By the time she found a parking space, Ian had completed his interrogation of the PC, and was waiting impatiently for her on the pavement. He gestured in the direction of the cop. 'He says the ambulance has been and picked up the body. There was a suicide note, which someone is going to scan and send to us, but apparently all it said was "sorry" and "I love you" so no great revelations there. And, he says he's been warding off journalists all morning, though most of them buggered off once the body was picked up.'

'Not surprising, I suppose, given that it's such a secret that it's been on the BBC website. Though I don't understand how it's made the news so quickly. Who told them?'

He shrugged. 'Who knows who Connington's partner phoned when he found the body? One of his so-called friends could have been straight on to the press. Or he could have phoned them himself. I doubt it was a leak. Not like someone from the HET shouting their mouth off about the meeting at the Museum.'

Fury engulfed her. 'That was nothing to do with the HET.'

'You're sure about that? Couldn't have been the disaffected staff member who's desperate to resign, or the one who is too young and self-absorbed to know any better, or the one who is so naïve he'd tell anyone anything if they asked nicely?'

'No.'

He smiled, a lazy, infuriating grin. 'Oh, well. Must have been you then.'

'Oh, fuck off.' She stormed into the building with a cursory nod at the PC, who shot her a nervous smile in return. As she marched up the stone stairs she tried to get her temper under control, mindful that in a few seconds' time she'd have to face the poor man who'd just lost his partner.

Jasper Connington's husband was slumped on his sofa.

'We're sorry for your loss, Mr Keaton.'

He was red-eyed and blank. Mona was pretty sure he was in shock. Fortunately, he wasn't on his own. A woman in her sixties was next to him, a protective arm draped around his shoulder.

'And, miss, can I ask who you are?'

'I'm Joyce Miller, Colin and Jasper's next-door neighbour. At least . . .' The unspoken past tense hung in the air. Colin Keaton rubbed at his forehead, his fingers going back and forth as his eyes fixed on a distant point across the room. Mona wondered if the paramedics had given him the once-over.

'Mr Keaton, could you tell us what happened this morning?'

He took a deep breath. For a moment Mona thought he wasn't going to speak, but he rallied and began. 'I was working all night – I'm a theatre nurse. We had a bad night of it, dealing with an RTA. A young driver with head injuries was brought in about 2am. We worked on him for about four hours but in the end it was no good, he'd taken too much of a hit.' He stopped and rubbed his forehead again. 'It was after eight when I got in so I was surprised to see Jasp still in bed. I thought he'd be long gone. He usually tries to get into the office by seven thirty at the latest. I thought he was ill, but when I went in,' his voice faltered, 'I could see vomit on his front.'

'Do you have to ask all this right now?' Joyce's tone was belligerent, which Mona thought was probably partly a cover for her grief.

'Sorry, ma'am, but we do. Mr Keaton, was Mr Connington still breathing when you found him?'

'He was cold.' His voice was flat. 'I screamed and Joyce came to see what was going on.'

'I'm so sorry, Mr Keaton, I understand this must be very distressing to talk about. Is there any chance that Mr Connington's overdose was accidental?'

'Accidental?' For the first time since they'd arrived, Colin Keaton looked directly at her. 'Jasp is – was – a nurse before he joined the civil service. He knew exactly what he was doing. He must have taken the tablets as soon as I left for work. He wasn't taking any chances of being found, he knew he'd be dead by the time I found him.'

'Surely you've asked enough questions now.' Joyce looked ready to punch someone, and Mona couldn't blame her. She must have had the shock of her life this morning.

'I'm sorry, just a couple more. The pills that Mr Connington took, what were they?'

'Anti-depressants. They were on prescription.'

'Had he been taking them long?'

'I didn't know that he was on them. He didn't tell me.'

'But you knew he was depressed?'

'I don't know, maybe, I suppose. I knew he was worrying about work, but I couldn't get him to talk to me about it. I should have tried harder.' He started rubbing his forehead again. 'I don't understand. I don't understand any of this.'

The phone rang.

'That may be a journalist,' said Ian.

'Yes,' said Joyce, 'the bastards have been phoning all morning.'

Mona pitied the journalist that got Joyce on the other end of the phone.

'How do they even have our number?' asked Colin. 'We're ex-directory because of Jasp's job.'

Mona reckoned it would take any hack worth his salt five minutes tops to locate an ex-directory number. 'Journalists have their ways, Mr Keaton.'

'But how do they even know about Jasp's death? The

only people Joyce and I spoke to were the ambulance service. Who told the press?'

That was a question she couldn't answer.

'That was odd,' Ian was absent-mindedly tapping the dashboard, which was putting her off her driving.

'What was? And please stop doing that.'

'Sorry.' He grinned, not altogether apologetically. 'The anti-depressant thing. If my wife was on them, I'd know about it.'

'People who are depressed can be secretive, you know, put on a brave face. For a man in his job there's probably a lot of stigma to saying that you can't cope with the stress of work. I mean, he was pretty near the top of the tree when it came to Virus stuff. He must have been under a ridiculous amount of pressure.'

'True. Not sure I could have done his job. But we only have Keaton's word for it that the depression was related to the job. Maybe it was something closer to home. Maybe he was unhappy in his marriage? Or was having an affair and couldn't cope with the guilt?'

'Possibly. Guilt does drive people crazy. But I'm still finding it a bit too much of a coincidence that he topped himself so soon after Nathan McVie jumped, and Helen Sopel went missing. I'd love to know what went on at that meeting at the Museum.'

'Well, there is someone we can ask.'

'Carlotta Carmichael?'

'We'd better speak to Stuttle.'

6

'I wonder what's in the package that Martine Galloway has for safekeeping,' said Bernard. 'Maybe it's a semen-stained dress, like Clinton.'

'Ew, yuck.' Maitland's expression moved from disgust to confusion. 'Why would Hilary Clinton have a semen-stained dress?'

'Not Hilary! Bill!'

Maitland face did not look any less confused by this explanation.

'How old are you, Maitland?'

'Twenty-four.'

Bernard sighed. 'Never mind, it's all ancient history to you.'

'Anyway, we'll know when Ms Galloway drops off the stuff. Although if there are any dresses in there, you can be in charge of examining them.'

'We're nearly there. It's this turning.'

Maitland sighed. 'Well, the trip to see Ms Galloway turned out to be a lot more interesting than I expected, but I'm pretty sure this is going to be dull as f . . .'

'Maitland! A visit to the Plague Museum is never, ever, dull.'

'You really are a sad little man.'

The Edinburgh Museum of Plagues and Pandemics occupied a full three-storey townhouse in Edinburgh's

90

New Town. It was rare to encounter a townhouse that hadn't been subdivided, and rarer still to find one which had been in the same hands since 1863. The Plague Museum, as everyone called it, had been established by a hefty donation from Archibald Cunninghame Esq, a childless chemist. His will, much to the annoyance of his many cousins, had left his entire estate to the establishment of a museum focusing solely on infectious diseases. After a brief sojourn on Leith Street, the Museum had moved to its current premises in the New Town, and with the exception of the interruption of a couple of world wars, had remained open ever since.

Bernard followed Maitland up the broad stone steps, which were lined on each side by a row of pot plants.

'I love this place,' he said happily.

'I know, you're a member, you said.'

'It's the attention to detail that I love. I mean, these plants, for example, they're not just any old pot plants, they're *plague* pot plants.'

Maitland put his hands together as if he was praying. 'Please God, don't let Bernard launch into a long explanation of the significance of the potted plant in tackling the plague.'

Bernard was an atheist. 'Can't you smell the lovely fragrance coming off them? Back in the seventeenth century people thought the plague was caused by a miasma of bad air. People started carrying around Plague Bags filled with herbs and sweet-scented plants because they thought it would protect them.'

'Is that nursery rhyme not supposed to be about the plague? A pocket full of posies and we all fall down, that one.'

'Actually, that's an urban myth.'

91

'Oh.' Maitland looked almost disappointed. 'Thought I knew a Bernard-type fact there. Anyway, the only plants I am interested in are the ones that can be harvested, dried and smoked.'

'Maitland.' Bernard was horrified. 'You're a former policeman. You can't advocate the smoking of illegal drugs.'

He grinned. 'Even the Police don't ban tobacco. What drugs were you thinking about, you badass?'

Bernard remained silent.

'Shall we go in, badass?'

'Shut up.' He pushed the front door. 'Oh, it's locked.'

Maitland pointed to a sign entitled 'Opening Hours'. 'They close at three on a Tuesday.'

'I phoned ahead, though. There should be someone here.' He pressed the ornate Georgian bell, and a deep dong sounded somewhere in the heart of the building. After a second or two's delay, the door opened a crack, and a female face peered nervously out.

'Are you the gentlemen from the Health Enforcement Team?'

'Yes. We're here to see Corinna McFarlane.'

The door opened a little further. 'She's not here.'

Maitland slowly but firmly pushed the door open and stepped into the entrance hall. Bernard followed him. It was a tight fit, due to a pile of brown cardboard boxes that stood as tall as he was. He looked at the labels on them. *Ebola. Yellow Fever. Crimean-Congo Haemorrhagic Fever.* With a shudder he stepped as far into the room as possible.

'What do you mean she's not here?' Maitland scowled. 'My colleague phoned ahead to arrange a time that was suitable to meet with her.'

Bernard looked at the woman. She was thirtyish, with long lank hair, and an unfortunately large nose. She was looking extremely uncomfortable at Maitland's questioning.

'Yes, I know, but something came up so she had to go out and she asked me to help you and,' she paused for breath, 'I'm Lucy, by the way.' She stuck out a hand. Bernard shook it. It was warm and moist to the touch. 'The assistant curator.'

Maitland also shook Lucy's hand, then rubbed his palm less than discreetly on his trousers. 'Well, you'll have to do, but tell your boss we're not impressed about her absence. Hindering the search for a Health Defaulter is a criminal offence, you know.'

Lucy's eyes almost popped out of her head. 'I'm sure Corinna isn't . . .' She stopped, confused. 'Who's missed a Health Check? Not Corinna?'

'No, and we don't need to go into all of that.' Bernard glared at Maitland, who was throwing his weight around rather more than Bernard thought was necessary. 'It can wait until we catch up with Ms McFarlane. But there is something you could do to help us – could we have sight of your meeting room booking diary? Or your online calendar, or whatever it is that you use.'

'Oh, I can do that.' She ducked behind the reception desk, reappearing with a large, leather-bound book. 'It's paper, I'm afraid. Some of our older volunteers are quite resistant to technology.' She dropped it onto the counter, where it landed with a thud that echoed around the room.

Maitland immediately started flicking through it. Bernard caught Lucy's eye. She smiled back, a full and, he thought, guileless smile which made her look quite pretty.

'Is it a particular meeting you're looking for?'

As she stepped toward Maitland, Bernard took the opportunity to shoot a glance at her ring finger, which was gratifyingly bare.

'We're looking to see how often there was a meeting of a group of civil servants in your premises.'

'Do you mean the meetings organised by Nathan McKie?' Her face clouded over. 'Poor Nathan.'

'You knew him?'

'Only through Corinna. He's an old university pal of hers. Nathan came to all the fundraisers that we held for the Museum, and I used to chat to him. He was a lovely man. And of course, I sometimes met him when he came here for meetings.'

'So he was Corinna's friend?' said Maitland. 'Boyfriend? Or just good friend?'

'Friend,' she said, firmly.

Maitland returned to leafing through the bookings journal. 'I'm not finding any Scottish Government meetings here.'

'Really?' She gently eased the book back out of Maitland's hands. 'Oh, I see the problem here. Corinna's been a bit lax noting who was meeting here. See.' She pointed at an example. 'Wherever she's booked the room, she's just written "Corinna" instead of saying who the meeting was for. Which will make it very difficult for us to know how many sessions to charge them for.'

'You'd charge the Scottish Government for using the room?'

'I assume so – we charge everyone else who books them. Corinna deals with all the finance stuff, so you'd really have to ask her. We're a small museum, and every penny counts. Although . . .'

'What?'

'Well, I hope I'm not talking out of turn, but I get the impression that we don't seem so badly off financially this year. I've been here coming up for five years, and a big part of my role has been organising fundraisers, you know, after-hours events, or membership drives. But Corinna hasn't even asked me to apply for any grant funding this year, never mind organise fundraisers.'

'But we'd have to ask Corinna about that?'

'Yes, absolutely.'

'OK, one last thing. Seeing as the book can't tell us, could you estimate how frequently the civil servants met here?'

'Maybe every couple of weeks, for the last six months? But they usually met in the evening, so I only saw them if I was still at work.'

'Well, thank you, Lucy, for your assistance,' said Bernard.

'Such as it was,' muttered Maitland.

Lucy's smile faltered. 'I'm sorry that your journey wasn't more useful. Can I offer you a tour of the Museum to make up for it?'

'What have you got in there?' asked Maitland. 'Any two-headed dogs or anything like that?'

She looked confused. 'We're an infectious diseases Museum, why would we have a two-headed dog?'

'So, no deformed animals of any kind then?'

'Please ignore my colleague,' Bernard stepped in. 'He's a philistine. He's confusing the concept of a museum with that of a freak show. I'm, ehm, I'm actually a member of the Museum.'

'Are you?' She beamed. Her smile really did make a huge difference to her looks. 'Would you like the full "behind the scenes" view?'

'I'd love to . . .'

Maitland coughed, noisily.

Bernard sighed. 'But I'd better get back to the office.'

'Maybe some other time, then? When you're not so busy.'

'I'd like that. Ehm, take my card, just in case, you know, your boss wants to contact us, or anything like that. Or if you have any questions. Anything at all, in fact.'

'Tell your boss we will be back to see her,' said Maitland, sternly.

Bernard smiled to himself as they exited the Museum, retracing their steps past the sweet-smelling plants.

'I saw that, you know,' said Maitland.

'Saw what, exactly?'

'You slipping Lucy your business card . . .'

'That was legitimate HET . . .'

' . . .and seeing as she's got a big nose and a bad hairdo, you might even be in with a chance.'

'Shut up!' He felt irrationally annoyed at Maitland's comments. 'I did not "slip her my business card", it was a work thing.'

'Whatever. Badass.'

The stairs that led up to their office were blocked by the large and unmoveable shape of Marguerite. Marguerite was by far the most outgoing of the team of admin assistants that the HET shared with the other departments in their building. Although 'outgoing' was only one way of describing her personality. Loud, might be another, or perhaps opinionated. She tended to hold forth on a narrow range of subjects including soap operas, pop music, hairstyles, make-up, nail art, ineffective diets and the best place in Edinburgh to get cheaply and efficiently drunk on a Saturday night. Suffice to say, Bernard had not yet encountered much common ground with her.

'Well, you pair made in back just in the nick of time.'

'What?' Maitland ground to a halt.

'Another five minutes and I'd have been out of here. Kev's got us tickets for the cinema tonight, and you know what he said last time I turned up late?'

'Marguerite . . .' began Bernard, hoping to head off one of Marguerite's very long tales about her boyfriend's shortcomings.

'He said if he'd had to wait for me to turn up late again, he was going in and I could pay for myself. Get that – pay for myself!'

'OK, but we're kind of busy . . .'

'So, I was planning to leave here at 4.30pm so that I could get home, have a bath, do my . . .hoi!'

Maitland had had enough of listening to Marguerite's plans for the evening and shoved her out of the way. She tutted, and manoeuvred herself more firmly in the way of Bernard.

'Please let me past.'

'I can't. I've got a parcel for you.'

Maitland ran backwards down the steps until he was level with her. 'From Martine Galloway?'

'Yes. And she made me promise I would deliver it *personally* into your hands. I said she could wait if she wanted, but she was a bit, you know, nervous or something and she said she'd just leave it with me. Made me give her a receipt and everything. So, that's why I'm still at work instead of halfway through a nice relaxing bath.'

Maitland threw an arm around her shoulder, and kissed her noisily on the cheek. 'Marge, that Kev doesn't know how lucky he is. You are truly an angel fallen to earth.'

'Tell that to Kev when I'm late. Anyway, the parcel's hidden under your desk.'

Maitland took the stairs two at a time. Keen to not miss out, Bernard ran after him.

'Thanks, Marguerite,' he called over his shoulder. 'Have some popcorn on us!'

'So, what is all this crap?'

Maitland had unloaded the contents of the box onto his desk, none of which, thankfully, were items of clothing with traces of the DNA of Helen Sopel's mystery boyfriend. The three items in the box had been set out across Bernard's desk.

On the left-hand side, there were several pages of itemised calls relating to a Virgin mobile. Someone had gone through the phone bills and highlighted a particular recurring number with a fluorescent pink pen.

In the centre of the desk, resting lightly on the computer's keyboard, was a face mask, which looked to Bernard like some kind of Native American folk art. It was painted black on one side and a powdery white on the other, and the mouth of the mask was distorted to one side. When Bernard picked it up, he was surprised at how light it was. He'd guessed it was reproduction, rather than the real thing.

On the far right, there lay a black-and-white photocopy of a photograph of a woman. She was wearing a full-skirted, knee-length dress, decorated with a floral print. This was topped off with a short, boxy jacket, and a hat. Her fashion sense placed the picture firmly in the 1950s.

'I don't know what it all means, Maitland, but I still think we should have waited until Mr Paterson was here before we opened this up. And shouldn't we be wearing gloves or something? Not getting our fingerprints all over it?'

'Relax, this is the HET, not a CID investigation.'

'But I thought this was a joint investigation with Police Scotland?'

Maitland stopped flicking through the papers. 'Oh, I suppose it is.' He pulled his jumper over the end of his fingers, and continued flicking. 'But finding Helen Sopel's important. We can't wait for the Guv or that Ian bloke to personally OK our every move.'

'But . . .'

'Shut up and look at this. These bills are all for Helen Sopel's phone, and she's highlighted the same number over and over. Do you reckon this is lover boy's mobile?'

In spite of his misgivings, Bernard focused in on the paperwork. 'It could be, couldn't it? We should probably ask Mr Paterson what to do with it.'

'Yeah, but he's not here, is he? And we could be wasting valuable time sitting on our hands, waiting for a grown-up to come along and say it's OK for us to play with our toys. I say we seize the day.'

'Oh, I really don't know about this.'

'Stop being such a wuss. I'm phoning it.'

Bernard opened his mouth to protest further, and for want of a half-decent argument closed it again. Maitland was right that they were wasting time, and if he was completely honest with himself, he was dying to know who Helen Sopel had deemed important enough to highlight to her best friend in an open-in-an-emergency package.

Maitland grinned at him, then punched the number into his phone. His expression froze, and he ended the call, dropping his phone onto his desk as if it was on fire.

'Shit, Bernie. We are so screwed.'

7

Stuttle was wearing a very sharp suit and appeared to have spent the last hour bathing in aftershave, if the smell permeating his office was anything to go by. Mona had to try very hard not to cough every time a whiff of it wafted in her direction. Stuttle sat behind his huge mahogany desk with an expression that suggested he was very annoyed to have his evening interrupted by the North Edinburgh HET. On the other side of the desk were Paterson, Mona, Ian and Bernard, with expressions that ranged from mild exasperation to heightened fearfulness.

'So, the gang's all here then? Where's the one that's threatening to sue me?'

'Carole?' said Paterson. 'She left the HET on the dot of five o'clock, and persuaded Maitland that he should do the same. She's not a very good influence on that lad at the moment.'

'All very interesting, but can you cut to the chase of why you all absolutely had to see me? I've got twenty minutes until I'm due at the Sheraton for a charity event . . .'

Mona turned to look at Bernard. She knew he'd be intrigued by this, as he was a strong supporter of charity. He'd be desperate to know which particular charitable endeavour Stuttle was a supporter of, but at the same time his fear of the SHEP boss was strong. Would curiosity or nerves win?

Bernard's mouth opened. 'Which one?'

'What?'

'Er, which charity?'

'I don't know, Bernard.' He waved a sheet of paper at them. 'I've not even had time to read the briefing notes yet. All I know is that I want to be there sharp at seven, eat whatever over-cooked, mass-produced hotel food I'm offered, say how strongly SHEP supports whatever charitable endeavour I'm actually at, then get home to Mrs Stuttle. So whatever supposed crisis involves all four of you being in my office, can you make your ask, I'll say no, then we can all get on our way.'

Ian smiled. 'I'll go first, shall I? There were four people at the meeting at the Museum, two are dead and one is missing . . .'

'And you want to talk to Carlotta Carmichael? Well, you can't. She's currently on a fact-finding mission to Tallin, Estonia, in the company of a range of health service staff, several trade and industry bods and her ever-loving husband, Jonathon.'

Paterson looked curious. 'Do you memorise her calendar so that you know where she is at any given time?'

Stuttle snorted. 'In my position, wouldn't you? Anyway, she's back tomorrow. I'll get something sorted. Shouldn't be a problem as we have a legitimate reason. What do you want to get out of the meeting with her?'

'We want to know what they talked about in their un-minuted meeting.'

'Yes, you, me and the whole of Twitter wants to know that, but I wouldn't bank on her telling you anything. There's always a danger that she turns up with her lawyer as well, who I think she's got on bloody speed dial, by the way. But I trust you guys not to mess it up. OK, who's next?'

Everyone turned to look at Bernard. 'Right, ehm, OK . . .'

'Clock is ticking, Bernard. The sick children slash animals slash historic buildings are waiting.'

'OK, right, Helen Sopel's best friend thought that she was having an affair, and was worried about this. She left a package with her friend in case anything bad happened . . .'

He looked intrigued. 'Like Monica Lewinsky and her dress?'

'Exactly like that! In that package was a selection of Ms Sopel's phone bills all with the same number highlighted.'

'The boyfriend's number?'

'We assumed so. So we phoned it and . . .'

The room was suddenly very silent.

'Jonathon Carmichael answered.'

Stuttle stared at him. Without taking his eyes off Bernard's face he reached over and picked up his phone. 'Katherine? Can you put in my apologies for that charity thing? Something's come up.'

8

Bernard trudged wearily in the direction of his new flat. The day had been exhausting, although not altogether unsatisfying. Professionally, it was disappointing that they didn't seem to be any closer to tracking down Helen Sopel, although on a positive note there was nothing in their investigation that suggested they'd be finding her body imminently, with or without a suicide note. On a personal level, he felt a modicum of pride in how he'd handled himself today. Maitland hadn't been barking completely up the wrong tree about him passing his business card to Lucy. He had pulled off something not a million miles away from asking a woman out, and he had a pretty much open invitation to go back to the Museum. After all he *was* a member.

He had also got all the way through a meeting with the supremely scary Mr Stuttle without humiliating himself, which was more than could be said for Maitland, who really ought to have been there. After all, he had been the one who made the call. But Carole had appeared when they were debating what to do, and persuaded Maitland that his best option was to clock off at five and worry about it in the morning. When Bernard had protested, she'd told him he was a jobsworth and flounced out, a grinning Maitland hot on her heels. So, it had been left to Bernard to phone Mr Paterson, who'd laughed solidly for a full minute when he'd explained about Jonathon Carmichael, before telling him to 'get his arse along' to the meeting with Stuttle.

And now, at long last, he was heading home, a bag of mixed vegetables in his hand. In round about fifteen minutes he'd have a lovely stir-fry to eat in front of whatever tonight's documentary was on BBC4. Or maybe he'd spend a while hunting for the *Guide to the Edinburgh Museum of Plagues and Pandemics* that he'd bought on one of his earlier visits. He'd familiarise himself with their range of exhibits, just in case, well, you know.

He turned onto the driveway for his flats, and was so lost in his thoughts that he didn't see a figure detach itself from the shadows and step toward him.

'Bernard.'

He jumped a good six inches in the air, his shopping bag swinging against his knees.

'I need to talk to you.'

'Now?'

'Now.'

For a man who was desperate to talk, Bryce was taking a long time to say anything. He'd remained stumm all the way up the stairs, then sat silently in the living room while Bernard made them both tea. As Bernard plonked a mug of tea in front of his mute friend, he decided to hurry matters along a little. He'd like to get the stir-fry cooked and eaten, and still have a good long bath before bed.

'You needed to talk?'

This provoked a long sigh, and a burst of head-shaking. 'This just feels really, you know, disloyal?'

'Are we talking about Marcus?'

'I probably shouldn't say anything . . .'

Bernard resisted the temptation to agree. He sneaked a look at his watch. He'd have to forget about the bath. At this rate he'd be eating his tea in front of *Newsnight*, while the next hour was going to be spent dragging information piece by piece from Bryce, information that he wasn't sure he even wanted in the first place.

'No!' Bryce banged a fist on the table, making Bernard jump for the second time that evening.

'No?'

His friend seemed to be having some kind of argument with himself that Bernard wasn't party to. At least he appeared to have come to some decision.

'I've decided. I have to speak up.' He took a deep breath. 'I think Marcus is in trouble.'

'What kind of trouble?'

'I think he's got himself addicted to online gambling.'

'Really?' Bernard couldn't imagine Marcus doing anything quite that stupid.

'I'm afraid so.' Bryce gave a sad shake of his head. 'He invented what he described as "an infallible system for winning" at online roulette, based on what he thought were predictabilities in the programme's algorithms.'

That did sound more like Marcus. 'And was it infallible?'

'Nope. And he's lost a fortune, used up all his overdraft and maxed out his credit cards.'

Bernard sighed. 'That's really, really stupid.'

'You don't have to tell me. But what really worries me, is that I think he's still gambling.'

'How? He can't have any money.'

'Well, possibly.' Bryce looked uncomfortable. 'Marcus and I, as you know, spend a lot of time in different forums, and every so often we may, carelessly, let slip that we work for the government.'

'That's super stupid.' Bernard redoubled his sighing and added a tut for good measure. 'And could probably get you both sacked.'

'Probably. But we don't use our real names, obviously, or say anything that could identify us.'

This still sounded ridiculously risky to Bernard. He never told anyone he worked for the HET if he could possibly avoid it, although to be fair, that was less about security and more about the ever-present worry that he would be ranted at about the HET's infringement of civil liberties.

'And from time to time people make approaches to us, offering us money for information . . .'

'Who?' It was news to him that they had anything worth selling. 'Why?'

'The why varies with the who. We get approached by people who want to sell IT services to SHEP, people who are looking for evidence to undermine SHEP, conspiracy theorists who want to know what's really going on, journalists . . .'

Bernard thought about the recent leaks at the HET. 'You think he might . . .be tempted?'

'I'm afraid that there's a very real possibility that he's already given in to temptation.'

Bernard slumped back in his chair. 'What can we do? Should I speak to him?'

'No.' Bryce shook his head vigorously. 'He'd only deny it. I'm going to try to keep track of what he's up to but if you notice anything untoward at work, try and cover for him.'

'I'm not sure I can do that,' said Bernard, doubtfully.

106

He wasn't sure that ethically he was prepared to cover for someone who might be leaking HET secrets. More practically, he wasn't sure that he had the deceptive ability to participate in a cover-up. His woeful inability to lie convincingly was one of the many things that Maitland berated him about.

'He's our friend, Bernard. We need to try to help him.'

'I know, but . . .'

'At the very least can you tell me if you spot any leaks, or anything else that? And let me know if you think Paterson or Stuttle are on to him? Then I've got a chance to warn him, if nothing else.'

He sighed. 'OK.'

9

There were three missed calls on Mona's mobile, all of them from Elaine. Hell would freeze over before she phoned her back. For all that she'd met Elaine on a dating site, she was and remained, a member of the press. There was only one reason that a journalist would be getting in touch with her – she would be making contact to see if she could get any more gossip out of Mona about the current state of the HET, and God knows she'd already been indiscreet enough. If she got out of this without providing featured content for a Cassandra Doom column she'd be lucky.

'Do you want a cup of tea, Mona?' Her mother's voice drifted up to her. 'I'm putting the kettle on.'

'No, thanks.'

An hour ago she'd sat through a full meal of pork chops, roast potatoes and veg, followed by apple tart and custard. There was a vague feeling at the back of her mind that this might have been her favourite meal at some point in her childhood. She'd been touched by her mother's efforts, particularly given the current state of her health, but had also been extremely keen to get back to her room to plan what she was going to do next. It would take more than the offer of tea to lure her downstairs.

She put her mobile with its accusatory missed calls

back into her bag. Oh God, what a mess. What had possessed her to sign up to Internet dating? At the time it had seemed easier than meeting people face-to-face. She'd been unable to picture herself making small talk in a bar, or over dinner, with a group of women that she might have nothing in common with except her sexuality. Internet dating had seemed a good way to get to know someone before committing to meet. When she'd met Elaine in person her critical faculties should have kicked in, but the amount of alcohol she'd consumed on their date meant that she'd lost whatever common sense she had in the bottom of a wineglass. At least she could go back and check what she'd said when they'd chatted online.

You heard all these scare stories about people being unwittingly infected by talking to people they didn't know over the Internet. Could Elaine have unleashed some tracking device onto her laptop or her phone that let her read her files? Had she given her a route into eaves-dropping on current activity at the HET? Was that even possible, or was she having a massive bout of paranoia? She really needed to talk to someone who understood computers, but she didn't fancy confessing to Marcus or Bernard or the other geek from IT what she'd been up to. It would have to involve starting from the first principle of explaining why she'd been on a date with a woman, for one thing. She was pretty sure that would come as a revelation to her colleagues.

Maybe she was just being paranoid but given the sensitivity of what she had planned for the rest of the evening, she wasn't willing to take the risk. If she couldn't use her laptop or her mobile, her evening's activities were going to involve a library and a call box, two things that she hadn't used since she was a teenager. Time to find out if such things still existed in her neighbourhood.

Morningside Library was an oasis of calm after the stress of her day. The librarian, a well-heeled woman in her late fifties, had been delighted to assist with her request for a library card. It was very important, she'd said, that people continued to use the library, as funding for the service was always under threat. Mona had nodded a little guiltily. The only time she'd been in a library recently was when they'd tracked an elderly male Health Defaulter down to Blackhall Library, where he'd been sound asleep under a copy of the *Scottish Daily Express*.

Her temporary library card secured, she relocated to a computer terminal. The paranoia she'd experienced over the past few days was still in full flow; she gave a furtive look round to make sure that no one had followed her here. There were two teenage boys huddled round a computer on the other side of the table from her, and three older ladies who were browsing the stacks. Unless she was being pursued by a master of disguise who could carry off a convincing Morningside matron, she could probably assume that nobody was interested in her and her Internet surfing.

After all the preamble, she had an answer to her question in only a couple of Internet searches. She needed a phone number, and the power of Google had presented her with three possible options. Now all she had to do was locate a payphone. She considered asking the librarian, but given the high level of customer service she'd experienced so far there was a danger she'd be offered the use of a phone, and what would she say then? No thanks, I'm trying to contact someone without leaving a trace?

Picking up her printout, she headed out on to Morningside Road. Payphones were few and far between. Should she start walking in the hope she stumbled across one, or should she ask a passer-by? The most likely place would be at Morningside Station, she guessed, unless . . . something on the other side of the road caught her eye. Unless there was one very close by indeed.

She stood on the kerb to allow a bus to pass, then ran over the road to confirm her suspicions that this was a phone box. With one hand she pulled the door open; her other hand had its fingers firmly crossed in the hope that this one contained a fully functioning phone. A deeply unpleasant smell hit her nose. Looking down she could see a large puddle, the origins of which she decided not to dwell on. Placing a foot on each shore, she pulled out the list of numbers and dialled the first one. It returned a dead tone, which was unhelpful but at least conclusive. She could strike it off the list. The second number put her in touch with an elderly and apparently quite deaf man who couldn't make sense of her request. He got a question mark next to his number. She sighed and dialled for the last time. A woman answered.

'Is that Theresa Kilsyth?'

There were a few seconds of silence. 'Who is this?' The voice was imperious, posh Edinburgh and unmistakeably Mrs Kilsyth.

'This is Mona Whyte.'

Another silence followed.

'From the Health Enforcement Team.'

'I know who you are.' Theresa's voice dripped with irritation. 'I don't know why you are ringing me.'

'I rang the university but they said neither you nor the Professor was working there now.'

'So you thought you'd harass me at home instead. I'm hanging up now.'

'Don't!' Mona realised she'd have to dive right in. 'Did the Professor really have a heart attack, or did someone get to him?'

'Well, you would know more about that than me, Mona. I left him with your people. I trusted you all to take care of him.'

'Believe me, Mrs Kilsyth, they are *not* my people. I don't trust any of them, and I don't think Professor Bircham-Fowler did either.'

'A bit late in the day, Mona, for these discussions. Good . . .'

'Don't hang up! They're asking me about the Professor. They want to know what he told me when we were in London.'

The phone sighed. 'Where are you phoning from? Are you on a mobile?'

'No.'

'Your landline? Your office landline?'

'I'm at the call box on Morningside High Street.'

There was a dry laugh. 'Well, at least you've learned something. If you want to come round here immediately, I'll talk to you. I assume you know where I live.'

The phone went dead.

Theresa placed an unasked-for cup of coffee in front of Mona. 'I don't have any milk, I'm afraid. I don't take it myself.'

'Black is fine.' After only a couple of sips she felt her heart racing. Mrs Kilsyth liked her coffee strong. 'Thank you for agreeing to see me.'

'I'm not sure this is a good idea.' Theresa sat down

opposite her. She looked as small and trim as Mona remembered, but the events of the last couple of months had taken their toll. She seemed to have lost some of her energy, and now looked like a woman on the verge of retirement, which, Mona supposed, she actually was. 'I very much doubt I'm going to give you whatever it is you want.'

'What I want to know more than anything is that the Professor is OK. Is he?'

'Is Sandy OK?' She seemed to mull this over. 'Well, he's still alive, still breathing, which he could very well not be. There were a few scary moments in the hospital where we nearly lost him.'

'I tried phoning lots of times, but I could never get anyone to answer his mobile.'

Theresa waved this away. 'Yes, yes, everyone and their dog was phoning to speak to him. Colleagues, students, journalists, well-wishers of all kinds. I turned the phone off and stuck it in a drawer. He'd didn't need that kind of nonsense in his condition. Oh, and thank your boss, Cameron Stuttle, for the lovely bunch of flowers he sent. That was a very nice touch.' She glared at her.

'Theresa, I . . .'

She held up her hand. 'Before you go on, I think there are a few things you need to know. The first thing is that I haven't actually seen Sandy since he was released from hospital. Since he came home he hasn't answered my calls and he won't come to the door when I attempt to visit.'

Mona was shocked. 'But you two were so close.'

'We both worked sixty-hour weeks at the university. We shared an office. We went on holiday together. There is nothing I do not know about that man. Which is why I can say I am not surprised that he has cut off contact.'

113

Mona frowned, trying to take this in. 'You might understand that, Theresa, but I don't. Surely he needs you now more than ever?'

'Sandy has never been one to put his own needs first. But we'll come to that. The second thing you need to know, as the events of the past few months have made crystal clear, is that Sandy has made some pretty powerful enemies in the course of his work.'

'Like Carlotta Carmichael?'

Theresa snorted. 'That self-important little trollop? She was the least of his worries. She's very much a sideshow, the real circus is elsewhere.' She shook her head at the thought. 'And the third thing you need to know is that the jaunt that Sandy was sent on to London worked a treat.'

'Really? I thought the whole thing was a disaster for both SHEP and Police Scotland.'

'Oh yes, it was a cock-up from start to finish for them. But the darker forces that were out there got exactly what they wanted. Overnight Sandy went from being a fusty old workaholic professor, without wife or children or grandchildren, to a happy family man.'

'I don't get it.'

'He went from being a man with nothing, or at least very little, to lose, to a man who was susceptible to pressure. He became a person who could be manipulated, leaned on to not discuss certain unfortunate topics.'

Mona's face must still have been portraying her inner confusion because Theresa leaned forward and started speaking very slowly, as if she was spelling out a difficult lesson to a child.

'He would have done anything for his daughter. He'd spent years looking for her. My guess is after his "heart

114

attack" certain people suggested to him that they know where his daughter lives, they know she is pregnant, and that if they can give the Professor a cardiac episode, think what they could do to an expectant mother.'

'Do you know who these people are?'

'I have my suspicions.'

'We need to help the Professor.'

'How, dear? Do you have a plan?' There was an air of sarcasm to her tone.

'No, but, well . . .' She stopped, flustered. 'But I think the Professor wants me to help him. He gave me a hug when I left him with the Police Scotland guys, if that's who they really are . . .'

'I doubt it very much.'

'And in the course of the hug he slipped a business card into my pocket which he'd written something on.'

'What did it say?' Theresa contemplated her fingernails, feigning indifference.

'"Follow the orders of Mrs Hilda Milwood", all in capitals. I don't know what it means but . . .' She tailed off as she caught the expression on Theresa's face. 'You know what this means, don't you?'

She didn't respond.

'Theresa, are you Hilda Milwood? Is it a name that Professor Bircham-Fowler uses for you? I thought perhaps he was trying to get me to speak to you.'

'It is absolutely nothing to do with me,' she snapped.

'I'm sorry, I just . . .'

'Mona,' Theresa reached over and took hold of her hand, 'listen to me and take the advice of an old woman. Leave all this alone. Messing around with this will get you and yours into all kinds of trouble.'

'My only relative is my mother, Theresa, and she's

lucky if she's got six months left. I've got no partner, and no children. I'm not sure I've got anything to lose either.'

'You stupid girl!' She dropped her hand. 'The Professor is extremely high profile, which makes him difficult to kill. You, on the other hand, are a junior functionary. You can have an accident any time they want, and they won't even have to worry about your grieving widower.'

'But . . .'

'Forget about Sandy. Forget about whatever nonsense he has told you and get on with living your life.' She stood up. 'And please don't come here again.'

WEDNESDAY

CHIMPS

I

Bernard had awoken, refreshed and rejuvenated, after a good night's sleep in his new flat. The only thing that had prevented him getting his full eight hours was the fact that he'd woken just before six, and Bryce's comments about Marcus had started playing over and over in his head. It was hard to imagine his friend being so idiotic, but then Marcus did possess the particular brand of stupidity that came from continually being the cleverest person in the room. It was the kind of stupidity that made him immune to sarcasm, rendered him incapable of recognising signs of boredom on other people's faces and prevented him from realising that you were never, ever, going to get one over on a website that was probably run by the Russian mafia.

At five past six he'd got out of bed. Bernard knew from bitter experience that lying awake imagining the worst that could happen was generally more unpleasant than getting up and actually facing the music, so he'd decided to steal a march on the day and get into work early. A peaceful walk through deserted streets, followed by an hour of clearing his emails before everyone else turned up would be a pretty good start to his morning. Marcus notwithstanding, he had a good feeling about the day. Today could be the day that they found Helen Sopel, alive and well, and escorted her to her Health Check. And he would have a perfect excuse to nip round to the Museum and thank Lucy for her help.

The streets around his flat were as quiet as he'd hoped, although the nearer he got to the town centre, the more other early birds he encountered. There were a surprising number of people on the streets near his work. For some reason everyone seemed to have decided to come in early. The little park opposite their offices was full of people, students from the look of them. He wondered if this was the remnants of some outdoor party that had taken place overnight. There were at least twenty of them, which was clearly breaking the prohibition on meeting up in large groups. They'd be attracting the attention of his colleagues at SHEP if they didn't move on soon.

There was a lone student sitting on the bottom step of the small stone flight that led up to the front door of the Cathcart Building.

'I'm afraid we don't open for another hour.' He smiled, apologetically.

The young man just stared back at him.

Bernard was still mulling over this silent visitor as he pulled the door carefully shut behind him. He heard footsteps clattering down the stairs and wondered which of his colleagues had also made it into work for 7.30. As the footsteps drew nearer he realised it wasn't anyone from the HET. A tall dark-haired man was heading toward him at some speed. Bernard was about to challenge him when he realised that he looked familiar, although he couldn't immediately place him.

'Ehm, hello?'

The man ignored him, and rather than going out the front door headed down the corridor to the fire exit.

'Don't open that, you'll trigger the alarm!'

120

His warning was ignored. The man pushed the emergency bar and left without looking back. Bernard braced himself for a high-pitched electronic wail, but nothing happened. The door slammed shut, the noise echoing round the empty stairwell, leaving Bernard staring at it in confusion.

His confusion deepened when he made it to the HET office. Paterson was already there, locked in conversation with Stuttle. The sight of the Head of SHEP jogged his memory and he realised where he'd seen the mystery man before.

'I just saw Paul Shore leaving.'

'No, you didn't,' said Stuttle.

'No, I really did, he . . .' Bernard stopped. He realised from the expression on his boss's, and his boss's boss's face that he'd got it wrong. This was one of the times when HET reality was at odds with actual reality as he perceived it, and he hadn't just seen Carlotta Carmichael's parliamentary secretary leaving their offices after a secret meeting.

'Well, whoever it was he left via the Emergency Exit.'

'Tut, tut,' said Stuttle, grinning to himself. 'A visitor leaving via the tradesman's entrance. Better check the silverware's all still there, John.'

'Don't worry about it, Bernard,' said Paterson.

'I am worried. The alarm didn't go off when he opened the door. Should I phone the Facilities Manager and get him to check it?'

Stuttle's face, unlike the Emergency Exit, registered alarm. Bernard realised, with slight embarrassment, that the SHEP boss had been responsible for the security breach, no doubt so that Paul Shore could sneak into the building. The door system forced you to present

121

your Green Card on entry, providing a neat register of everyone who had been in the building. No doubt this would have interfered with Stuttle's intention to pretend the meeting had never happened.

'No, don't go doing that. John, er, you'll get that sorted out?'

'Of course. What are you doing in so early anyway, Bernard?'

Wishing I'd stayed in bed, he thought. 'Work. Finding Helen Sopel.'

'Good, good. Dedicated team you've got here, John. Perhaps we can continue our discussion in the cafeteria and give Bernard here some peace?'

A welcome silence filled the room. As soon as Paterson and Stuttle were out of sight he hurried to Maitland's desk and retrieved the key to the office cupboard. With a glance over his shoulder in case his bosses had returned, he opened it. To his relief, the box with Helen Sopel's emergency information was still there. Although he remembered putting it on the second shelf, it seemed to have migrated overnight to the third. Almost like someone around 5'8" tall had put it away last night, only for someone taller to put it back this morning. Paterson, Stuttle and Paul Shore were all, by his estimation, at least six foot tall.

Bernard pulled the box out and leafed through it, and had a second burst of relief when he found all the contents were still there. He quickly repacked it, then paused for a moment deciding which shelf to put it back on. He opted for the second. He leaned against the cupboard and tried to work out what Shore had been doing there. Was he there so he could go back and warn Ms Carmichael about its contents, or there so that he could help identify the

122

significance of the items? If they *were* significant, would anyone even bother to tell them?

The sound of voices drifted in from outside. He walked over to the window and saw that the number of people in the park seemed to have increased. This ruined his theory that it was the remnants of a student party; this wasn't the dying embers of an event, this looked like something just about to start. A few of the 'students' were wearing scarves over their faces. What was going on?

'Hello.' Marcus was standing in the doorway.

'Hi! Have you seen what's going on out there?'

'I certainly have. I actually came to warn you that there were plans on the Twittersphere for a demonstration outside your office, but I appear to be a little late.'

'So it's a demonstration. I thought it was some kind of student party.'

'Alas, no.'

Marcus gave his usual goofy grin, and Bernard's thoughts turned from the demo to his conversation with Bryce. This opportunity to talk to Marcus had been unexpected but the empty office did make this the perfect time to offer some support.

'So, how are you?' Bernard smiled at his friend. To be honest, he didn't look like a man deep in debt and doing dirty deeds. He could, of course, also be deep in denial.

'Fine, fine. Missing my house guest, of course, and our cosy late-night chats.'

'Oh, right. Yes, I'm missing you too,' he lied. 'But you're OK? Not worrying about anything?'

'Actually, right now I'm mainly worrying that Mr Stuttle will somehow see the demonstration outside as my fault. He has a worrying tendency to blame whoever tells him bad news for actually causing it.'

'Mr Paterson does exactly the same thing! He always shoots the messenger.' Realising he was heading off-topic he resumed his theme. 'But personally, you're OK?'

'Is this about Mona?' Marcus looked suspicious. He'd had a crush on her for as long as Bernard had known him. 'Are you trying to tell me some bad news? She's got a boyfriend, hasn't she?'

The news on the Mona front was much, much worse than Marcus could imagine, but this probably wasn't the time to tell him. He was saved from making a decision by the arrival of the woman herself. She walked straight past them and headed for the window.

'Have you seen the crowd out there? Does the Guv know?'

'He's downstairs having coffee with Stuttle, so he's going to find out pretty soon.'

'Oh well, they can sort it then.' She turned her attention to Marcus, who had been busily engaged in staring at her. 'My computer is making a terrible noise. Any chance you could, you know, while you're here...?'

'Delighted to help.' He reached into his pocket and, with a flourish, produced a small screwdriver. 'When did you last dust the hard drive?'

'Ehm, never?'

'Tsk, tsk, Mona. No one ever takes proper care of the hardware.' He knelt down at the side of her desk, a move which led her to back her chair quite rapidly away. He burrowed underneath it and started dismantling.

'I've been keeping an eye on the hashtag I mentioned,' Marcus's voice was slightly muffled. 'There's a lot of people out there who are convinced that the HET are up to something. Consensus is that these civil servant deaths are sinister and you lot are covering something up.'

'What is going on out there?' Stuttle and Paterson had returned from their plotting session in the canteen. Stuttle wound his way through the office and stood staring out the window.

'It's a Twittermob, Mr Stuttle,' said Bernard.

'Twitter? I thought we paid that prick from IT to monitor these things?'

Marcus popped up from underneath Mona's desk, screwdriver in hand. He'd been bang on the money about getting the blame. Stuttle looked surprised to see him, but not particularly apologetic for the insult.

'I have been, Mr Stuttle. The hashtag started going really crazy about 2am so I thought I'd better pop in and warn everyone that they might have a bit of difficulty getting into the office this morning.'

'One of the tools out there is carrying a placard with "What Do They Know" on it,' said Stuttle. 'Like that bloody hashtag thing you were rabbiting on about.'

Paterson stood by the window looking out at the scene below. 'You know how you said that if word got out about McVie's death and Sopel being missing there would be panic, Cam?'

'Yes.'

'That doesn't look like panic to me. That looks like a pretty damn well-organised demonstration.'

Stuttle thought this over for a second. 'Marcus, you follow all these Internet nutjobs. Who's responsible for this?'

'Hard to say, Mr Stuttle. There's a lot of people posting against that particular hashtag. There are a couple of particularly prolific tweeters but none of the ones who were calling for this illegal demonstration were using their own names. Obviously.'

Bernard raised his hand. 'I have a question.'

'As always,' muttered Paterson.

'Why are they doing this? Are they genuinely concerned or is there some other motive? And why North Edinburgh HET and not SHEP's offices?'

'I can answer the second question,' said Stuttle. 'They'd never get near our place with the level of security we have.'

'Yeah, God forbid that the masses should storm the magnificent staircases of the City Chambers.'

'Shut up, John. And as for the why, I don't think we know that yet.'

Maitland and Carole appeared, giggling.

Stuttle looked at his watch. 'Glad you could finally make it.'

Carole's expression changed to a look of fury. Bernard winced. He hated confrontation. Sympathetic as he was to Carole's feelings, he didn't think there was a lot of point in having a showdown with her ultimate boss. She appeared to feel differently and walked over until she was inches away from Stuttle. Bernard thought that this was far, far closer than he would care to risk. Getting that close to Stuttle was like putting yourself within mauling distance of a grizzly bear. Legend had it that the front benches in the British Houses of Parliament were two sword-lengths apart. This seemed to Bernard to be an appropriate distance to keep from the Head of SHEP. Two sword-lengths would give you time, if not to draw a weapon, at least to start running.

'We've both just risked life and limb fighting our way through an aggressive mob of protestors.' Her voice was quiet, but extremely firm. 'And when we got here, what do we find? Certainly not any concern from senior

126

management about our well-being. No, instead we get a telling-off for being late, as if we were naughty school children, rather than two employees who have just run the gauntlet of protestors out there. What are you planning to do to keep your staff safe?'

'I'm on the case, Carole.' Stuttle aimed for a reassuring tone, one that implied that he was on top of the situation and normal service would be resumed imminently. He didn't quite carry it off.

'And *exactly* what are you planning to do, Mr Stuttle? We can't safely get back out of the building. We're trapped in here. We don't know what their plans are; they could be about to start lobbing Molotov cocktails, for all we know. What's your immediate advice?'

Stuttle didn't respond.

'It's not just the HET, either. What about the other staff in the building? Some of the girls in the admin team are very upset.'

A vision of Marguerite ramping up the amateur dramatics downstairs went through Bernard's head. Stuttle probably had more to fear in getting past the admin office than from the protestors.

The sound of singing started outside.

'Oh, God, there's more of them.' Stuttle peered out of the window. 'Right, I take your point, Carole. No one is to venture out there until we get this sorted. John, can I borrow your office? I need to make a few calls and get that lot shifted.'

2

Mona was shrouded in a fog of irritation. Her colleagues were being very annoying.

She'd phoned Ian, as a courtesy, to warn him not to come into the HET office. He'd responded with a slightly impatient comment about not intending to come over that morning anyway, followed by his opinion that the protest was all a bit of nonsense and the HET should just man up and get on with things. She'd hung up at that point.

Bernard, who had the ability to irritate her just by breathing, was obviously fretting about the situation. She could see he was busily flicking between the BBC News website and various self-help websites suggesting how to protect yourself against a potentially armed and angry mob, interspersed with anxious trips to the window. Her one consolation was that Stuttle had sent Marcus off somewhere, so that at least she didn't have to listen to him prattle on.

But most of her ire was directed at Maitland and Carole. They were making no pretence at work, and seemed to be playing some kind of tennis-type game with balled-up bits of paper. Mona caught Paterson's eye. He was already annoyed enough at being evicted from his own office, without having to witness his staff's blatant work avoidance.

'Maitland, do you not have something you could be working on?'

'Bit tricky, Guv, what with us being stuck in the building.'

'Well, find something to do.'

Carole tutted. 'We're both still stressed about getting into work this morning. This is very threatening, been trapped in here. I don't think we're calm enough to work.'

'Yes, I thought that,' said Paterson. 'I was listening to you both giggling over there and I thought the two of them sound exactly like they're too stressed to work. Maitland – find something to do, before I find it for you.'

Maitland reluctantly slid over to his own computer, while Carole sat and glared at Paterson. Mona hoped she had a really, really good lawyer, because if she did end up remaining at the HET, there was no way Paterson would forget all this.

There was silence for all of two seconds, before Bernard piped up. 'I think that's the police here.'

There was a roar from the crowd.

'Oh, that's bad. They're throwing things at the police.'

The office abandoned any pretence at work and joined Bernard at the window. By Mona's estimate there were now between seventy and eighty protestors in and around the park, predominantly male, many of them with their faces covered by scarves. To her mind, this didn't signify a commitment to peaceful protest.

'Oh no! They're ripping up the flower beds.' Bernard looked outraged.

'Not just the flowers – look!' Maitland pointed at a group of protestors who were doing their level best to throw a park bench at the police.

'I'm glad we didn't venture out there,' said Bernard. 'At least the police have got riot gear on.'

'You'd still get your arse kicked, even if you were in riot gear,' said Maitland.

'Don't be mean,' said Mona.

'It's a fact!' Maitland grinned. 'You'd be fine though, Mona, what with you being a bit on the butch side.'

One of these days she would snap and throttle him. 'I'm not butch, I'm just tougher than you are, loser.'

'Yeah.' He upped the grin to a full-blown smirk. 'Must be the lesbian thing.'

She frowned. Was he just being his usual annoying self, or did he actually know? 'The what?'

'The you being a lesbian thing. We know about it.'

Mona's head whipped in the direction of Paterson, who was looking so uncomfortable he could have been seated on hot coals. She knew exactly who to blame for this. 'This is bloody Ian Jacobsen, isn't it? Outing me!'

'Well, actually . . .' began Bernard.

'Mona,' said Paterson, loudly. 'The important thing is that it is out there now. Everyone knows . . .'

'I didn't until just now,' said Carole.

'So, now it's out there we can all just get on with life.'

'I suppose so,' she said, doubtfully. In truth, it wasn't the end of the world that everyone knew. It saved her having some awkward conversations. 'But I'm still going to kill Ian.'

The door to their office flew open, and Marguerite rushed in and straight into Paterson's office. 'Mr Paterson . . .'

'He's not in there!'

'Oh, Mr Stuttle . . .' She reappeared again, looking even more flustered.

'I'm here, Marguerite.' Paterson stepped forward. 'What's the panic?'

'We just took a phone call downstairs. Someone said there's a bomb on the premises! He says we've got fifteen minutes to get out.'

3

'This is total bullshit.' Maitland peered round the side of a fire engine. 'There's no way that there's actually a bomb in there.'

'I know,' said Paterson. 'But Stuttle wasn't going to take the risk of you lot being blown sky-high. Me, I'd have taken my chances.'

It had been a busy hour. Bernard thought that he might have scored himself some brownie points with Stuttle, as he had been the only member of the team – including Paterson – who had been able to immediately lay his hand on the building's evacuation policy. (It was nestled in a plastic pocket, three documents along from his contract.) Stuttle had snatched it out of his hand and set about putting it into action.

With an efficiency that Bernard could only admire, Paterson had managed to get all the staff out of the back door of the building and evacuated to a safe distance without anyone being trampled, while Stuttle had yelled loudly and authoritatively to one of the riot police at the front of the building until they'd got sufficient reinforcements to drive the protestors back to a safe distance. Bernard might not have the fondest feelings toward his line management structure, but he had to admit they came into their own in a crisis.

Stuttle appeared in Bernard's line of sight, deep in

conversation with a police officer Bernard didn't recognise but whose epaulette silverware declared her to be Someone Very Important Indeed.

'Oh. My. God,' Marguerite's distinctive tone interrupted his thoughts. 'That was worse than the whole bomb thing.'

'What was?'

'Talking to Stuttle and that woman.'

Paterson smiled. 'I'll tell him that, shall I? Marguerite would rather get blown up than talk to you and Assistant Chief Constable Callachan?'

'Don't you dare, Mr Paterson.' She waved an admonitory finger at him. 'Enough of your joking. My nerves are shot.'

'So, what did you tell them?'

She sighed. 'Well, they wanted to know all about the phone call. I said it was a man.'

'And what else?'

She looked embarrassed. 'I couldn't really remember. I got such a fright when he said there was a bomb that I wasn't really paying attention.'

'Was he Scottish?'

'Yes,' she said, confidently. Her face clouded over. 'At least, I think so.'

'Young, old?'

She shrugged. 'I'm not sure.'

'Excellent work, Marguerite. They'll be able to narrow down the search to fifty per cent of the population.'

'Coffees, as requested.' Mona had returned from her quest, bearing four cups. 'Sorry, Marge, I didn't know you were back.'

Marguerite tutted and walked off.

'I really didn't know she was here,' said Mona.

132

'It wasn't you,' said Maitland. 'She's got the hump because the Guv complained about her bomb hoax message-taking skills.'

'Where's Carole?' asked Paterson.

'She decided she was too stressed by events to come back. Sorry, Guv.' Mona passed him his coffee.

He rolled his eyes. 'Probably for the best. Well, there's no point you lot hanging around either. Maitland and Bernard – you go back to the Museum and try and door-stop the Director.'

'Oh, Bernard, you're in luck.' Maitland made kissing noises.

'Why is he doing that?' asked Paterson.

'Because I love museums so much.' He glared up at Maitland. 'Shut up.'

'Anything I can be getting on with, Guv?' asked Mona.

'Plenty. First you can track down Ian Jacobsen, and ask him if he's got a meeting room he can borrow, so that the three of us can do some preparation.'

'What for, Guv?'

'An interview that is going to require more tact and discretion than anything you've ever done before.' He stopped for a slurp of his coffee. 'Stuttle's got us an interview at four this afternoon with Carlotta and Jonathon Carmichael.'

'*Together?*'

'As I said, tact and diplomacy are going to be essential.'

Mona looked at Bernard, and he smiled sympathetically. Tact and diplomacy. Not Mr Paterson's skill set.

4

'So, this time are you going to actually grow a pair and ask the big-nosed bird out?'

'Her nose wasn't that big, and no, I'm not planning to ask her out.'

'Why not? The woman is so dull that not only does she have membership of a museum, she actually works in one. You're a perfect match.'

'People who work in museums aren't dull, they're just not ignorant like you. Anyway, she might not be there.' He wondered if, somewhere beneath Maitland's appalling phrasing, he was right. Was he in with a chance? Should he be making some kind of 'move'? He wasn't sure his nerves were up to any more excitement today, and he was absolutely certain that he wasn't going to make any advances to Lucy with Maitland standing by, so he decided to focus on the investigation.

'What are we going to say to this woman anyway?' he asked.

'Well, I think, given that she's friends with one of the people attending the meeting, she knows more about this than she's saying. And why didn't she acknowledge in the diary who was meeting here?'

'Don't know.'

'And add all that to the fact that she stood us up, I think she's dodgy.'

'Well, we're here, so try to keep that feeling under wraps.'

Bernard was pleased to see that the Museum door was wide open this time. He hurried through and stopped at the reception desk, which had a very elderly woman sat behind it.

'We're here to see Corinna McFarlane.'

'Who?'

'The Director?'

'Oh, I don't know anything about that.'

'Could you ring her?'

The woman gazed at them. Bernard thought for a second she was going to query that, but very slowly and, it appeared, painfully, she got up from her seat. 'I'll find Lucy. You two sign in.'

Maitland waited until her back was turned and elbowed him in the ribs. 'It's your bird.'

'Do not say anything to her, Maitland.'

'I'm promising nothing.' He smirked.

'Oh, it's you two.' Lucy came bustling in. 'Hello again. I'm sorry Mrs Cartwright couldn't help you.' She lowered her voice. 'I don't think she quite heard what you were asking. Can I ask you to . . .' She gestured at the Green Card box on the wall.

'Of course.' In turn they presented their cards and waited until the machine beeped.

'I'll take you upstairs. I'm sure Corinna will be delighted you've caught her.'

The look on Corinna McFarlane's face when they appeared in her office doorway conveyed many emotions, none of which corresponded with delight. She quickly recovered herself. 'Thank you, Lucy.' She stood up to shake their hands. 'Sorry about the confusion over our previous meeting.'

'No problem,' said Bernard. 'We do have a few questions, though.'

There was a brief pause. 'Lucy, you'd better get back downstairs. I don't like to leave our entire front desk security to Mrs Cartwright.'

'Oh, OK.'

She waited until Lucy left, then closed the door and turned to them both. 'You had questions.'

'We do,' said Bernard. 'We want to talk to you about a series of meeting that were held here at the Museum, particularly one on Friday 4 September.'

'I'm not sure how much help I can be.'

'Why were the civil servants meeting here? They have a number of buildings of their own that surely they could have used.'

She shrugged. 'I understand there was a certain amount of pressure on their meeting rooms.'

'But Lucy said the meetings were mainly in the evening. I can't imagine that the Scottish Government would be short of meeting rooms out of hours.'

Maitland's phone pinged. 'Excuse me, I need to take this.'

Bernard felt a sense of alarm. He was mildly perturbed at the thought of carrying on with the interview solo, and deeply disturbed at the thought that Maitland was roaming around the building with an imminent risk of him bumping into Lucy. He tried to focus.

'So, they were fully booked for evening meetings?'

'I don't know if it was a capacity issue, or if it was more difficult to get someone to open and close the building after hours. You'd really have to talk to the Scottish Government directly.'

'I'd like to, Ms McFarlane, but as you are probably aware, two of the people who attended those meetings are now dead, and Helen Sopel is missing.'

Her hand went to her mouth. 'Helen is missing?'

'Didn't you know? She missed her Health Check, hence our involvement.'

'I didn't realise, I thought you wanted to talk to me because . . .never mind. I can't believe Helen missed her Health Check.'

'Yes, a career-ending move. Not something she would have done if she could possibly help it, therefore as you can imagine we're very worried about her. So, if you have any information about these meetings it would really help.'

This was met with silence. He decided to nudge her.

'We're meeting Carlotta Carmichael to discuss her involvement in the meetings.'

This provoked a furious hiss. Ms Carmichael seemed to cause that response in a lot of people. 'That woman won't be able to help. She only attended the last meeting before . . .' She leaned back in her chair and folded her arms. 'You know Nat was a good friend of mine?'

'Lucy said. Do you think his death was suicide?'

'Yes, of course.' She nodded. 'That's what the police are saying, isn't it?'

'Yes. Do you have any idea what might have driven him to that?'

She sighed. 'I don't suppose any of this can hurt him now. I'll tell you what I know, which, frankly, isn't much. I know that Nat had been really unhappy for the past few months.'

'Unhappy at work?'

'I'm just not sure he was cut out for all the pressures involved in dealing with the Virus.'

'How well did he get on with his colleagues?'

'Fine, I think.'

'And Mrs Carmichael?'

'I really wouldn't know about that.' She pushed her chair back, and stood up. 'Why don't you ask her when you meet her?'

Maitland was sitting on the front steps of the Museum, a cigarette in his mouth.

'Does Kate know you're still smoking?'

'No,' he said, getting to his feet. 'And if you tell her, I'll kill you. Anyway, you owe me one.'

He felt a cold, icy hand grasp his heart. 'Oh, God, what did you do?'

He grinned. 'First of all, I played the old make your phone ring trick, to get out of that extremely tedious interview. Then I wandered down to see your future girlfriend, and had a very cosy chat about the Museum's accounts.'

'Accounts?'

'Yup, I was thinking about her comments the other day. So she tells me that Corinna keeps all that stuff very close to her chest, password-protected files on the computer etc. But she did reiterate her comments about what good shape the Museum is in financially. Is that unusual? I thought these places all survived from one government handout to the next?'

'It's not a "government handout", it's a government investment in culture and heritage. But yes, they do tend to have quite precarious funding arrangements.' He thought for a moment. 'It's all useful information but I don't see how it constitutes me "owing you one".'

Maitland held out a scrap of paper. 'I told her that my

138

colleague was keen to ask her out but he'd never have the nerve, left to his own devices.'

Bernard looked at the paper. 'That's her phone number.'

'Yup, her home number. And she said she'd love to hear from you.'

'Really?'

'Yup. And I told her your herpes was back under control since that last set of tablets from the doctor.'

Bernard blinked. 'That's a joke, right? You didn't say that?'

He laughed. 'Relax. All I actually said was that my colleague Bernard might need to speak to her again, and could I have her number.'

Bernard looked at the paper and smiled. A thought struck him. 'This is unusually nice of you, Maitland. What are you up to?'

'I'm thinking of our investigation. That Museum boss is well dodgy. And considering how much I got out of Lucy in a five-minute conversation, I reckon a posh restaurant and a couple of drinks inside her, she'll have told you everything there is to know.'

'That's another joke, right?'

He shook his head, solemnly. 'Phone her and get that date set up. Time to take one for the team, Bernie.'

5

'Is this the best you could do in the way of meeting rooms? We're practically sitting on each other's knees.' Paterson shifted awkwardly on his seat. They appeared to be in the most compact meeting room that Police HQ at Fettes had to offer.

'This is all I could find at short notice,' said Ian, mildly. 'And maybe you lot could stop antagonising people so much that they want to blow you up, and then we could use *your* meeting space?'

'I'm not even going to rise to that one. They're only targeting us because SHEP are so mollycoddled they've got police crawling all over their building and the slack-arsed protestors aren't up that kind of challenge. Anyway, they've got until three o'clock to certify that our building is clear of bombs, otherwise we're going to have to relocate the meeting with the Carmichaels to a hopefully slightly larger meeting room here.'

'No problem. Worst comes to the worst one of the senior brass will relocate and offer up his office. There's nothing we won't do make our MSPs comfortable.' Ian turned to Mona. 'You're very quiet.'

She glared at him, her arms folded.

'What did I do now?'

'You know perfectly . . .'

140

'Mona,' said Paterson, firmly. 'Let's move on. Let's focus on the task in hand – the Carmichaels.'

'At the risk of sounding like Bernard, Guv, I have some questions.'

'OK.'

'First of all, what does Jonathon Carmichael actually do for a living?'

'He runs his own marketing consultancy,' said Ian.

'I'm not sure that makes it an awful lot clearer.'

Ian laughed. 'If you check out his website, you'll see that he specialises in branding, project management, helping organisations develop strategies, that kind of thing. Still not clear?'

'Not desperately, no.'

'To put it another way, he does a lot of behind-the-scenes fixing for his wife and her cronies. You want something sorted out quickly and discreetly, he's your man. He's very well connected. And he knows where all the bodies are buried.'

'Which leads me neatly to my second question. I don't understand why we're being allowed to deal with this. I thought Stuttle would lead on this, or someone senior from Police Scotland.'

Both Paterson and Ian laughed.

'Stuttle's not going anywhere near this. Whatever we say to them, Mr and Mrs Carmichael are going to want to complain to someone more senior about the appalling way they've been treated etc. etc. If Stuttle's here, the only person more senior is a Scottish Minister, and nobody wants to be involving them in this. So, we do as full an investigation as we can, they complain, and Stuttle mollifies them, says he'll have us disciplined, retrained, hung, drawn and quartered or whatever else she's asking for.

The Carmichaels are happy, Stuttle's happy and we just keep our mouths shut.'

'All right.' That did make sense, although she wasn't delighted at her role in the scenario. 'But why are we interviewing them together? Isn't it all a bit, you know, delicate, Guv?'

'I know, it's weird. But it was their suggestion, not ours.'

'They actually want to be interviewed together? Do they know what it's about?'

'I don't know. SHEP contacted both their offices separately. They must have spoken to each other, because Carlotta's PA phoned back and said they'd both see us at the North Edinburgh HET office at four.'

'That's going to be fun, isn't it?' said Ian. 'Asking Jonathon Carmichael about his girlfriend with Carlotta sitting there. I mean, he must know there's a possibility that we've found out?'

'Probably planning to brazen it out. Let's just hope that he's updated Mrs Carmichael that he's been playing away from home before we broach the subject. Anyway, I suggest we start with me welcoming them, Ian asking about what went on at the meeting, then Mona going in for the kill regarding Mr Carmichael's love life.'

'Thanks, Guv.'

'It'll be better coming from a woman.'

'I'm really not sure that it w—'

She was cut off by the sound of Paterson's phone ringing. She sat impatiently while he took the call, his side of the conversation consisting mostly of yes, right and OK. When he finished he stood up. 'That's Facilities Management to say we got the all-clear to go back. Marguerite's been given a script to memorise in case we get any other nutters phoning up. The Facilities Manager wants to meet with me tomorrow morning, and from the tone of his voice I'd say he was holding me personally responsible for today's events.'

6

'Please stop glaring at me.'

'I don't see why I should,' said Maitland, scowling harder than ever. 'If you hadn't insisted on checking your emails, we could both be sitting on a bus right now heading home. But, oh no, you had to log on.'

'Paterson would have our guts for garters if we just clocked off now, seeing as we can safely return to the office,' said Bernard. He stopped to let Maitland catch up. He was taking dawdling to a whole new level.

'No, he wouldn't. He doesn't know that we got the message to go back.'

'Even the Guv is aware that we can check our email when we're out of the office.'

'We could just say that we couldn't find secure Wi-Fi to log in. The Guv never challenges anything to do with technology. You could tell him anything so long as you mention some technical term – doesn't even have to be a real one. I once got an afternoon off because I told him the optical thread in my home-to-work connection needed to be reworked. He just nodded like this,' Maitland stroked his chin thoughtfully, 'as if he knew what I was talking about.'

'If you put half as much energy in to actually working as you did into skiving you'd be running your own HET team by now.'

'Perish the thought.'

'Anyway, you need to watch yourself.' Bernard stopped again and gestured at his colleague to hurry up. 'Carole's getting away with murder right now, but Mr Paterson's not going to take the same nonsense from you.'

'Whatever.'

They turned into the street that housed the HET's offices.

'They're still here,' said Maitland, pointing to a small group of protestors who were hanging around the park.

'Are they the same ones as earlier?'

'Dunno. Hard to tell when they've got their faces covered.' Maitland looked round. 'Looks like they've stood down the police protection.'

'No, that's the Thin Blue Line over there.' He pointed in the direction of a solitary policeman who was standing in the entrance to the building.

'I don't think you can call one person a line, Bern. He's more of a Thin Blue Dot. Hey!' He waved to the cop, who looked slightly nervous as he headed in his direction. 'We're HET officers. I believe it's all clear to go back into the building?'

They both held up their HET ID cards, which the PC looked at in turn. 'Yep, you're good to go in.'

'What do you make of this lot?' asked Maitland, gesturing a thumb in the direction of the park. 'I thought you moved them all on?'

'We're keeping an eye on it. They've been drifting back in ones and twos for the past hour. If I had my way, I'd have their arses kicked right into touch, but you know what it's like at the moment for manpower. There's just me, another guy round the back and the promise of a Rapid Response Team if it all kicks off again.' He paused and watched one of the protestors leave the park and head off down the road. 'And, to be honest, I'm not sure that the promised response will be either rapid, or much of a team. You two ex-cops?'

'I am, he's not,' said Maitland.

'Well, keep an eye on that lot, and get yourself down here at the first sign of trouble. If it all kicks off again, I'm going to need all the help I can get.'

'Well, that was reassuring,' said Bernard, returning to his desk. He was almost wishing that he'd followed Maitland's advice and not checked his email.

His colleague had resumed his earlier position at the window. 'I reckon there's an even dozen of them out there. One cop's not going to be able to stop them if they decide to rush the building.'

'You think that's what they're planning?'

'Don't know. But they've got to be hanging around there for some reason. The plod downstairs was right – we might be needed to help out.'

'We?'

'Yeah. If the building's under threat we're all going to have to step in. What do you say, Bernie? If it all gets a bit physical out there, can we rely on your backup?' He clenched both his fists and started shadow-boxing.

Bernard's phone started to ring. *Saved by the bell.* 'I'd better get that.'

'Bernard.' He heard the bark of his boss at the other end of the line. 'We're all on our way back to meet with the Carmichaels. Cameron Stuttle is meeting us at the office, so he can have another look at the box of tricks that Helen Sopel's pal left with you before Mona and I go into the meeting. Can you get them set out for us? We'll be there in ten minutes.'

He hung up without waiting for Bernard to agree or disagree with his proposal.

'Mr Paterson and Mr Stuttle are on their way.' He spoke to Maitland's back, but he was busy staring out of the window. 'Stuttle wants to see the paperwork Martine Galloway left.'

'It's locked in the cupboard,' said Maitland, without turning round. 'Key's in my top drawer.'

'I know.'

Maitland didn't move.

'I'll get it then, shall I? Don't you bother lifting a finger.'

'I'm doing important work here. I don't want the Guv and Stuttle walking into some kind of ambush.'

Bernard headed over to Maitland's desk. He opened the top drawer and rooted around in the sweet wrappers until he found the key. The lock on the metal cupboard was stiff, so he jiggled it up and down until it turned. When the door swung open, he had to step back to avoid being hit. He looked at the shelves one by one.

'It's not there.'

'What?' Maitland made it to his side in one long bound. 'It must be.' He did the same top to bottom sweep that Bernard had made. 'Would somebody have moved it? Has Marguerite tidied up?'

'Unlikely that she'd do it without being asked. She's not generally that keen.'

'The Guv could have taken it for some reason. . .although I suppose he would have mentioned he'd moved it on the phone.'

Bernard grunted. If this had been down to Paterson or Stuttle the box would have vanished early this morning, rather than just being returned to the wrong shelf. 'There is one other possibility. We did have a bomb hoax that meant this building was completely empty.'

'You think someone has stolen it?'

'Well, it hasn't just vanished. And I reckon we've got about seven minutes to come up with an explanation for where it is, before Mr Stuttle rips our heads off.'

7

In the months that she'd worked for the North Edinburgh HET, Mona had witnessed Stuttle in a state of absolute fury several times. In fact, she had provoked this response on at least one occasion herself. Similarly, she witnessed her immediate line manager moved to anger on at least a daily basis. She'd observed on these instances that when incensed Paterson's face would move through a range of pantones on the red spectrum, before ending on a rage-induced crimson. Stuttle, on the other hand, grew paler and paler the angrier he became.

She'd seen them individually enraged often, and from time to time, in a state of fury with each other. But until now, she'd never seen them murderously angry in unison. With Paterson puce of face, and Stuttle spectral-white, it was as if a bar of coconut ice had become sentient, and decided it was one deeply pissed off piece of confectionary.

'What do you mean it's not there? They're supposed to be confronting the Carmichaels with the evidence in . . .' Stuttle stopped to look at his watch, 'less than fifteen minutes and you're telling me you don't have it?'

'We think someone took it,' said Bernard, apologetically.

'Yes, well, we gathered that, Bernard. But *how* did they manage to take it?'

'The bomb hoax,' said Paterson, slapping his head. 'Empty building, someone could have been in and out.'

'Not that easy,' said Ian. 'You wouldn't be able to get past the Green Card machine. It wouldn't be difficult to trace anyone who'd accessed the building.'

'Although currently the Emergency Exit isn't alarmed,' said Bernard.

'Isn't it?' said Maitland.

'Yeah, but you'd have to know that . . .' Stuttle stopped, a look of realisation passed across his face. Mona guessed he'd found his culprit.

The Guv seemed to know who he was thinking of. 'And you'd have to know we had it, and there's not many people who knew that. Also, it was under lock and key, wasn't it? And there are only two keys. I've got one and the team have got the other.'

'Yes.'

'So they broke in?' Stuttle pushed the door of the cabinet shut. 'I don't see any sign of forced entry.'

'Actually,' Maitland's voice was unusually subdued, 'we think they took the key out of, ehm, a desk drawer.'

Mona's money was on the drawer in question belonging to Maitland.

Stuttle's face paled even further. He looked like he should be on life support. 'You keep the key to your evidence cupboard in the same room as the cupboard? Jesus Christ, it's like having a bloody bunch of chimps in charge! I would sack the lot of you if there was any chance at all that I'd be able to replace you. Right, well, we'll deal with this stupidity later. Our immediate problem is what do you say to the Carmichaels, who I suspect may well know of our predicament.'

He exchanged a glance with both Paterson and Bernard. What did Bernard know about all this, Mona wondered? She'd get it out of him later.

'OK, let's recap – what was in that box?' asked Stuttle.

Bernard nervously held out a piece of paper. 'Here's the inventory.'

'Monthly telephone bills for Helen Sopel's mobile,' he read aloud. 'April to August. Right, well, we all know what that one was all about. One folk mask, possibly Native American. One black-and-white photocopy of a photograph picturing a woman in 1950s dress . . .what is this stuff? Does any of it make sense to you?'

'No, Mr Stuttle. But it must have been significant to Helen Sopel.'

The phone rang. Mona picked it up. 'They're here. According to Marguerite, there's only two of them.'

'No lawyer then. Let's be thankful for small mercies.' Stuttle shook his head. 'Well, you better not keep them waiting.'

Paterson didn't move. 'What exactly are we going to say to them?'

'Well, you've got things you want to ask Carlotta about that meeting, and when it comes to Mr Carmichael you'll just have to improvise.'

'Improvise?'

'Yeah. Don't mention the box unless they bring it up.'

'And if they do?'

Stuttle ducked the question. 'I've every faith in you guys. You can do this.'

'Oh God. Let's get it over with.'

The Member of the Scottish Parliament for Upper Lithdale and her husband had been installed in one of the larger meeting rooms on the ground floor. Marguerite was fussing around with a flask of coffee. The good chocolate biscuits – the ones with shiny foil wrappers

– had also made an appearance. Mona was grateful for Marguerite's efforts, but it was going to take more than quality snacks to get through this meeting.

She'd only ever seen the Carmichaels in the Scottish Parliament before. Carlotta was an attractive woman in her forties, with immaculately coiffured red hair. She seemed smaller than she did when she was commanding the attention of everyone at the Scottish Parliamentary Virus Committee. Her husband was slightly older, tanned, with receding grey hair, and oversized glasses with tortoiseshell frames. Both of them seemed intent on watching Marguerite fluttering around, rather than making eye contact with the HET officers.

Paterson swung into action. 'John Paterson, Team Leader here at North Edinburgh HET. We've met before.'

Jonathon Carmichael's face registered a brief look of annoyance. One of the previous times the two of them had met was when the then Police Sergeant Paterson had arrested Mr Carmichael for speeding. Neither man had a great regard for the other.

'This is Mona Whyte from my team, and Ian Jacobsen from Police Scotland.'

'Police Scotland?' Carlotta raised an eyebrow. 'What's your interest in this interview?'

'Potential links to a couple of our ongoing cases, Minister,' said Ian, without batting an eyelid. Mona felt a grudging admiration. He appeared to be a good deal more practised in dealing with politicians that she was.

Paterson began the proceedings. 'So, Mrs Carmichael, the HET is looking for a senior civil servant who has missed her Health Check, a woman called Helen Sopel.'

Carlotta looked surprised. 'I've worked closely with

Helen for the past couple of years. Has something happened to her?'

'We don't know yet, I'm afraid. As you are well aware, under the terms of the Health Defaulters (Scotland) Act . . .'

She waved a hand to stop him, her irritation palpable. 'I understand the confidentiality aspect, Mr Paterson. I helped to draft the legislation.'

'Of course. And I'm sure in your role as Chair of the Parliamentary Virus Committee you'll also be aware of the deaths of both Nathan McVie and Jasper Connington?'

Both sets of Carmichael eyes strayed in the direction of Ian Jacobsen. Mona guessed they were wondering if these were the criminal cases he had alluded to.

'You wouldn't have to be head of a Parliamentary Committee to be aware of that, Mr Paterson, the deaths have been all over the news. Both suicides, I have been led to believe?' Her eyes rested on Ian again, who refused to be drawn.

'Were you aware that Ms Sopel was missing?'

She inclined her head. 'I had a meeting yesterday with the Permanent Secretary to discuss staffing issues. As you can imagine, we're suffering a severe leadership crisis in Virus policy at the moment. We also discussed the continuing leak of information about those staffing issues to Twitter.' She shot Paterson a glance.

'None of which is coming from this office, I can assure you, Mrs Carmichael.'

She looked away in a manner that managed to convey disbelief.

'Anyway,' he continued. Mona could sense that any nerves he had had about the interview were rapidly being replaced by irritation. 'Mrs Carmichael, on the day

Mr McVie died, he was in a meeting with Helen Sopel, Jasper Connington and yourself. Two of those people are now dead, and one is missing. You can see, therefore, Mrs Carmichael, that it is very important that we know what was discussed at that meeting, and you are the only person who can tell us.'

'I believe you also wanted to speak to me about something?' asked Jonathon Carmichael.

Annoyance flashed across Paterson's face. 'Yes, Mr Carmichael, but I'd like an answer to my question to your wife first.'

Carmichael held up a hand to stop him, which Mona could see was enraging Paterson further. 'You'll have an answer in due course, but I think you need to talk to me first.'

He thought about this for a second. 'OK, OK, if you insist.' He turned to her. 'Mona . . .'

Thanks, Guv. 'We wanted to ask you about Helen Sopel, Mr Carmichael. How well were you acquainted with her?'

He nodded in a manner that suggested he had been anticipating this question, then looked at his wife. She sighed. To Mona's surprise, Jonathon took Carlotta's hand in his. 'I met Helen through my wife's work. We collaborated quite closely on a couple of projects I was working on and, ehm, unfortunately I did not maintain the level of professional distance that I should have done.'

'I'm not sure what you're trying to say here, Mr Carmichael.'

'Helen and I had an affair. A short-lived one. I soon realised my mistake. But Helen, unfortunately . . .'

There was a pause. Mona wondered if he was waiting

for someone to help him out. After a second or two, when no help was forthcoming, he continued.

'Helen was very angry with me for ending our relationship and made a number of accusations about me to close colleagues.'

Carlotta pulled her hand out from under her husband's. 'Hence the meeting at the Museum. It wasn't about work, as such, more about Ms Sopel and her colleagues making some rather veiled threats about my husband.'

'Threats?'

'They were requesting his removal from any future Virus work.'

'What did you say to that?'

'I said I would have to think it over.' Carlotta had not made eye contact with her throughout the interview. Her eyes now flicked briefly in Mona's direction. 'But I haven't been able to give anyone an answer as, obviously, we've been overtaken by events.'

Mona wondered what to say next. In her head she'd prepared lots of gently probing questions, lots of ways in which she could slowly reel in an uncooperative Jonathon Carmichael. She'd been prepared to give him enough space to ramble on, in the hope that he would trip himself up. She'd been prepared to ask him outright about his marriage and had thought of a few tactics to leverage the advantage of his wife actually being in the room. The one eventuality she hadn't prepared for was a full and frank admission of adultery. Jonathon Carmichael had completely taken the wind from her sails. *No further questions, Your Honour.*

Ian stepped into the breach. 'Well, thank you to you both for coming in. I appreciate this can't have been an easy afternoon.'

They both looked a little surprised that they were being released.

'Obviously we'd like a little discretion on this issue.' Jonathon Carmichael got to his feet. 'Can we assume that it won't be all over Twitter by tomorrow?'

'Absolutely, you have my word.' Ian said. 'I'll just show you back to reception.'

The Carmichaels both followed his lead, and left the room without any further eye contact or attempts at farewells.

Mona pulled the door shut tight behind him. 'I wasn't actually done there, Guv. I had a few more questions for them,' she lied. 'But Ian got them out the door pretty damn quick.'

'Yes, but I think we got everything that we needed from them.'

'Did we?' asked Mona, doubtfully.

'Oh, yeah.' He nodded, solemnly. 'Now I can believe that Carmichael was shagging around. I'd heard rumours in the past that he had a bit of a roving eye. I could also believe that Helen Sopel was annoyed with him for ending things. I could equally believe it was the other way round, and that she dumped him, and he was making a nuisance of himself. But I struggle to imagine a Minister being summoned to a meeting by a group of civil servants, however senior, so that they can tell her off about her man's behaviour.'

'Well, we should have dug a bit deeper.'

'They're not going to tell us, Mona. But you explain this to me. Why is Carlotta 'fessing up all this to dogs-bodies like us? I mean, why is she not insisting on a discreet meeting with Stuttle? Or sitting there with her lawyer threatening us with all sorts? Why would the pair of them be so open about the affair with an organisation that they suspect of being responsible for a number of recent leaks?'

'They want this story out in the public domain.' Mona thought for a second. 'But that must be completely humiliating for Carlotta.'

'Yup. I also don't believe a word of this affair. I think he's being meeting Helen Sopel about something, and suspects we have evidence. But I don't think it was an affair. And now the box has done a vanishing act I think that we can assume that the phone numbers were the least incriminating thing in it. We need to work out what that mask is all about, and who that woman is.'

'I agree.' She thought for a moment. 'But what could they have been meeting about that is so embarrassing that you'd rather pretend publicly that it was an affair?'

Paterson leaned back, his hands behind his head. 'I don't know. But I'm looking forward to finding out.'

8

Bernard was pacing. There were only ten steps between the door of his 'open-plan' living space and hitting the sink and cooker on the other wall. He'd added in further walking potential by detouring into the bedroom, but that floor space could be covered in six large strides.

Pacing helped him think. He was revisiting a conundrum that he hadn't thought about since he'd been twenty-one. The age-old dilemma – what to say to a girl when you phoned up to ask her out.

He'd not had a huge amount of practice. He could remember doing it only twice during his high school years (once asking Maria McDonald out to a film, and one high-stakes phone call to Catriona Henderson to try to score himself a date to the end of term dance. It was some small consolation that he had been successful on both occasions, although he did seem to remember that at the time he'd sworn never again due to the levels of stress it had caused him.) The only other time he could remember was a call to Carrie, which had led several years later to their marriage. So he was well aware that phone calls could lead to great things. But you still had to get up the nerve to pick up the phone.

He paced from the front door to the far side of the bed and back. How to play this? Was he phoning Lucy to take up her offer of a tour of the Museum, or should he go straight to a less ambiguous invitation out to dinner?

He repeated the thirty-two strides. Did he actually want a date with her? His marriage was only just over, maybe not even broken beyond repair. And what if he'd misunderstood the situation and Lucy already had a boyfriend?

He made the trek from door to bed twice more, then decided he was ready. A woman who liked museums as much as he did was just too good a proposition for him not to at least attempt to secure a date. Standing next to the cooker, he could feel the cold of the tiles rising up through his socks, he dialled the number, the card with her number on it propped up against the washing rack. As soon as he'd made the call he'd go and dig out his slippers.

She answered after a couple of rings.

'Lucy?' he said, just as disaster struck. He'd underestimated how slippery his palms had become as he'd paced and fretted round the apartment. The phone slipped straight through them. He made a grab for it, and in his haste knocked the ceramic pencil holder off the work top. It broke into pieces, and in the middle of the fragments Bernard saw something small and silver.

He picked it up and rolled it round between his finger and his thumb. He assumed it was a bug, although he'd never seen one before. Though why anyone would bug his home was beyond him. Anything of interest he had to say about the Virus would generally be done on the work phone or mobile.

Which, of course, were also probably bugged, or hacked, or whatever it was you did.

Why he was being bugged might remain a mystery, but the 'how' was simple. He assumed that the bug had already been present when he'd been given a super thoughtful gift by a friend. A friend who had some financial difficulties.

What had Marcus got himself into?

9

Mona drank her tea, trying not to scowl. Since leaving work, she'd been home, loaded up a bag with enough clothes to last a few days, and headed round to her mother's. Her mother's twisted ankle appeared to have had a variable impact on her ability to do household chores. She'd happily cooked them a meal consisting of chicken in white wine sauce, followed by rice pudding, but had then claimed to be 'absolutely worn out'. Mona had put the bins out, stuck a load of washing on and was sulking in the living room while her mother watched *Coronation Street*.

Her phone bleeped, and a text message flashed on the screen. *Elaine*. She quickly turned her phone off, glancing guiltily at her mother, who remained engrossed in her soap opera. After a second's reflection she realised she was being stupid and turned the phone on again. Her mother would be delighted to know that Mona was dating. Of all the many people who would be annoyed about Mona's current love life, her mother really wasn't one.

She swiped back to her text messages. It was the second time today that Elaine had texted. The first one had been a message to say how much she'd enjoyed their date. Mona assumed that this was good Internet dating etiquette but hadn't replied. The lack of response didn't appear to have put Elaine off, as the more recent message was short and to the point. *Drink later?*

The text provoked a range of emotions in Mona, the uppermost one being fear. She knew she'd messed up. Some vague memories of the evening were coming back, and she was pretty sure she'd made all kinds of indiscreet comments about the HET office to Cassandra Doom. Loose lips sink ships, and her career was in serious danger of beaching on a set of rocks of her own making. Her only hope was that her comments had been lacking in detail, that she'd just voiced the usual drunken complaints everyone makes about their boss and colleagues with a bottle of red inside them. Or maybe she'd spilled chapter and verse about the Sopel investigation, and Elaine only wanted to meet her to pressure her into going on record about some of them.

Underneath the worries that she'd compromised her professional integrity, there was another deeper fear. She'd enjoyed getting to know Elaine, both over the Internet, and then in their date, right up until the point when she'd ripped off the mask to reveal the right-wing pundit she really was. Mona had been invested in the relationship. She'd been hoping to see her again and take things further. That, too, was scary.

She looked up to see her mother watching her.

'If you have to go out to work, Mona, just go. I'll be fine here.'

There was a slight accusation in the tone. *You can't even make it through one evening in my company, Mona. Always running off to work, just like your father.*

'Well, if you're sure, Mum. I really won't be long.'

She started typing.
Pear Tree, half an hour?

The Pear Tree pub was an Edinburgh institution, located bang in the middle of student-land. The pub occupied a mansion house that had been built in the eighteenth century, and had moved through various occupancies and near-dereliction until it re-opened in 1982 as a public house and beer garden. What the ghosts made of the behaviour of the modern-day students was anyone's guess.

Mona had chosen it because it was a ten-minute jog from her mother's and, more importantly, as she wasn't a student she thought it very unlikely she'd meet anyone she knew in there. Her intention was to have one (soft) drink, try to establish if she'd said anything indiscreet on Monday, then to suggest apologetically to Elaine that it might be for the best if they never saw each other ever again.

She marched into the beer garden, heading for the wide set of stairs that led up to Pear Tree House.

'Mona.'

Elaine was sitting on a bench, stubbing out the remains of a cigarette. 'Filthy habit, I know. Shall we head inside?'

'Yes, OK.' Mona could feel her heart starting to race. She took a breath. *In, find out what she said, deal with it, home listening to her mother moan by 9pm.*

Elaine took the initiative and offered to go to the bar. Mona grasped the opportunity to choose a corner table, and to have a good look round the room to make sure there was no one there that she knew. By the time Elaine returned with Mona's requested Coke, and a pint of cider for herself, she had reassured herself that they were as good as alone, and she began to relax.

'Do you usually drink cider?' asked Mona.

'No, but when in Rome . . .' Elaine waved a hand at the room. 'Actually, I haven't been in this pub for years. My show isn't too popular with a lot of your more liberal-minded students. Too young to know any better, most of them.'

'Yeah, about your writing . . .'

'I really enjoyed our meal together, Mona.'

Mona could feel Elaine's ankle brushing against hers, accidentally she assumed.

'It was the first time in years I'd actually had intelligent conversation on a date.'

Elaine's calf was now pressed against hers. She considered it unlikely that this was accidental. She should probably move if she was going to keep all this professional, but on the other hand she didn't want to antagonise her. The soft warmth against her leg was making it quite difficult to concentrate.

'How was it for you, Mona? I do hope you had fun.'

'Ehm.' For the second time that day, Mona felt as if she were in an interview that she wasn't really in control of. 'The thing is, Elaine, I think I may have said some things I shouldn't about life in the HET.'

'Like what? Do you mean the things you said about the attitude of your manager, Paterson, was it? Or the fact that SHEP starved you of the resources to do an even halfway decent job, while maintaining, what did you call it, "their fuck off massive office suite on the High Street"?'

Mona cringed.

'Relax!' She laughed. 'You weren't telling me anything that I didn't already know. Obviously I'd love it if you wanted to go on record about some of these issues, but really, I'd rather have another date with you. What do you think?'

Mona said nothing. Another date would be a very bad idea, for many reasons. She wasn't exactly a world authority on dating, but she did know that successful relationships were invariably built on mutual trust and respect. She had very little respect for some of the views Cassandra Doom espoused and was extremely clear on exactly how little she trusted her. But on the other hand, now that she was here, a large part of her very much wanted to reach under the table and run her hands right up under the ridiculously figure-hugging skirt that Elaine was wearing.

'Do you believe all that shit you say when you're being Cassandra Doom?'

'Every word, darling!'

Mona moved her legs firmly to her own side of the table.

'You look so disappointed.' Elaine laughed. 'Come on, nobody believes everything Cassie says.'

Mona disagreed. She thought there were some people who hung on Cassandra's every word and were more than happy to turn her words of hatred into deeds. 'So, why do it if you don't believe it?'

'I do believe some of it. I do think that your Health Checks are an invasion of our civil liberties. And I do think that Cameron Stuttle is a self-serving arse. But Cassie's been good to me. I've got a profile that most journalists would kill for.'

Mona didn't say anything.

'I do also write sensible investigative journalism as well, if it makes you feel any better. Although nobody reads that. Cassie just seems to be what people need in these difficult times.'

'I should probably go.' Mona reached for her bag.

'How's the investigation into Helen Sopel's disappearance going?'

She froze. 'I . . .I didn't tell you about that.'

'You didn't.' Elaine grinned. 'But your reaction to my question just confirmed my suspicions. The answer should have been, "Who is Helen Sopel?"'

Mona wondered if she should resign, then remembered she couldn't. Stuttle and Paterson were going to make her life a misery.

'You didn't tell me, Mona, but you did mention you were looking for a civil servant. I just put a few calls in to civil servant friends to see who hadn't turned up for work recently. Sounds like a cracking story. Two suicides and a Missing Person.'

'She's a Health Defaulter. You can't mention any of this in the paper.'

'Ha! We might not be able to print chapter and verse, but Cassie's lawyers are very adept at advising what we can and can't allude to. I could run home right now, and dash off 200 words of pure innuendo about trouble at the top of the Scottish Virus tree, and the lawyers would have it OK'd in time for my column tomorrow. But don't look so worried.' Elaine's legs were pressed against hers once more. 'I want to see you again, Mona. I want you to trust me. I'm not going to breathe a word of your little investigation. Not unless you tell me that I can.'

'Hello – I thought it was you.'

Mona jumped. There were two girls standing by the table. One of them had short spiky hair, which seemed to have been decorated with a bluey-silvery dye, and a nose stud. The other, with long brown hair falling in spirals, looked slightly familiar. Then she said, 'I'm Kate, Maitland's girlfriend?'

165

'Oh, of course.' *Shit, shit, shit.*

Kate looked over at Elaine, obviously expecting an introduction.

'This is, ehm, Elaine.'

'Elaine McGillvary?' Kate's friend stepped forward. Mona took in the nose ring, then the blue hair. If she'd drawn a picture of the very opposite of a Cassandra Doom fan, Kate's friend was pretty much exactly what she would look like. And she appeared to know exactly who Elaine was, which meant that before the night was out, Maitland would know about the company she had been keeping.

'Guilty as charged.' She raised her glass to them.

'I hate your column.' Kate's friend stood with her hands on her hips. 'You do nothing but spout hate for everyone and everything. You should be ashamed of yourself.' She pulled at Kate's arm. 'C'mon. Let's find somewhere else to drink.'

Kate looked confused but let herself be led away. 'Bye, then.'

As she walked off, Mona could hear her asking her friend what all the fuss had been about.

'Oh God.' She rested her head on her hands.

'Don't worry about it, it happens to me all the time.'

'I am worried! That was the girlfriend of one of my colleagues. What if she tells him who I was with?'

'Well, I dare say you will lie and say that you had no idea who I was until Kate's friend made a scene.'

'But your column tomorrow . . .'

'Mona, I can assure you, I am not about to mention anything that we discussed.' She reached across the table and stroked Mona's cheek. 'Relax.'

She brought her other hand up, gently pulled Mona toward her and kissed her.

She tasted of apples.

166

THURSDAY

BENEATH THE MASK

I

Bernard strode purposefully into the office, having
stopped en route to purchase the smallest, sturdiest
screwdriver that the 24-hour Asda had on offer. For the
second day running he had made it to work by 7.30am,
and he was confident that today at least he would have
the place to himself. He'd do what he had to do, then
treat himself to a well-deserved large egg and spinach
roll to celebrate. He dropped his bag by his desk, pulled
off his coat, and was raking in the pocket for his new
purchase when he heard a cough. He spun round to see
Mona watching him with the slightly amused grin that
she often wore when eyeballing him.

'Morning, early bird.'

'What are you doing here?' Bernard was trying not to
look irritated at her presence in what should have been a
completely deserted space, and was, he suspected, failing
miserably.

'I work here. And I have a lot to do, seeing as we seem
to be no nearer to finding Helen Sopel than we were on
Monday. Not surprising, given that we've had to deal
with a bomb hoax and our evidence seems to suddenly
have grown legs and scarpered, but nonetheless I'd like
to get the whole thing wrapped up and move on to something a bit less controversial.'

He turned his back on her and walked to his desk,

cursing the fact that everyone suddenly seemed to have developed a taste for early starts. 'You sound a bit on the grumpy side, Mona. Maybe you need to go and get a cup of coffee?'

'Way ahead of you.' She waved a takeaway cup at him. 'And the grumpiness is all natural, not the result of caffeine deprivation.'

He was unwilling to have his mission thwarted. Another half-hour and Mr Paterson would come storming in, and he'd stand no chance of a moment's peace. He positioned himself in a way that prevented Mona seeing what he was up to, and got out the screwdriver. He slowly slid the metal tip in between the plastic seams.

'What on earth are you doing?'

Bernard jumped and narrowly missed impaling himself on his Hyper-Tough Soft Grip Flat 3.5mm.

'Jeepers, Mona. Why are you sneaking up on me?'

'Because you were being weird! I wondered what you were doing.' She paused. 'Actually, what *are* you doing?'

'Nothing.'

'Yeah, right. You're in here at the crack of dawn, and obviously well peed off to see me here.' Her eyes narrowed. 'You're not the evidence thief, are you?'

'Of course not!' He sighed, giving in to the inevitable. Opening his hand he showed her the screwdriver. 'I found a bug in my flat.' He returned to his levering. 'I want to see if there's one here as well.'

'Don't!' Mona grabbed his hand.

'What? Why?'

She gestured toward the door, and he followed her. Once in the corridor she stopped and looked round.

'If you take the bug out, whoever planted it there will know that you've found it.' Her voice was low.

170

'True.' Taking his cue from her, he whispered back. 'But why is that a problem?'

'Because this gives us an opportunity to try to find out who put it there.'

Bernard thought he probably knew the answer to that.

'And, if we put some misinformation out there, I'd be really interested to see where it ended up. This could be the source of our Twitter leaks.'

'OK.' He had to admit that was a good idea. 'Why are we discussing this out here?'

'Because if there are bugs in the phone, there's also a possibility that there are other bugs in the office. Don't mention this to a soul, Bernard, until we can work out what's going on.'

'I don't know. Maybe we should tell Mr Paterson if we find something?'

'No, not a word to the Guv until we know what's going on.'

'But . . .' Bernard wasn't a natural rule breaker, and he was pretty sure that if you found a listening device in your workplace phone you were duty-bound to report it. But Marcus, despite his current idiocy, was a good friend, and if he was behind the bugging then he didn't want to get him into trouble. Maybe he should talk to Bryce again. Maybe he should talk to Marcus . . .

'Earth to Bernard!'

'Sorry, OK, OK. I'll keep mum, and I won't do anything that will alert him that we've found his bug.'

'His bug?' Mona hissed. 'Whose? Bernard, do you know something?'

'Morning, troops.' Paterson swept past them. 'Why are you skulking in the corridor?'

Mona leaned in close to him. 'I want to know everything.'

171

Paterson reappeared. 'Are you two not coming in today?'

'Yeah, Guv, we're coming.' She shot Bernard a look then followed their boss in. He cursed himself for his stupidity. No one should ever trust him with a secret. Although, maybe telling Mona about Marcus wouldn't be such a bad thing. She could usually be relied upon to come up with a solution to any given difficulty. While he saw a problem from so many different angles he ended up unable to make a decision, Mona was usually good at getting right to the heart of it and suggesting a plan of action. He might actually tell her. Although maybe he shouldn't involve anyone else in this. There was a lot to think about.

'You're in early, Guv.'

'Yup.' He headed into his office, and they could hear the sound of the kettle being put on. 'The Facilities Manager wanted to meet me at 8am to point out my many failings in response to yesterday's events.'

'*Your* failings, Mr Paterson?' said Bernard. 'The HET are only tenants of the Cathcart Building. If anyone is at fault I personally think the Facilities Manager is. I've been working here nine months and we've never had a single evacuation drill. As far as I'm aware the admin team have never been given any training on how to deal with bomb calls or other hoaxes, and we've obviously become a bit more high profile over the past week or so, so really SHEP should have given some consideration to security concerns . . .'

Paterson emerged from his office. 'Stop there, Bernard.'

Once again his views seemed to have upset his boss. 'Sorry.'

To his surprise, Paterson waved his regrets away.

172

'You've absolutely nothing to apologise for. I just came out to tell you it's your lucky day.'

'Really?' Given that so far he'd nearly stabbed himself with a sharp implement, had almost ratted out his friend to Mona and was now so hungry he could hear his stomach impersonating a lion, he couldn't say he'd seen any evidence that today was shaping up to be particularly auspicious.

'Yes, congratulations.' Paterson took his arm and shepherded him in the direction of the door. 'You just won a visit to the Facilities Manager.'

Lady Luck returned to her usual place in his life and resumed filing her nails. 'I didn't, did I?'

'You certainly did. When we meet him, I want you to spout all that guff again, as firmly and authoritatively as you can.'

And he still hadn't had any breakfast. 'Oh dear.'

Barry Gifford, Facilities Manager for a number of NHS properties in Edinburgh, did not look like a man to be trifled with. He was short but sturdy, with dark brown hair and moustache, and was wearing a blue short-sleeved shirt with a tie.

'Nice to meet you, Barry, I'm John and this is Bernard from the HET team.'

He gave Paterson's hand a cursory shake and nodded in Bernard's direction. 'Well, I have to say I'm not happy about this situation. Not happy at all.'

'Neither are we, Barry, I can assure you. Now, our main concern is what you are going to do to rectify it?'

Barry's moustached quivered up and down with outrage. 'What am I going to do? *Me*?'

'Well, you *are* the Facilities Manager . . .'

Bernard suspected Paterson was enjoying this.

' . . . while my Health Enforcement Team are only tenants of the Cathcart Building.'

'Yes, but—'

'And as tenants, we have certain expectations about the way things are done. I'm a little bit concerned that we haven't to the best of my knowledge had an evacuation drill . . .'

'Now, wait a minute . . .'

'I have to think about the safety of my staff. Has your admin team ever had any training on how to deal with threatening communications such as calls about bombs on the premises?'

Paterson was really getting into his stride. Bernard wasn't sure whether he should feel proud of inspiring his boss, or worried that he'd created a monster, some kind of Facilities Manager-baiting behemoth.

'I mean, I don't have to tell you that we've become pretty high profile over the past week or so, so really you should have been reviewing your policies in light of these security concerns . . .'

'You're damn right you don't have to tell me that!' Barry Gifford's patience had run out. 'I never wanted you people here in the first place. I said to management, once you've got police moving in, you need a police level of security in place.'

'We're not actually Police Scotland,' said Bernard.

'You might as well be! You're staffed by ex-coppers, you attract student protests and hoax calls. We never had that before you lot moved in.'

'Barry, I . . .'

Bernard didn't get to hear Paterson's response to Barry's assessment of the situation, because the door to the meeting room flew open. Marguerite was standing there, a sheet of paper quivering in her hand. 'It was a young woman, I mean, really young sounding.'

'What woman? What's this all about?' asked Barry.

'She didn't have any kind of accent that I could hear—'

'Marguerite!' Paterson managed to get her to stop. 'What are you talking about?'

'The phone call, Mr Paterson. We've had another one. They're saying there's a bomb.'

'There's not really going to be a bomb in there, is there, Guv? I mean, we had all this rigmarole yesterday, and it turned out to be nothing.'

Bernard trailed after his colleagues as they evacuated the building under the no-nonsense direction of Barry Gifford. He couldn't help but notice that people weren't hurrying quite as fast as they had been yesterday.

'I'd have to say I agree, Mona. But every time we get a phone call, we have to go through this. How often do you think they're going to pull this trick? We're never going to get any work done at this rate.' He sighed, all his earlier good mood vanishing. 'At least there's nothing left for them to steal.'

Bernard hurried after him. 'Who do you think is making the calls, Mr Paterson?'

'Well, I had this down as part of a conspiracy to interfere with our evidence. Our visitor from yesterday swears blind it was nothing to do with him, although I have to say I'm not entirely sure I believe him.'

'Who visited yesterday?' asked Mona.

'Mind your own business.'

Bernard caught her eye and got the message loud and clear that she'd have that piece of information out of him as well. People really should stop involving him in secrets.

'I remain open-minded about whether yesterday's hoax was a deliberate attempt to get us out of the building so that the box could take a walk, or whether we were all being evacuated, and someone saw their chance and took it. And if you are about to say "who", don't bother, because I have no idea.'

'And today's call?'

'No idea, but I wouldn't be surprised if it's linked to that lot.' Paterson jerked a thumb in the direction of the straggly band of protestors who had returned to the park. None of them looked to Bernard as if they were the type to phone in a bomb threat. One of them saw him staring and made a rude gesture in his direction, further confirming his view that they were all about direct action. Spray-painting the building, brick through the window, yes. Complex plots involving bomb threats as a cover for stealing evidence in a health defaulter case, not so much.

Paterson continued with his theory. 'Either they did them both, or saw yesterday's palaver and thought it looked like a good wheeze. And I'll tell you something else. That Barry Gifford had a good point this morning. We should have the same level of security on that building as you'd have on a police station.'

'Although it's not like you can just walk in off the street, Guv. You need to go through the Green Card barrier, then reception.'

'Yeah,' Paterson said, 'but what background checks do they do on the people who work in the building? How much do we know about who's working in the other offices?'

'True, Guv.' She turned to Bernard, and he knew her

176

mind was going back to their earlier conversation about bugs.

'You'd better let Ian Jacobsen know that there's no point in rushing over here.'

Mona pulled a face.

'What?'

'He was a pain in the arse when I told him about the previous bomb threat. I can do without another set of smart alec comments.'

'Why don't you text him?' said Bernard.

Her face brightened and she immediately began tapping on her phone. 'Cheers, Bernard.'

'Where are Carole and the idiot boy?' Paterson eyed up the crowd of office workers milling around.

'I don't think either Carole or Maitland has shown up yet.' Mona checked her watch. 'Although it is only a quarter past nine.'

Paterson snorted. 'Which is a quarter past when they're supposed to be here.'

Bernard looked round for any sign of his errant colleagues, but saw only a young man in a slightly scruffy grey suit walking straight toward them. Bernard didn't recognise him, but the man seemed to know Mona. He tapped her on the shoulder, and she spun round, her face registering surprise.

The young man spoke. 'I need to talk to you.'

2

Simon, Mona's civil servant contact, piled two lumps of sugar into his tea, stirred it vigorously, then sat gently tapping the spoon against the red vinyl tablecloth.

'Nice caf, Guv. I've never been in this one.' Mona regarded their surroundings. They weren't what you would describe as fine dining, in fact they were definitely on the greasy spoon side of things, but, in her opinion, none the worse for that.

'They do a great bacon roll.' Paterson's eyes flicked in the direction of the kitchen. 'Maybe later.'

'Anyway, Simon, you had something to tell us?' Simon's arrival had intrigued her, but she was trying not to get her hopes up. Their investigation seemed to have stalled, but in her experience the more you hoped for a breakthrough to land in your lap, the less likely it was to actually happen.

'Yeah.' He fiddled with his spoon some more. 'I mean, I don't want to keep you if you need to get back to . . .whatever that was?'

'It was a bomb hoax, and we've got it covered.' Bernard had been left in place, with strict instructions to come and get them if required. He'd made some protest about not having had breakfast yet, which had been swiftly overruled by Paterson, on the operational grounds that someone had to keep watch and it wasn't going to be him. Maybe she'd take him back a fried egg roll. 'Say what you need to say.'

'Anneka is being a nightmare.'

'She is your boss. She's allowed to be a nightmare.' She smiled. 'Making their staff miserable is a boss's job.'

Paterson raised an eyebrow.

'I know, I know. And it's not like she wasn't a pain in the arse before all this kicked off, but now it's like she's morphing into Helen. She's doing all the same kind of secretive stuff.'

'Like what?'

'Phone calls. Ones which she doesn't want to take in the office.'

'Could be lots of reasons for that. Boyfriend, hospital test results . . .'

'In theory, yes, but I know there's more to it.' He played nervously with the spoon again, and Mona had to resist the temptation to rip it out of his hand. 'I may have done something stupid.' He dug into his coat pocket and pulled out a mobile phone, which he placed next to his teacup.

Paterson and Mona eyed it. 'Is that Anneka's?'

'Yes.' He pushed it toward them.

She was itching to pick it up but forced herself to keep her hands on her lap. 'Technically, that's theft.'

'I see myself more as a whistle-blower than a thief.'

'Whistle-blower? Is there something of public interest on it, son?' Paterson's fingers were inching toward it.

'I think so. In fact I'm pretty certain that there's stuff on there that's relevant to your investigation.'

'Isn't it password-protected?' Mona was now actively sitting on her hands.

'It is, but I guessed it. The pin code is Helen's birthday.'

179

He looked pained. 'Which I find kind of creepy.'

'It is a little.' She didn't even know Paterson's exact age, never mind his date of birth. 'So, what did you find?'

'She's got a whole lot of calls and text messages from this one number over the past couple of days. It doesn't say who the number is but I can guess from the context.'

'Helen Sopel?'

'Yup.'

Paterson's hands were either side of the phone. 'Does it say where she is?'

'I haven't looked at them in detail...'

Mona wasn't sure she believed this.

'There are lots of texts about picking up food and supplies, but I didn't see anything like an address. But I thought you'd have IT specialists and if I handed it over to you, you might be able to figure it out.'

'What do you think, Guv? Can we take it?'

Paterson's hands were edging closer to either side of the phone, like an army of fingers performing a pincer movement. 'I think we can make a public interest defence for our accepting it.'

Mona reached out and pocketed it before he changed his mind.

'So,' asked Simon, warily, 'I'm not under arrest or anything for taking it?'

'No, but please talk to us before pinching anything else,' said Paterson, his stern expression not quite masking his excitement at getting the phone.

'Will Anneke be under arrest if it turns out she is hiding Helen?' Simon asked, with a cadence to his voice that was distinctly hopeful.

'We'll see,' said Mona.

Bernard's face appeared at the window. He gave her

a thumbs up, then pushed open the door and headed swiftly in the direction of the counter.

'Looks like we can go back, Guv.'

'I'll be off then.' Simon stood up.

'Thanks for your help.' Mona stuck out a hand. He shook it, bobbed his head at Paterson, then slunk furtively out of the café.

'Have we had the all-clear, Bernard?' asked Paterson.

'Yeah. Egg roll, please.' He put his order in to the bored-looking woman sitting behind the Formica tabletop.

'To go,' shouted Paterson to the kitchen. 'What's the story?'

'Barry Gifford interrogated poor Marguerite about the call. She'd filled the call sheet in faithfully, noted that the caller was a young girl and everything, but there wasn't a box that asked if she could hear all the caller's pals giggling away in the background.'

'So it was just teenagers mucking around?'

'Looks like it. Ooh, thank you.' He bit into his roll with delight. 'This tastes so good. Anyway, Barry Gifford was furious with Marguerite, which in my opinion is a little bit unfair, because she was doing her best. I think you got him all riled up this morning, Mr Paterson.'

'Good! He needs to get all this nonsense knocked on the head. I'm not getting kicked out of my office every time some bored teen wants a bit of a laugh. Anyway, Marge will be getting tea and sympathy from the rest of the admin team. She'll be fine.'

Mona eyed Bernard's sandwich. 'Couple of bacon rolls for the road, Guv?'

'Why not?'

The office was already occupied when they returned. She couldn't see what was on Maitland's computer screen,

181

but Carole's browser was open at Facebook. She didn't rush to close the page, and if Paterson saw it he opted not to comment.

'Colleagues, glad you could join us. Eventually.' Paterson pointed in the direction of the metal cupboard. 'Anything else go walkabout while we were out of the building?'

'Nothing left for them to take, Guv.' Maitland yawned, a wide-open affair that afforded everyone a fine view of half a dozen fillings and a set of tonsils.

'Late night?' asked Paterson.

'Yup.' He sat up straight. 'Interesting story, Guv. I was out with Kate last night . . .'

Mona sensed where this was going. She sat down at her desk, bracing herself for the full wrath of her colleagues when they found out the story about Cassandra Doom and her unlikely drinking buddy.

'Thanks for sharing, Maitland, now step to it.'

'No, Guv, you need to hear this. It relates to these leaks we've been having. I think I might just have found the source.'

Paterson stopped in the doorway to his room.

'So, I caught up with Kate about ten o'clock last night. She'd been at some Christian nonsense or other with her leftie mate Lyndsey, who does my head in, so I told Kate to give me a call when Lyndsey went home. We had a great night in the pub, but once we get back to my flat, Kate starts talking about seeing my colleague Mona out on a date. With a woman.'

'Good for you!' said Bernard. 'That's not news, Maitland, that's Mona's private life.'

'Bernard's right. That's absolutely none of our business.' Paterson finally went into his room.

182

Mona wondered whether to make a break for it. Maitland could spill the beans, she'd give them time to digest the news, and then she could come back all guns blazing in an hour or so. It was totally up to her who she dated. Or in this case didn't date.

Maitland raised his voice so that Paterson could still hear him, whether he wanted to or not. 'And Kate said that Lyndsey had been all upset because the woman Mona was with was some right-wing nutjob commentator. Of course, Kate couldn't actually remember the name of the woman, but after a long, long, Internet search I find out that my colleague is dating none other than Cassandra Doom.'

The room was silent. Mona spun round on her seat and stared Maitland out. He glared back.

'That can't be right,' said Bernard, his tone wavering between confusion and hope. 'Mona?'

The silence stretched on excruciatingly, until she gave in. 'I've seen her twice.'

Paterson went into his office, slamming the door of his office shut behind him. Almost immediately he reappeared. 'Give me the phone.' He beckoned to her.

'What?'

'Give me Anneka's phone.' He stretched out his hand. 'Now.'

She slowly reached into her pocket for it and handed it to him. 'Why?'

'As far as I'm concerned you're a security risk.'

'Damn right,' muttered Maitland.

She felt a wave of fury rising up from her feet. 'You can't be serious.'

'I'm deadly serious, I can assure you. Bernard, check out the contents of this phone. See if it says anything relevant to Helen Sopel's whereabouts. Report anything you find directly to me.' He pointed at Mona. 'And not to her.'

She looked round at her colleagues. Maitland and Paterson were still glaring at her like she was Public Enemy Number One. Carole and Bernard were avoiding catching her eye. She stood up. 'I'm going out.'

'Good.'

As she walked down the corridor she could hear Bernard's voice.

'Ehm, whose phone is this, Mr Paterson?'

3

'That's awful.'

'I know.'

'No, Maitland, I mean, really, really awful.'

His colleagues were huddled round Maitland's computer. Bernard didn't know what they were up to, but he'd put money on it not relating in any way, shape, or form to the search for Helen Sopel. He wondered if he should point out to them that Paterson was in an extremely bad mood at the moment, not likely to be improved by coming out of his office and finding them messing about.

'Bernard, you have to see this,' said Carole.

'What?'

'Cassandra Doom's columns.' Maitland joined in. 'They're appalling. I was up until 3am reading them. I just couldn't stop, Bern. Each one was worse than the one before.'

'I'll look at them later, once I've got some work done.'

'*Why are we spending millions trying to keep our prisons free of the Virus? We should be encouraging it. If it wipes out a few free-loading criminals, that's a saving to the public purse . . .*' Maitland read aloud from the screen.

'It doesn't really say that, does it?'

'It does.' Maitland yawned. 'And that's one of the more liberal headlines.'

Bernard was sorely tempted. Paterson was bunkered down in his office. Before retreating he'd barked some instructions about the phone, which Bernard hadn't really understood. He had thought he would be able to work out who the phone belonged to and what he was supposed to be doing with it once he turned it on, but fell at the first hurdle when he discovered he needed a pin number. He'd have to risk Paterson's wrath and ask some follow-up questions before he could do anything useful with it, but thought he'd give him ten minutes to calm down before braving his lair. He might as well have a look at the articles. He turned round, but he'd spent too long thinking about it, and Maitland and Carole were now giggling about something else.

Suddenly Maitland got up and headed out. Bernard saw that his jacket was still there, hanging on the back of his chair. Carole, on the other hand, was putting her coat on.

'You're going out?' he asked.

'Good guess, Bernard.'

'What do I say if Paterson asks where you are?'

'Don't say anything. Or tell him a complete lie, I really don't care.' She smiled, giving him a wave as she left.

As the door shut behind her, the office felt unnaturally quiet. After a second's adjustment, he decided he was quite happy with the peace, so he could process what he'd just learned. Mona, the colleague whom he highly respected, if not actually entirely liked, was dating one of the people that he most despised on the planet. With a quick eye to Paterson's office to make sure he wasn't about to appear, he typed Cassandra Doom into a search engine and watched as a string of articles popped up.

It's called the NATIONAL health service – time to clamp down on Virus tourism

Enough is Enough – we need to cut back on the so-called 'refugee orphans' claiming that their parents are Virus victims

The articles went on and on. There was no aspect of Virus policy that Cassandra appeared to think was immune to abuse by benefits claimants, foreigners, or left-wing, Britain-hating politicians. Carlotta Carmichael was a 'sock puppet of righteousness, committed to protecting the citizens of Scotland from the idiocies of her own policies'.

'Ouch,' he muttered to himself.

Cameron Stuttle was 'an over-promoted plod, who shouldn't be in charge of a country hospital, never mind a national health emergency'.

'Oh dear.'

He could see why Maitland had spent so long surfing the articles. They were quite addictive. As well as her feelings about the HET, she was quite consistently vitriolic across a wide range of topics, with a particular emphasis on the shaming of people who were overweight or under-white.

He took a deep breath and entered *Cassandra Doom HET* in the search engine.

Big Brother Health Police Planned – a new agency is being created to police people's health behaviour. Under the pretext of the Virus . . .

What a cock-up! The Keystone Cops staffing the Health Enforcement Teams messed up big time today . . .

He cast a further eye in the direction of his boss's office and typed: *Cassandra Doom John Paterson.*

It only returned one response, relating to a

187

particularly rough time that his boss had had at the Parliamentary Virus committee. He read the article from beginning to end, and sincerely hoped that Paterson wasn't making the same Internet searches as him. The many derogatory comments about his boss's intelligence, competence and commitment in the article would no doubt annoy him, but Bernard reckoned it was the several references to his weight that would really have him spitting tacks.

He tried again to bend his mind around the situation. Cassandra Doom would love to have an inside source on the HET. But if Mona was passing information to her, why wasn't she using it in her articles? If Cassandra wanted information about HET disasters, he was sure that Mona could supply her with daily evidence of incompetence, and there was nothing in any of the articles that he'd read that seemed to be based on North Edinburgh HET investigations. And the current leaks had ended up posted anonymously on Twitter. If there was one thing that you could be sure about with Cassandra Doom it was that she wasn't shy about people knowing her opinion. So, while he might not approve of Mona's taste in women, it was a bit of a leap to her being a mole.

A part of him felt almost disappointed at that thought. When Maitland had accused Mona of leaking the information to Cassandra Doom, his first thought had been relief that the leaks weren't coming from Marcus after all. He could go back to thinking of his friend as a slightly unworldly geek, instead of a bankrupt gambler, willing to sell his colleagues down the river for the chance of one more round of poker. Guilty as it made him feel, if one of his colleagues was leaking information, he'd rather it was Mona than Marcus.

The door to Paterson's room flew open. 'How did you get on with the phone?'

'Actually, Mr Paterson . . .'

'And this Mona stuff.' He stood in front of Bernard's desk, frowning down at him. 'What do you think? Is it true?'

'Well, Mona didn't exactly deny she was seeing Cassandra Doom, or whatever her real name is.'

'Uh-huh.'

'But,' Bernard continued, 'I don't see Mona leaking any information to her. I think she is really loyal to the HET, well, loyal to you at least. I could imagine Mona getting fired up about some real injustice, but not leaking the kind of low-level innuendo Cassandra Doom specialises in.'

Paterson didn't exactly nod, but inclined his head to one side to show that he didn't entirely disagree. 'It could be stuff she's said by accident, you know, pillow talk.'

This provoked a mental image that Bernard swiftly pushed aside. 'She did say she'd only seen her twice.'

He grunted. 'Well, we'll see. Anyway, the phone. It belongs to Helen Sopel's deputy.'

'You didn't tell me what the pin code is.'

'Apparently it's Helen Sopel's birthday. I assume we know that?'

'I can get it from her Green Card. But is it just the day and month, or day, month and year? And if the year is included is it four digits or two?'

'I don't know. Give them all a try and tell me how you get on.' He looked toward the door. 'Do you think Mona went to the canteen? I should maybe go and speak to her.'

'I think she was a bit upset when you called her a

security risk. She might have gone a bit further afield.'

He grunted. 'Well, I'll give it a try anyway.'

Bernard listened to his boss's footsteps recede, and be replaced by complete silence. He had a brief opportunity here to complete the task that he'd started last night, before he'd become distracted by phone bugs. He picked up his phone, remembered again about potential bugs, and pulled out his mobile instead. He contemplated it for a second, wondering if it was any more secure, then decided he had to use some method of communication, and before he could change his mind, quickly typed in Lucy's number.

'Hello?'

'Oh, hi, ehm, Lucy, this is Bernard from the Health Enforcement Team. We met yesterday?'

'Oh, yes, I thought you might be in touch.'

He smiled. She remembered him at least. Maybe she'd been waiting for his call? 'I was wondering if you'd be available to meet up tonight, maybe get some food? I was thinking The Stuffed Pepper at 7pm?'

'Yes. I can do that.' Her tone was solemn.

Delighted as he was to hear the word 'yes', it wasn't quite the joyful acceptance he'd hoped for.

'Is there anything I need to bring with me, Bernard?'

'How do you mean?' He'd been intending to pay, so she didn't need to bring any cash. Unless she was the kind of woman that liked to pay her own way, which he could totally respect. Or did she mean something else? Oh, God, how much had dating changed since he'd last swum in that particular pool?

'For your investigation,' she clarified. 'Is there anything I need to bring from work?'

Oh no. Oh no, oh no, oh no. She hadn't realised this

was a date. He desperately tried to think of a way to correct her, but nothing sprang to mind. 'No, no, just yourself is fine. See you at seven.'

He hung up and sat staring dejectedly at his phone. Maitland made this kind of thing look so easy. He'd have to tell her about the misunderstanding as soon as he got there. It would be completely unethical to do otherwise. He could be accused of misusing the power vested in him as a HET officer. Although, now that he thought about it, it would take some of that 'first date' pressure off. Maybe he'd consider what to do over the rest of the afternoon.

With renewed vigour he returned to Anneka's phone and put the pin code in successfully. 'Now, what's your secret?'

4

Mona rode out of the building on a tidal wave of fury. *Security risk*. She'd done nothing wrong. The HET had the right to her full attention between the hours of nine and five and nothing more. It didn't have the right to police how she spent her evenings, and it certainly didn't have the right to tell her who she could and couldn't become romantically involved with. Although, if she was honest, if Maitland had walked in one day saying he was dating Cassandra Doom, she'd have questioned his judgement. She'd have questioned his sanity. And Cassandra's.

She jogged out of the building, dimly aware of several heads in the admin department turning to see who was going past in such a hurry. She wondered if Maitland had got round to passing the news on to them yet. That would be a joy to deal with. Although she suspected they'd be far more interested in the fact that she liked a woman, than who that woman actually was. She could picture a future conversation with Marguerite involving a lot of questions that she really didn't want to answer.

As soon as she was out of the building she picked up her pace and sprinted round the corner to the newsagents.

'*Daily Citizen*, please.'

The middle-aged Asian woman behind the counter handed it to her. 'You in a hurry, love?'

'Little bit. Thanks.'

She opened the paper on the counter and flicked directly to the Cassandra Doom column. Cassandra was on fine form, ranting about the NHS, the new double yellow lines on the street near her house and the state of education in Scotland. She had nothing, however, to say about the Health Enforcement Teams in general, and not a word about the North Edinburgh HET in particular. Even more importantly, not a single line referenced missing civil servants. Mona heaved an inward sigh of relief and started to laugh.

'Must have been a good joke.' The shop owner peered at the page in an attempt to see what her crazy customer was finding so funny.

'Something like that.'

She waved goodbye to the shopkeeper and headed out, pausing only to pull out her mobile and turn it off. Bernard might be right about the phones being bugged or he might be being completely paranoid, but either way the leaks had to be coming from somewhere. Who knew what tracking software had been included in her HET-issue mobile phone? She didn't want anyone cyber-stalking where she was, or who she was talking to, so for the next couple of hours she was going AWOL.

She headed to the main street in nearby Newington. She passed the charity shops, off-licences, takeaways, vintage clothes emporiums, and the other retailers meeting the needs of the local student population, ignoring them all until she saw what she needed on the other side of the road. Dodging through the traffic, she dived into a shop selling mobile phones. The buzzer sounded as she pushed open the door, and the young guy behind the counter, all tattoos and piercings, looked up. Something about him struck her as familiar. His eyebrows shot up when he saw her, suggesting that he recognised her too. If there was a mutual connection, he didn't acknowledge it. She suspected they'd crossed paths in her former life at Police Scotland.

She approached the counter. 'I'd like a pay-as-you-go phone, just a cheap one, and a SIM card.'

He reached behind him. 'How about these?' He placed a slightly battered-looking phone and a pre-packaged SIM card in front of her. 'The phone's recycled.'

He watched her nervously as she picked up the phone and gave it the once-over. 'OK, I'll take it.'

She placed two ten-pound notes on the counter, sincerely hoping she hadn't just bought stolen property, and got out as quickly as possible. She peered back through the window. The shopkeeper was leaning against the back wall of the shop, one hand on his head, the other hanging limply at his side, radiating relief. He definitely had her down as Police; he'd have to be insanely stupid to have sold her a dodgy phone. If the day ever came when she returned to CID, she'd be asking a few questions about this particular shop.

Putting the transaction out of her mind, she ducked down a side street, looking for a quiet place to assemble her new purchase. After a minute's walk she spied an empty bench. The SIM card was duly inserted into her new old phone, and she dialled Elaine's number.

'It's me, Mona.'

There was a moment's pause. 'Well, hello. I wasn't sure I was going to hear from you again after the speed with which you galloped out of the pub last night. I thought you might be the kind that smooches a girl then never calls.'

The memory of kissing Elaine's soft, cider-drenched

lips came in to her mind. 'Can we not talk about that? Anyway, I wanted to say I read your column.'

'And I kept my promise. Are you phoning to say thank you?'

'Do you want to see me again?'

She laughed, a throaty rasp that Mona remembered from their first date. 'Of course, darling! I thought I made that clear enough yesterday.'

'Then I'm going to need a favour.'

There was a moment of dead air. 'I'm not sure I work like that.'

Mona was silent in return, and after a second Elaine gave in. 'What is this favour?'

'I need an address for someone.'

'Who?'

'Alexander Bircham-Fowler.'

'The Professor? Interesting. Any chance you could tell me why you want to speak to him?'

'No.'

'This is a little bit one-sided for my liking, Mona.'

She felt a sudden burst of anger. 'Forget it then. Sorry I asked.' She ended the call and threw the phone into her bag.

Almost immediately she regretted it. Talk about a bull in a china shop. Elaine owed her nothing; in fact, she'd already sat on a story just to save Mona's blushes. It was a bit much to phone up and demand that she do her another favour. And what had made her think she was such a great prize that the promise of a date with her would get her a no strings attached act of kindness from a journalist? She groaned. Her hand hovered over her bag, as she considered phoning back. Maybe later, she thought.

It was nearly an hour since she'd stormed out of the office; was that enough time for her colleagues to have calmed down? She didn't feel entirely composed herself, but then maybe while she was still fired by fury she should go back and stand her corner with Paterson, and follow that by finding Maitland and telling him where to shove it. She'd tell them both that she didn't need to run her romantic choices past the HET staff, she could date who she liked without permission from her co-workers. She wasn't sure that she did either like Elaine or want to date her, but they didn't need to know that.

If she was going to confront them, it was time to get it over with. She started walking back in the direction of the office, retracing her route through Newington, although this time she crossed the road to avoid going past the phone shop. A police car shot past, sirens blaring, and turned into the street where her office was. She picked up her pace, changing to a slow jog. It was probably nothing to do with the HET but given the events of the previous day she was a bit twitchy. A minute later, a further police car shot past, and this time Mona started to seriously worry. Given the Police Scotland manpower crisis, police cars travelling in pairs was a rare sight, and unlike magpies it was rarely two for joy. Something was up. Another bomb hoax? Something worse? Her jogging turned into full-blown sprinting. She turned the corner at speed and crashed straight into Bernard.

'Mona, thank God.' For a moment she thought he was going to hug her, but he settled for a pat on her shoulder.

'What's going on?'

'Bomb hoax.' He jerked his head in the direction of the group of people from their offices who were being shep-herded away from the building by the police. 'Yet again.'

'Again? Probably more teenagers messing about. Shall we get out of here until we get the all-clear? Head to a café or something?'

'No!' He looked surprisingly distraught at her suggestion. 'We can't go. I need your help to get back in there.'

'There's been a bomb threat! You can't just nip back in.' She regarded him suspiciously. 'Why do you need to get back in there, anyway? What have you done?'

His expression resembled that of a schoolboy caught smoking behind the bike sheds. 'I was looking at Anneka's phone when the threat came in . . .'

'Oh, God, please tell me you secured it before you came out?'

'The Facilities Manager was shouting at me, and I panicked, and . . .'

'Bernard!'

He looked miserably at his feet. 'It's lying on my desk. I really, really need to get back in there. Help me sneak in somehow.'

'You can't go back in, you could die.'

'It's not going to be an actual bomb threat, is it? It's much more likely that it's a ruse so someone else can get into the office and steal the phone.'

'Which only you, Paterson and I know about.'

'What about the bugging? It's probably all over Twitter by now that we have it.'

'Possibly, but even if it is you can't chance going back in.'

'Negligible risk of death in there.' He pointed at the building. 'Out here, odds on certainty of me being executed when Stuttle and Paterson find out I've lost another piece of evidence.'

'Still, Bernard . . .'

He pointed at the building again. 'I repeat, negligible . . .'

His voice was drowned out by the noise of an explosion, and two of the windows on the first floor blowing out. There were screams from some of the crowd as broken glass rained down on the heads of the bystanders. Even above all the noise, Mona could make out the caterwauling coming from Marguerite.

'What just happened?' She looked round at the crowd, as if there was someone who could actually answer that question.

'They blew up the HET office.' Bernard's complexion had paled to the colour of milk. 'We're obviously a target now. We've upset someone very important and now there's a vendetta against us.'

'But we're on the second floor. It's the first floor that's on fire.' She did a quick calculation in her mind and worked out which room had been targeted.

She felt a large hand on her shoulder. 'You two OK?' asked Paterson. His eyes were darting between the building and the crowd.

'We're fine, Guv. Any sign of the others?'

'I haven't found them yet. Either of you know where they went?'

'They both went out earlier,' said Bernard. 'But, look!' He pointed over Mona's shoulder. 'Here's Carole coming. She looks pretty upset.'

'Maitland, is he here?' Carole shouted, as she ran toward them.

'No.' Mona looked at her in surprise. 'We assumed he was with you.'

Carole shook her head vigorously, her long hair shaking around her. 'I think he's still in there.'

'Not possible,' said Paterson. 'They evacuated the

building when we got the phone call. He would have heard to come out.'

'No, he wouldn't.' She bit her lip. 'He went for a sleep in the third-floor conference room. He was going to lie under the table so that no one could see him, and I said I'd cover for him if anyone asked where he was. I thought it would be OK if I nipped out for half an hour.'

'For what? A meeting with your lawyer? Anything happens to that boy I'm holding you responsible. This is your fault.' Paterson started running in the direction of the fireman at the building entrance. He shouted back over his shoulder. 'You and your bloody attitude.'

Carole buried her face in her hands. 'Oh, God. What have I done?'

Mona put an arm round her shoulder, and watched Paterson gesticulate the story into the face of the fireman. There was a flurry of action, and three firemen disappeared into the building.

Her new phone beeped. With her free hand she pulled it out of her pocket: she had a text.

Elaine had sent her an address.

5

'Bernard, I need to do something.'

'Now?' He was only half-listening to Mona, too busy staring at the mess on the first floor. Smoke was pouring out of the broken windows, but there were no visible flames. It looked like the firefighters had it all pretty much under control. If Maitland really had been on the third floor when the explosion happened, surely he was in with a chance.

'Yes, sorry. Can you handle things here?' She gently shoved Carole in his direction, and he took over half-heartedly comforting her, patting her on the shoulder.

'Yeah, yeah, OK.'

'Text me the second you hear about Maitland.'

'Of course.' He suddenly realised that Mona was leaving. 'Where did you say you were going? Will you be long?'

He looked round but she'd vanished.

'What's taking them so long?' Carole sniffed. 'They know exactly where to look for him.'

'They might need to put out the fire before they can get to him, which will be causing a lot of smoke in the stairwell. And we only know where he was when the explosion took place. He could have tried to get out, hit the smoke, got disorientated . . .' He stopped, sensing that he wasn't being as reassuring as Carole would like.

'Oh God, the smoke could kill him before they get to him.'

'If he's any sense he'll barricade himself in somewhere and wait for help to arrive. I'm sure Maitland has well-refined self-preservation skills. He probably trained for all this at Police College.'

Carole clutched his arm, her eyes big and wet with tears. 'What if the smoke killed him before he even woke up? Paterson was right. It *is* my fault, all of it. I've been egging Maitland on these past few days, encouraging him to mess about. It was my idea that he should skive off to the conference room. I said I'd cover for him and then I went and left the building without telling him.' She buried her head in his shoulder. 'I feel terrible.'

'There was an almighty explosion, Carole. They probably heard it all the way to the Scottish Parliament. Even Maitland wouldn't sleep through that.'

A tall thin figure appeared in the doorway to the building, supported on either side by a firefighter.

'Is that him? Yes, it is, it's him all right. He's here, Carole, and he looks OK. He's upright at least.'

'Oh, thank God.' She removed her face from his shoulder. 'Do you think he'll hate me for this?'

'Maitland is a grown-up. The only person responsible for him being in that building was him.'

'He might not see it like that.'

'Well, shall we go and find out? I think they're taking him over to a medic.' If Maitland gave Carole any grief about this, Bernard was going to have his say.

They made their way through the crowd, most of whom were still staring at the smoke in shock. A couple of policemen were trying ineffectually to persuade the gawkers that they might want to move slightly further

201

away from the building, in case there were any more explosions, but the lure of social media pics was just too great. Bernard took Carole's arm and shepherded her through the sea of camera phones to the ambulance where Maitland was being treated. He was sitting on the back step of it, wrapped in a blanket and with an oxygen mask on.

'Oh, Maitland.' Carole threw her arms round him.

The paramedic gently removed her. 'We're still running a few tests. Give him some space.'

'What the fuck happened there?' Maitland pulled his mask off, then started to cough.

'A bomb hoax that wasn't a hoax, I'm guessing,' said Bernard.

'Keep the mask on, pal. Your lungs have taken a bit of a hammering.'

Maitland waited until the paramedic's back was turned and took it off again. 'Please say you didn't tell Paterson I was asleep in the conference room.'

'I had to.' Carole dabbed at her eyes. 'We didn't know if you were OK. You could have been dead.'

'I was fine! I shut myself in the third-floor toilet, with a damp towel along the door. I knew you'd tell them to come and get me.'

Carole let out a small sob.

'Which is exactly what Carole did,' said Bernard, 'the first moment she could.'

Her head returned to his shoulder and he patted the top of it.

'Couldn't you have lied and said I was working up there for some peace and quiet?' asked Maitland.

'I couldn't think that fast.' Her voice was muffled. 'We were worried. And I thought they might not look under the table if I didn't say that's where you were.'

'You said I was under the table? Oh God. I am so screwed.'

He wasn't wrong. Maitland's powers of self-preservation might have been well enough developed to save him from deadly smoke, but they were going to have to work overtime to get him out of a meeting with his line manager unscathed.

'Paterson would never have bought you disappearing off there for "peace and quiet" anyway.' Now that Maitland was safe and well, Bernard felt happy to resume hostilities. 'He knows you're bone idle.'

'Bernard, I'm going to . . .' He started coughing, and the paramedic reappeared and pointedly snapped his breathing apparatus back into place.

'Oh, crap,' muttered Maitland, underneath his mask.

Bernard followed his sightline and saw Paterson and Stuttle hove into view. He took an involuntary step backwards. This wasn't going to be pretty.

'You.' Paterson pointed at Carole. 'Get out of my sight.'

After a final anguished look at Maitland, she hurried off.

'Give us a minute, will you?' Stuttle said to the paramedic.

He placed his hands on his hips and let out an exasperated sigh. 'I'm not sure he's fit to talk.'

'He'll be fine. I'll take full responsibility.'

The paramedic debated for a second whether to pursue this, then seeing the expression on Stuttle's face, decided not to. 'Keep it short. I want to get him to the hospital.'

Stuttle leaned in toward Maitland, and gestured Paterson and Bernard to join him. He spoke very quietly. 'This will be all over the Internet by now. I already have

203

a press conference set up to discuss the two hoaxes in less than an hour's time, and now this . . .' he struggled for a word, 'fiasco. People will want answers from me and I don't know what's going on. Tell me what's happening here.'

'What makes you think we know anything?' Paterson put as much grievance as he could into his tone while still whispering. 'It wasn't even our offices that were blown up. Are you certain it was aimed at us?'

'There's nothing else going on in the building that is remotely controversial, as you well know, John. Unless there's someone out there with a grudge against NHS statisticians, or the staff of the national breastfeeding campaign . . .'

'Actually, people do object to . . .'

'Shut up, Bernard!' whispered Stuttle and Paterson as one, in both timing and level of irritation.

'OK, sorry.'

'Anyway,' continued Stuttle, 'the fire was in the room housing the server, which a pretty restricted number of people have access to . . .'

Like IT staff, thought Bernard. But surely Marcus couldn't be behind this. It wouldn't make sense. Selling information about the Virus or the HET might be lucrative, but what was to be earned by blowing up the server? And although it looked like the explosion wasn't aimed at hurting anyone, there was so much potential for it going wrong. Marcus wouldn't be so cavalier with the health and well-being of his colleagues and friends. He just wouldn't.

' . . .but they have successfully banjaxed the entire computer system for the building, which may not be unrelated to whatever they are trying to achieve.'

Paterson gave Bernard a punch on the shoulder, which he probably intended to be gentle. 'Seeing as we can't get back into the building, why don't you go and chat to your daft prick mates over at IT and double-check they haven't blown them up as well.'

'OK.' He was going to give Marcus a good grilling about all this. A thought occurred to him. 'Will we be able to retrieve anything from the building?'

'Depends what it is. I think you need to assume that any personal effects you left behind are trapped in there for the moment.'

'Helen Sopel's phone is in there.'

Stuttle raised an eyebrow at him. 'Secured in the metal, bombproof cupboard, I trust? With the key to said cupboard stored somewhere else?'

'I didn't quite have time for that, but it is secure.' He could feel himself blush as he lied.

'We're going to have a proper talk about the storage of evidence when this is over.' He pointed at the building. 'Talk to the head fireman. Say I authorised it. And John, you're coming with me.'

'To the press conference? Since when was I an asset at those?'

'You're not an asset. I just want someone to blame when it goes tits up.'

6

Mona hailed the first taxi she saw.

'Quite a commotion back there, love.' The driver grinned at her in his mirror.

'Yeah.' She suspected some conversational misdirection was going to be called for. The last thing she wanted was to have information about the blast spread across Edinburgh through the ever-effective cab driver gossip network.

'I heard it was an explosion on the first floor of the Cathcart House. Must be some nutter with a grudge against that Health Check team.'

Her skills of evasion obviously weren't going to be required. This guy possibly knew more about what had happened than she did.

'I mean, I'm not a fan of the Health Checks myself, love, but folk are just doing their job, you know what I mean?'

'Yeah, agree, totally. Ehm, how did you hear about the explosion?'

'Heard the kaboom sound.' He took both his hands off the wheel to illustrate his comments with a mime of an explosion. 'So I had the radio on to see what the story was. BBC Scotland is all over it.'

'Really? News travels fast.' She wondered what the journalists' take on it would be. Cameron Stuttle was probably busy telling anyone from the press who'd listen about a gas leak, or an overheated server. Twitter, on the other hand, would have a full range of opinions tending to the view that the explosion was a top-level conspiracy. Somewhere in between, the truth was lurking.

'Certainly does these days. It's the Internet, isn't it? People will have had pictures of the explosion on the Facebook as soon as it happened.'

Given that there was a park full of protestors opposite the bomb site, that was pretty much an inevitability. She'd have to get Bernard to give her the rundown on who Twitter were holding responsible for the attack. The thought of how she'd deserted him sent a dart of guilt through her. She scrabbled in her bag to find her work mobile. As soon as she turned it back on, two text messages arrived from Bernard.

Maitland walking wounded
But still being very annoying

She smiled. Maitland's ego appeared to have survived intact – at least until Paterson dealt with the whole issue of him nipping off for a kip in the middle of the working day. She breathed a huge sigh of relief. She'd be the first to admit that Maitland was annoying, and she wasn't done with him over the whole Cassandra Doom thing, but still she'd have hated to see any of her colleagues hurt.

She checked her phone for other messages, and was surprised to see that she had multiple missed calls from a number she didn't recognise, all of which had arrived in the last hour. Someone must have heard about the explosion and was concerned about her well-being.

'All right if I cut through the park? It's the quickest way at this time of day.'

'Yes, whatever you think.'

She puzzled over the number. She hadn't given Elaine her work number, although, as a journalist she was sure she could get it, but, then, why bother when she had other ways to contact her. With a burst of conscience she wondered if they could be from her mother, who she really should have phoned to tell her she was OK. Not that her mother possessed a mobile, or actually understood how they worked. Perhaps she'd heard about the explosion when she was out and about, and had persuaded some random stranger to phone on her behalf.

She hit her mother's name in the address book. After several rings her mother picked up the call. 'Hello?'

'Mum? It's Mona, I'm fine.'

'Of course you are.' Her mother's voice was a mixture of surprise and irritation. 'Why are you phoning just to tell me that?'

The taxi slowed down. Scanning the rows of stone-built terraces, she searched for a street name, and realised she'd reached her destination.

'Watch a news bulletin, Mum. See you later.'

She pressed long and hard on the doorbell, and in response a chime sounded somewhere inside the building. This was followed by rapidly approaching footsteps, and a second later the door was yanked opened.

'Hello, Professor.'

His face showed no surprise at all at her arriving unannounced on his doorstep. 'Mona, thank God.' He stepped forward and enveloped her in a bearhug. 'You're not hurt.'

Over his shoulder she saw Theresa in the hall.

'I thought you hadn't seen him in months?'

'People lie, Mona. A person of your age and intelligence should have figured that out.'

Theresa pushed the Professor to one side and gave her a hug, albeit a much more restrained one than Bircham-Fowler's. 'I'm very pleased to see you. We've been phoning you but you weren't answering. We heard about the explosion at the HET offices, and this silly old fool thought he'd got you killed by involving you in things that he really shouldn't.'

'What things? Do you mean Hilda Milwood?'

The Professor answered by closing the door behind them. 'Come through to the kitchen. I'll make some tea.'

'Was anyone hurt in the explosion, Mona?' asked Theresa.

'One colleague was still in the building, but not badly hurt. I don't think the bomb was aimed at loss of life though. It seems to have been located in the room that houses the server.'

'To disrupt your IT?' asked the Professor.

'Well, that would be pointless, Sandy.' Theresa gave him a look. 'These things are all backed up off-site. Like it was at the university.'

'You're right,' said Mona. 'We wouldn't have lost more than a few hours of work.'

'So why blow it up?'

'The important thing, Sandy,' said Theresa, impatiently taking over the tea making duties, 'is that it wasn't targeted at people. So, despite your unfortunate comments to Mona, she wasn't in any danger from the blast.'

'But you do think the explosion was connected to Mrs Milwood?' she persisted.

The Professor and Theresa looked at each other. The Professor appeared to be silently asking her permission for something which, from the look on Theresa's face, was being firmly denied.

'At least tell me what the phrase means!' Mona was completely losing patience. 'When you heard about the explosion, you thought that it might have been targeted at me because you told me something you shouldn't have, but even now you won't even tell me who Hilda Milwood is – how do you know that you're not putting me in more danger through my ignorance?'

'Oh, Sandy, why did you start all this?' Theresa slammed the lid onto the teapot.

'If I'd delivered my speech, if I hadn't taken ill . . .'

'Ill? Ha!'

He sighed. 'All right. If I hadn't been stopped from making my speech, either by nature or by human intervention, everyone would have known about it. Milwood would have been on the front page of every paper, and on all of these Internet sites. When we parted, Mona, I didn't realise that I was putting you in a difficult position.' His eyes, surprisingly blue and clear, gazed into hers. 'But if you want to know, I will tell you.'

'Sandy—'

'Shush, Theresa. I'm not the man I was, we both know that. Whatever brought it on, I did have a heart attack. And I have responsibilities and commitments that I didn't have when I was going to make my stand. I'm not going to go public with what I know, not while Maria is pregnant, and these people,' he spat out the words, 'could do her harm.'

Theresa slammed two cups down in front of them but didn't try to stop him speaking.

'I will tell you what I know, and what you choose to do with it is up to you.' He paused, as if expecting her to speak.

'Thank you.'

'So . . .the most important thing that you need to know about Hilda Milwood is that she doesn't exist, at least not in real life. But over the years she has become a kind of shorthand, a motif if you like for—'

'Oh, for goodness' sake, Sandy, get on with it!' Teresa sighed irritably. 'If you must tell her all this nonsense, at least start with the film.'

'I was about to tell her about the film!' He gestured over his shoulder toward the kitchen. 'That woman is impossible. Anyway, back in the 1950s, when the Cold War was at its height, there was a suite of public information films about the situation, of which *Protect and Survive* is the most well known. If you were a very senior civil servant you would have watched a training film called *Thrive and Prosper*, which examines some of the eventualities that might arise if a nuclear attack was launched on Britain.'

'You can watch that kind of thing on the Internet.'

'I guarantee you that this particular film is not on general release. No, you had to be someone pretty high up to have seen this one. The main thrust of it was that the great and the good might not make it to the shelters on time, and some hoi polloi might actually survive, because of geographical isolation, or because of some genetic quirk that made them resistant to radiation. Crazy idea, of course, but it was a long time ago. So, *Thrive and Prosper* dealt with the scenario that when the world was being rebuilt the people in charge may not be of the same,' he paused for a moment, '*calibre* as the existing top brass. The film was to prepare them for a world that might be run by whoever was left. Like Hilda Milwood.'

'A *woman*, Mona.' Theresa's voice came from the

211

depth of the kitchen. 'Imagine how terrifying that thought must have been for them.'

The Professor grinned. 'Mrs Milwood was a housewife with two young children, acted no doubt by some fine young RADA actress with received pronunciation. But all of that is but a footnote on history, important for one reason only. "Mrs Milwood" became a kind of in-joke for the members of the upper echelons of the Establishment. This developed into the concept of Milwood Orders, when, for whatever reason, decisions were taken by people much more junior than would normally be making them.'

'Like in a pandemic situation, if all the Cabinet were stricken, the civil servants would step in?' asked Mona.

'Exactly. At least that's how it started out. When the Virus first became a problem, there were certain emergency measures put in place, some of which continue, such as restrictions on the size of groups that are allowed to meet. Other restrictions such as the closure of schools, and the late-night curfew were so unpopular that they were abandoned as soon as possible. And some measures, such as the establishing of the HETs, were unpopular but tolerated as a necessary evil by most of the population.'

He paused again, and she nodded her agreement with his analysis.

'We live in a democracy,' the Professor continued. 'The government of the day, even in an emergency situation such as our current predicament, needs to take some heed of what the population will tolerate. Our approach is different from countries with a more, say, directive, leadership than our own. China, for example, has had some quite extreme restrictions on people's freedom of movement. But the Virus doesn't recognise governance structures. It doesn't care if you are a democracy, dictatorship or whatever. There is a body of thought within what you might call the Establishment that some extreme measures are called for.'

'Like further civil liberty restrictions? Banning people from meeting up? Closing the schools again? That kind of thing?'

'No. Because all those things are very public. There would be an outcry amongst the public, which they might follow through with at the ballot box. Normal electoral government still exists in this country. We haven't yet abandoned it for a National Government-type arrangement, so all the old political concerns about re-election remain.'

'But in private . . .'

'In private, politicians, civil servants and the like, all remain bound by the same ethical codes that govern their public work. Until someone tells them otherwise.'

'And did someone . . .?'

'Yes. The inner sanctum of the government decided that the time had come to delegate a certain amount of power to their senior civil servants, along with a number of not insignificant budgets. These powers and resources would allow them to do take a more, er, robust approach to tackling the Virus than politicians would feel happy defending in public. And both sides were happy with this. The civil servants could work with the NHS, universities, and so on, to do what needs to be done, and the politicians get plausible deniability if the civil servants get it wrong. A 21st century spin on "acting under Milwood Orders".'

'How do you know this? Were you part of one of these projects?'

213

'Goodness, no. Nobody would trust me to take part in something as cloak-and-dagger as a Milwood project. What actually happened was that some months ago I received an anonymous email alerting me to concerns about the government's response to the Virus. There was a certain reticence to the conversation, but we exchanged enough emails for trust to develop to the point where we met in person. My contact was the first to tell me about the term Milwood Orders, although I was aware that in a crisis situation, of course, the government would likely take extreme measures.'

'What were the extreme measures?'

'The one that I was made aware of was an unregulated anti-viral drug trial in one of the more impoverished areas of central Africa, using children, mainly street children, as the research subjects. The kind of experimental left-field research that would never have got through a university ethics committee in this country, with good reason. Within weeks of the research starting, there were child deaths.'

Mona stared at the Professor. 'That's appalling.'

'Absolutely, yes, to anyone with a conscience.'

A thought struck her. 'Your contact – was he or she a civil servant?'

He smiled. 'Jasper Connington, late of this parish. I'd had some dealings with him through my work at the university, which may have been why he chose to ask for my assistance. A lovely man, but probably not cut out for the politics of the Virus. He was appalled by what they were being asked to do but couldn't see a way out.'

'Were his colleagues equally appalled?'

'He said there was a difference of opinion between them. One of his colleagues shared his views, the other was much more committed to the project.'

'Which colleague?'

'I have no idea. Jasper didn't share any more than he absolutely had to with me. I didn't know the names of his colleagues on the project, but obviously I could make an educated guess who might have been involved. It would come as no surprise, for example, if poor Nathan McVie was also part of this project.'

It wouldn't surprise her either. She thought back to the box of evidence, locked away in their office. 'I think Helen Sopel's disappearance is linked to Milwood Orders. She left a box of evidence with a friend in case anything should happen to her, which it now obviously has. One of the things that was in it was a picture of a woman in a 1950s dress. I bet it was a still of Hilda Milwood. A great big warning to her colleagues of exactly how much she knew.' She frowned. 'Stuttle didn't recognise her though I'd have thought he'd know all about Milwood Orders?'

The Professor gave a loud, throaty, chuckle. 'Oh, yes. Mr Stuttle would most definitely be involved in that kind of thing. However, there's nothing to say he'd actually seen the film. I'm led to believe by my source that the film was a source of much entertainment to the upper echelons of the civil service. I'm not sure Mr Stuttle would be on the invite list for wine, cheese and a private viewing of *Thrive and Prosper*. Nor do I think he is of the persuasion to spend a lot of time debating where the Milwood in Milwood Orders actually derived from.'

'So, Mr Connington told you all about Milwood Orders – and what else?'

'What Jasper gave me was enough information to publicly denounce the project in my speech at the Parliament. If I'd been able to give it.'

'Do you think Mr Connington really took an overdose? Could someone have . . .?'

'I think he was depressed enough about the situation to have tried to kill himself. But then, I suppose I am old and unfit enough to have had a heart attack.'

'So, Mona,' said Theresa, 'this silly old fool starts poking around in things and has a heart attack, Jasper Connington unexpectedly takes his own life . . .can you guess what I'm about to say to you?'

'Be careful?'

'No!' Theresa looked furious. 'Don't be careful, don't get involved at all! Go back to work and get on with your day job, keep your head down until all this Virus nonsense is over and done with, and live your life. You're young. Sandy had no right involving you in any of this in London, and he has no right involving you now.' She glared at them both.

'You're right, Tess, of course you're right. You are always right. I'm sorry, Mona. You should probably leave now.' He opened the kitchen door and gestured to her to leave, following her back down the narrow corridor. 'Go back to work,' he said, loudly, 'keep your head down, find yourself a nice young man and go and have some babies.' He reached over her shoulder to open the door. 'And, Mona—' His voice dropped to a whisper. 'Be very, very, careful.'

7

Bernard hugged his rucksack to him, Anneka's phone safely tucked in the middle pocket. When he'd approached one of the firemen for permission to pop back into the building he'd been met with an outright no. The fireman had been adamant that no one was returning to the building under any circumstances, and it didn't matter how many times Cameron Stuttle's name was invoked. He had, however, proved remarkably amenable to retrieving the phone for him, and had been the recipient of much gratitude as a result. Now Bernard was not going to let the phone out of his sight until he had downloaded all the messages on it.

So, that was the good news. The bad news was that he had literally no idea what to say to Marcus. Surely no amount of debt could persuade someone to plant a bomb. Nothing short of a full-on radicalisation programme could change a mild-mannered computer technician into the kind of person who would explode government property. And surely he would have noticed some change in his behaviour? Bernard had spent enough nights on Marcus's floor to be convinced that his friend's sphere of interest had not strayed from its fairly narrow focus of *Buffy the Vampire Slayer*, *Serenity*, and the earlier works of George Lucas. Furthermore, where would Marcus have developed the skills to create an incendiary device?

He might be a whizz when it came to identifying why your printer wasn't working, but Bernard had first-hand experience of watching him cock up simple household tasks. Marcus's attempt to change the living room light bulb had ended up with a smashed glass, a broken step ladder, and Bernard running for his life to avoid being crushed by the flying body of an IT technician. The only person Marcus was likely to blow up successfully was himself. And possibly Bernard, sleeping unawares on his inflatable mattress.

Bernard walked slowly up the driveway to Fettes, lost in his own thoughts. It would be good to have another chat with Bryce before confronting Marcus. He had his fingers crossed that they were both in, and that he could somehow have a private conversation with Bryce before he tackled Marcus. There were some details he really wanted to pin down. Bryce had been very sure that online gambling was the issue, but perhaps he'd been wrong about that. It could have been a completely different issue. And exactly who was Marcus selling information to? Bryce had been completely adamant, but on little information that Bernard could see.

At Police Scotland HQ, he signed in at the reception desk and headed down to the IT unit. Peering through the small pane of glass on the door he could see Marcus's jeans-clad backside sticking out from under a desk, probably working on a hard drive. He scanned the room as best as he could with his limited field of vision. Unfortunately there didn't appear to be any sign of Bryce. He tapped gently on the glass. Marcus emerged, smiled and buzzed him in.

'Bernard! You are alive, unhurt, unscathed by the terrible events at your office!'

He looked genuinely pleased. If this was a bluff it was a good one.

'Is everyone else OK?' he asked anxiously. 'Mona all right?'

When all this was over he was really going to have to manage Marcus's expectations about Mona. 'She's fine. Everyone was out of the building in time, except for Maitland. And even he wasn't hurt.'

The phone on Marcus's desk started to ring.

'Do you need to . . .'

The phone on Bryce's desk also began to ring.

'There's no point in me answering them, Bernard. They're all phoning to say the same thing. "My computer isn't working," or "I can't log into the HET website." It's devastation out there. All our systems are down.'

'Because of the explosion?'

He shook his head. 'No, although maybe not unrelated to it. I think we've been infected with a virus, which is ironic, because the whole point of our computer system is to fight *the* Virus. Ha! I hadn't really considered until today that we have imported wholesale the language of illness into the world of computers. Viruses, bugs. And not unlike a doctor I make a diagnosis, then I take action.'

He started wandering round the room, stopping now and then to peer down the back of desks and cabinets. Bernard watched him. He certainly sounded like his usual self, talking the same nonsense he always tended to spout. The anxious pacing was new, though, and could be indicative of an unstable mind. He decided to push a little bit. 'Doctors have the Hippocratic oath. Do IT technicians also agree to Do No Harm?'

'Do no harm?' The pacing stopped and Marcus pivoted round toward him. He regarded him impassively from behind his little round specs, then looked over his shoulder. 'I don't think you closed the door properly when you came in, Bernard.' He strode over and grabbed the handle. The door gave a soft thump sound as it closed. 'We need to keep this room secure.'

Bernard experienced a slight feeling of unease. Whenever he visited, Marcus always buzzed him in and then showed him out. He'd never paid much attention to the mechanics of it before, but now that he thought about it he wasn't sure how you opened the door from inside the room. He had struggled to believe Bryce's take on the situation, but Marcus was behaving weirdly, and for good or for ill, Bernard was effectively trapped down here with him. Despite the lack of available exits, he decided to do a little more pushing.

'I don't know if you were aware of this, but the explosion took place in the room housing our server.'

'Really?' Marcus was pacing again, still, it seemed, searching for something hidden in the room. 'I'm beginning to think this was deliberate, Bernard. If they've knocked out both the server and the system then we're in real trouble. Bryce picked the wrong day to be off sick.'

'He's off sick? Today of all days?'

'I assume so, though I have to say it's not like him. I've never known him take a sickie before. But he went out yesterday, and he's not been back.'

There was a niggle at the back of Bernard's mind.

Bryce.

Bryce, who was uncharacteristically off sick on the day that IT hell had broken loose.

'How did they get access to the server room?' asked Marcus. 'That room is kept locked. Someone couldn't just wander in there.' All the time he was talking, Marcus was keeping up his relentless searching of the room. Bernard sincerely hoped that he wasn't hunting for a blunt object to aim at his head.

'I know.' He wasn't sure how to ask the question. 'Is there, ehm, anything you want to tell me, Marcus?'

Marcus stopped dead. His head dropped on to his chest, and he half-sat, half-leaned against a desk, as if he legs could no longer support him. 'Oh dear, oh dear.'

'Marcus?'

He looked back up at him, and Bernard was horrified to see the hugely guilty expression on his face. 'Sorry.'

'I was hoping you were going to deny it.' He started planning Marcus's defence. He must have been brain-washed, that was the only explanation. It couldn't have been a reaction to stress, as Marcus was generally the least stressed person on the planet. He'd certainly be happy to provide Marcus with a character reference. For what it was worth.

'I'm an idiot. You're not going to tell anyone, are you?'

Marcus really had lost the plot if he thought he could keep this to himself. 'I'll have to. I . . .'

His mobile rang, and Paterson's name flashed up on the screen. 'Bernard, are you with Marcus?' His voice was unusually soft.

'Yes.'

'OK, just listen, don't say anything. Stuttle has just had the results of the phone trace on the warning call for the bomb.' There was a sigh at the other end of the line. 'It came from a mobile registered to Marcus.'

Marcus was crawling around the floor, the locus of his searching now apparently focusing on the under-desk area.

'Bernard, are you listening?'

'Yes, yes, sorry.'

'Is he there with you?'

'Yes.'

'Just keep him talking. The Fettes guys are checking his locker, and someone's going to be down to arrest him.'

'But—'

'Don't tell him anything. Help is on its way.'

He ended the call and tucked his phone back into his pocket. Marcus was still on all fours in a footwell.

'Marcus,' he said quietly, crouching down beside him. 'Why did you do it?'

'Do what?'

'The bomb, Marcus, obviously. Why did you plant the bomb?'

'Ow!' Marcus banged his head in his hurry to retreat. 'Are you insane? I didn't do that!'

'But you said you had something to tell me!' Bernard was increasingly confused. 'And what are you looking so guilty about?'

'I've lost my keys, including the one to the server room. It's a disciplinary offence.'

'Have you also lost your mobile phone?'

'My whole bag has gone.' Marcus sighed, and sat back on his heels. He gave Bernard a long searching look. 'I'm only going to ask you this once, and if you say you didn't I'll believe you. Did you take my bag?'

'Me?' Bernard toppled over in surprise, and sat with his legs sprawled in front of him. 'Why would I take your bag?'

'To get access to the server. To plant the bomb.'

'Now who is insane? Why would I do that?'

'Well, Bryce said you were going through a few

difficulties, you know, with the break-up of your marriage and everything, and that you were maybe, you know, having a nervous breakdown.'

'Bryce said that?'

'Yes. He said it was probably just as well you were moving out, because he was a bit worried that you were going to do something stupid.' He contemplated him. 'When I heard about the explosion, I just had this moment of doubt that it might have been . . .might have been something to do with you.'

Bryce. Bryce, who was off sick. Fury started to burn within him, then he realised that they didn't have a lot of time. He glanced over at the door. No one had arrived yet.

'I don't suppose you've already reported your bag missing?'

Marcus shook his head. 'I was hoping to find it before I had to 'fess up.'

'Marcus, how well do you know Bryce?'

'Well enough. He's a colleague, and a friend.'

'Have you ever been to his house?'

'Well, no . . .'

'Met his family?'

'They're back in Ireland.'

'Met any of his other friends?'

'I don't think he has any.'

'Do you have a gambling problem, you know, playing online poker, casino games?'

Marcus was looking more confused by the minute. 'No, it's a mug's game. Virtual house always wins and all that. Why are you . . .'

'Shut up and listen. I think Bryce has set you up to take the fall for the bomb at our offices. Depending on which way things turn out, I think he was lining me up to be a potential patsy as well.'

'Bryce?' Marcus's eyes were almost as big and round as his specs. 'You think Bryce set the bomb?'

'Yes, I do. And you know how he told you I was having a nervous breakdown? Well, he's been making up stories about you too. He told me, and I suppose, quite possibly told other people, that you've been taking bribes . . .'

'Bribes?'

'And I think he used your phone to call in the bomb warning . . .'

'Oh, God. But why?'

'I don't know, I really don't. But I do know that the police are coming to arrest you.'

Right on cue there was a tap on the door.

'What do I do?'

'Tell them the truth. Tell them about your bag going missing, with your phone in it. Tell them as much as you know about Bryce, and that he's not turned up at work today. And I'll tell them what I know.'

The knocking on the door grew more aggressive. He stood up to see a pair of ferocious eyes staring through the glass panel, followed by a hand gesture suggesting that he opened the door *toot sweet*. He turned back to Marcus who was cross-legged on the floor.

'We need to open the door.'

Marcus looked up at him. 'It's a myth, you know.'

'What is?'

'*First Do No Harm*. It's not what the original Hippocratic oath says. It actually says "I will utterly reject harm and mischief." I'm not caught up in any mischief, Bernard, and I've certainly never harmed anyone. I just couldn't do that.' He reached under his desk and pressed a button. The door buzzed open, and the frame was filled by figures in black.

'I know,' said Bernard. He stepped back as a policeman and a policewoman pushed past him and hauled Marcus to his feet. 'I'm so sorry.'

8

Paterson looked up as Mona walked in.

'At last!' She had finally tracked him down to a meeting room at Fettes. It was a small room, with seating for only six people. Paterson seemed to have spread his belongings in such a way as to cover most of the table and several of the chairs. He was a grizzly bear, marking out his territory in an unfamiliar land. Despite the available seating options, he had opted to stay standing, a laptop in front of him.

'I was beginning to think no one had got my text. I was on the point of giving the entire team up as lost and heading off to the cafeteria to drown my sorrows in weak Fettes coffee.'

'Haven't you heard from anyone else?' Mona moved Paterson's jacket so that she could lower herself into a chair at the opposite end of the table.

'I've spoken to Bernard, bit of a story there, which I'll tell you later, but he didn't say if he was heading over here. Maitland is still in the hospital as far as I know, and no surprise here, Carole didn't respond to the message.'

'Kind of glad she's not here, to be honest, Guv. Maitland's an idiot . . .'

'Very true.'

'But I can't help feeling her attitude played a big part in him nearly getting blown up. He's got the excuse that

226

he's still young and stupid. She might not want to be at the HET but he's got his future career to think about. If she wants to mess about that's one thing but she should leave him out of it.'

Paterson grunted. 'I see why she's got a grudge, what with her boy, and getting kicked in the face, and everything. And I understand that she's bitter, I'd be exactly the same. But this ludicrous new no resignations diktat from Stuttle means we're all stuck with each other, and I'm just not sure I can see us working together with her in that mood. The woman's a liability.'

'No argument from me there, Guv.' They contemplated this in silence for a moment. 'Anyway, how are the computers?'

'Not looking good.' He spun the laptop round to show her a blank screen. 'Everything's down. The entire HET system.'

'What about IT? Can't they do anything?'

Paterson's face took on a most unusual expression, a grimace mixed with disbelief, with just a hint of sadness underpinning it all.

'What?'

'This is going to come as a surprise,' he shook his head, as if he was still processing some unbelievable thought, 'but the tall, speccy one from the IT department . . .'

'Marcus?'

'The one that has a crush on you, yes, well, he's been arrested on suspicion of being responsible for the bomb.'

'No!' She wondered if he'd got this wrong. 'Marcus? Big, geeky Marcus? They must have made a mistake.'

'Possibly, but they did have evidence that suggests he's involved.'

'But why would he do that?'

227

'I suspect at someone else's behest. And if you are about to say "whose . . ."'

She was.

' . . .don't bother, because I have no idea. But what I do know is that the box that Helen Sopel left vanished during the first bomb hoax, a bomb put paid to our server and God knows what damage is currently being done to our IT systems. Someone's done a pretty good job of destroying what evidence we've managed to accumulate.'

'Why?'

'I don't know! I was hoping that you might have some idea of what the hell is going on! Is Carlotta Carmichael behind all this, do you think? Are we're sitting on something dangerous to her interest, or maybe dangerous for other reasons, and we're all just too stupid to know what it is?'

Her conversation with the Professor had given her a pretty good steer on what that might be. She opened her mouth to tell the Guv about her findings, then some instinct for caution overcame her and she clamped it shut. Could she really trust Paterson? For all his bluster and supposed hatred of authority, the Guv was very much a company man. If she told him about Bircham-Fowler's information, he'd immediately want to tell Stuttle, and God knows where his actual loyalties lay. Chiefly to Stuttle, she suspected.

'You really think Carlotta would be up to risking the life and limb of HET staff, Guv?'

'No, but I think she'd be quite happy to delegate a task, and not take too much interest in how her underlings went about fulfilling her wishes.' He sat down opposite her. 'Stuttle and I had a private meeting with Paul Shore, her assistant, a couple of days ago . . .'

She remembered an earlier conversation. 'Was Bernard at it?'

'No! We're hardly going to invite Bernard along. What would he do – make the tea? Nah, the daft prick walked in on us.' He looked suddenly stern. 'I take it he's kept his mouth shut, as instructed?'

'Absolutely, Guv. Just me putting two and two together.'

'Anyhow, Shore says she's been in a terrible state these past few days. Thinks she's not coping with the workload, and these civil servant deaths are just the last straw. He seemed to think that whatever is going on, she's not in control of it any more. I think she might have started something that she's now regretting. Although Shore was totally adamant that he knew nothing about how or why the bomb hoaxes happened. And if he knows what or who might be behind it, he's not sharing.'

'The thing is, Guv, the actual evidence might have gone, but we all know what was in the box.'

He grimaced. 'Maybe that means that we're next in line for eradication.'

'Comforting thought! Oh, God, Guv, it's difficult to know who to talk to about this. I mean, if Marcus, the most boring man in the world, can turn out to be some kind of Virus terrorist, then there really is no one we can safely trust.'

'I know! Mona . . .' He paused. 'This friend of yours, Cassandra Doom . . .'

'Christ's sake, Guv!' She felt her earlier fury surging back. 'She's not a friend. I met her on a dating site where she was calling herself Elaine. I didn't realise who she was until I'd had dinner with her.'

'So . . .it's not you that's been leaking all the stuff?'

'Of course not.' She slumped back in her chair and wondered how the trust between them had disappeared so completely.

'I never seriously thought that it was . . .'

'Really? I thought I was a "security risk"?'

He sighed. 'OK, I had a temporary moment of insanity, but like you said things have gone crazy if the man who fixes my computer while chuntering on about science fiction is suddenly a terrorist.'

'I suppose. So, for the record, no, I have not leaked a single thing to Cassandra Doom, but . . .' She paused, as a thought hit her. 'Bernard found a listening device in his home phone and his office phone. I wonder if Marcus was responsible?'

'You found a listening device in the office? And you didn't think to mention it to me?'

'Trust is a two-way thing, Guv?'

'It's my bloody office! I had a right to . . .oh, you know, never mind. We don't have time for this. Just promise me you'll keep me in the loop from now on.'

'OK, Guv.'

'So, Marcus has been monitoring our emails and phone calls. Suddenly it all becomes clear.'

'Hello.' Bernard was standing in the doorway, with the expression of a man who had just had his world turned upside down.

'How are you doing?' Paterson pulled out a chair for him.

'Marcus—'

'I know, Bernard, it's difficult to take in,' said Mona.

'He didn't do it.'

'See sense,' said Paterson. 'His phone was used to make the hoax call.'

'That's a bit stupid,' said Mona.

'Exactly!' Bernard nodded enthusiastically. 'You'd have to be incredibly stupid to use your own mobile to commit a crime. And Marcus is far from dumb. In fact, he's hyper-intelligent and extremely IT literate. He would know how easy it would be to trace the call.'

Paterson's face had borrowed Bernard's earlier expression. 'You think someone set him up?'

'Yes,' said Bernard. 'And I know who. It was Bryce.'

Mona looked at Paterson to see if he knew who this was.

'The other IT guy!' Bernard looked exasperated. 'The one that never says anything.'

'Him?' Mona tried to get a mental picture of what Bryce looked like. She had a vague feeling of dark hair, a beard perhaps? 'But why?'

'I don't know why, but I do know it's him. The past few days he's been telling me things about Marcus that aren't true, like he's addicted to online gambling . . .'

'*Is* he addicted? Because that could explain . . .'

'No! It's all lies. Bryce disappeared off somewhere yesterday and hasn't come back. I couldn't get the police to take me seriously when I was trying to explain.'

Mona could see their point. Bernard was in a heightened emotional state, and frankly, sounding like a bit of a lunatic.

'And now Marcus is in *prison*.' Bernard threw himself into the chair.

'He won't be in prison yet,' said Paterson. 'He'll be in a room in Fettes somewhere, getting a stern talking-to.'

'Yes,' Bernard snapped. 'And he's exactly the kind of person who would confess to something he didn't do under duress. Or crack an inappropriate joke that makes things ten times worse.'

231

The look on the Guv's face suggested that he agreed with Bernard on this one. 'Leave it with me. I'll talk to Stuttle, see if we can find out more about this Bryce character before Marcus confesses to every unsolved crime CID has on their books. In the meantime, you two need to get Helen Sopel found, and see if she can shed any light on what's going on.'

'Take this.' Bernard pulled out what looked to be a large hanky. He peeled back the four corners of it to reveal a mobile phone. 'Anneka's. Pin code is 2309. I haven't had time to look at the messages, and now I need to go.'

'Go?' said Paterson. 'Where are you off to? I need you here.'

'I've arranged an, ehm, meeting with the woman who works at the Plague Museum, see if I can get some more information from her. Should take an hour tops, then I'll be straight home to see if I can find out anything else. I'll have access to the Internet at home, unlike here. Unless someone's blown up my flat while I was out.'

'I'm sure your flat is fine. OK. See you tomorrow.' Paterson was placated. 'But early, mind.'

'Bye, Bernard,' Mona said, absent-mindedly, her focus now entirely on the phone.

She heard Bernard speaking to someone as he left and looked up to see Ian entering the room. Without hesitation, she thrust the phone into her pocket.

'Rather an exciting day,' said Ian. 'Glad we could offer you some hospitality here until your building gets the all-clear.'

'Getting more exciting by the minute,' said Paterson. 'One of the IT guys has just been arrested on suspicion of placing the bomb.'

232

'Arrested? Really?' Ian's face showed no emotion, but Mona felt that there was some feeling that he was struggling to conceal. Was he incredibly shocked by this news? Or not surprised at all?

'Yeah, Bernard's pretty upset. He's good friends with Marcus.'

'Marcus?' Again, that look on Ian's face that Mona couldn't quite place.

'Yeah. Shocker, isn't it?'

'Remind me which one he is?'

'The tall one with the ponytail and the little round glasses.'

'Do you know who the arresting officer is?'

'No idea. Stuttle phoned me, and said he was sending a couple of plods down to arrest him.'

Ian considered this for a moment. 'I'll go see what I can find out.'

'I'll come with you,' said Paterson. 'I'm not getting anywhere with the IT system.'

Mona saw a slight hint of irritation cross Ian's face.

'The computer system is humped,' Paterson continued, shutting down his laptop and unplugging the charger. 'Shall we knock it on the head, Mona, come in fresh tomorrow?'

'Good idea, Guv.' She was grateful for the suggestion, wanting to get the phone out of Ian's grasp. 'Later, Ian.'

He didn't respond.

9

Lucy was already at the café when he arrived. He took a deep breath and tried to calm his fluttering stomach. He was far more flustered than he'd hoped he would be, and much less well groomed. His initial plans for the evening had been to leave work relatively early, go home, shower, and prepare two to three non-work topics of conversation that he could use. Instead he had run straight from his work to catch a bus, and was now a slightly sweaty nervous wreck.

Most of the bus journey had been spent debating with himself whether he should call the whole thing off. As he had climbed the stairs in search of a free double seat he was convinced he should cancel, he really should, and devote his time to trying to help Marcus. By the time the bus had hit Princes Street he was swinging the other way, because, after all, what could he usefully do? March into Fettes and tell him they had to let Marcus go and start looking for Bryce instead? Because he had tried that earlier without any success whatsoever. He could, of course, spend all evening on the Internet trying to look for clues. But if he was honest, if he didn't turn up some useful information by googling Bryce's name he wasn't really sure what to do. He usually relied upon Marcus for any complicated navigation of the world wide web. By the time the bus pulled up at his disembarking point, he'd decided to meet Lucy, keep it as business like as possible and be out of there within the hour.

Lucy had bagged a nice corner location, a discreet distance from the other diners. A candle was flickering away on the table, lighting up her face as she turned to smile and wave at him. All in all, the date could not be getting off to a more romantic start. Except that Lucy didn't know it was a date, and now he was going to have to have a very embarrassing conversation to bring her up to speed on the nature of his thought processes about the evening. He resolved to get it over sooner, rather than later.

'Hello, Bernard. I hope you don't mind but when I saw this seat was free I just grabbed it. I thought it was the best one for a,' she lowered her voice 'private conversation'.

'Yes, about this evening . . .'

'Would you like some menus?' A waiter appeared at their side, proffering two wooden clipboards with a list of dishes attached to them.

'Ooh, lovely.' Lucy immediately began scanning the options.

'So, about tonight . . .'

'Wine list?' A third wooden clipboard appeared between the two of them.

'Ehm, no, thank you,' said Bernard.

'It's a working dinner,' said Lucy, brightly, by way of explanation.

Bernard gave up. This was not going to be a date. He should never have imagined Lucy wanted to come on a date with him. They were going to spend an hour talking about work, they'd go their separate ways and he was going to die alone. Without even Marcus for company, who would be doing a thirty-year stretch for crimes he didn't commit.

'I'll have the lentil lasagne, and a Coke, please.' He handed back his menu. At least he was going to be fed.

'The polenta for me, and a mineral water.' She handed the wooden board over, shooting the waiter one of her lovely smiles; somewhere deep within Bernard a green-eyed monster awoke. He'd like one of those looks. 'I expect you work round the clock at the HET. You must have working dinners all the time.'

'Not exactly.' *Never, to be precise.* 'Anyway, how long have you worked at the museum?'

'Oh, just a couple of years. I did the MLitt in Museum and Galleries Studies at St Andrews, then got an internship at the Museum, which turned into a proper job, yay.' She made a little air punching gesture. 'Of course, when I started it was quite a sleepy little Museum, then the Virus hit and suddenly we're hugely popular. And you? How long have you been at the HET?'

'Nine months. Before that I was a professional badminton player, then I retrained as a health promotion specialist. A little-known profession, then the Virus hit and suddenly we're hugely popular.'

They both laughed. If this had been a date, it would actually have been going quite well. He thought about raising the issue, but didn't want to jinx the magic. The waiter appeared and placed their drinks on the table.

'Anyway,' said Lucy, suddenly businesslike. 'Fun as this is . . .'

She was having fun!

' . . .I don't want to keep you because I know you're super busy. What was it you wanted to know about the Museum?'

He kicked himself. If this wasn't a date, of course she expected him to actually have a meaningful question to ask her. And, with a guilty start, he remembered that he needed to get back and do something about Marcus. Something, still not sure what.

'It was about, I mean, an issue . . .to do with your Green Card machine?'

To his surprise, she nodded enthusiastically, the candle-shadows dancing around her face as it bobbed up and down. 'I'm so glad you brought that up. I was going to say something, but Corinna said it was just trivia and I shouldn't bother you with it.'

'I'm really interested to hear whatever you have to say,' he said, sincerely.

'OK. And I really hope this is of some use, because every time I think about poor Nathan, it just makes me want to weep. But anyway, the thing that I think is odd is that on the night he was in the building no one was there.'

'No one from the Museum? We knew that.' Possibly this wasn't going to be as interesting as he'd hoped. 'Although, now that I come to think about it, how did he get in?'

'I'm not sure. We sometimes give out the keys, but only to registered keyholders who tend to be long-term volunteers with us. But that wasn't what I meant. *No one* was there.'

'We know that – he was the only person in the building.' He didn't want to ruin the atmosphere, but the conversation was taking a circular turn.

Lucy put down her glass. 'I'm really not making this clear. Let me start at the beginning. The Green Card Box, as you know, records everyone in and out of the main door. On the evening in question no one was recorded as entering the building. Not even Nathan.'

He frowned, as he tried to work out how this could be. It was impossible to get past a Green Card box. They were generally wired into the door mechanism. If someone didn't get the all-clear – for example, because the HET was looking for them – the door just wouldn't open. Most systems allowed for a manual overwrite to allow the door to be opened in an emergency, but you couldn't erase the fact that a card had already been used because the data was transmitted in real time. In fact, the Green Card boxes were an extremely effective method of monitoring who had been where, and were either a huge infringement on individual privacy or vastly useful in tackling crime depending on your point of view. It might be that the boxes were susceptible to hacking. Could Bryce have used his skills in this area? But if so, why?

Lucy mistook his thought processes for disbelief. 'It's true – you can check the machine logs. Corinna was the last person out of the building at half past six. And there's nothing else recorded until Corinna comes back in the next morning. When she found, you know, Nathan's body.'

'I do believe you, Lucy. And it is a very interesting point,' he reassured her. He played absent-mindedly with the remaining bit of lasagne, moving his fork round and round the lentils. 'But the question now is how on earth did he get in?'

'I can't work that out. We have two fire doors, one on the ground floor and one which exits onto the roof, but I checked and neither of the alarms went off.'

He considered the other available options. 'A window then?'

'It's not that easy to open our windows. On the floors where we have exhibits – the ground, first and second

238

– we operate a climate-controlled environment, to protect some of our more delicate artefacts. There's a constant log of the temperature across the building. If a window was opened, we'd know about it.'

'Did you check the temperature logs?'

'Yes. And I'm ninety per cent sure nobody opened a window on any of the exhibit floors. And, to add to that, the windows are all locked, and even if somehow you had a set of keys, if you came in after hours you would set off the burglar alarm. And you would be captured on CCTV.'

'Could someone have let him in?'

'There would still be the same problems of showing up on the Green Card Box, or on CCTV. Aside from the issue of *who* would let him in.'

Corinna McFarlane seemed the obvious candidate to him. She'd obviously been very unhappy about their investigation, missing a meeting and then trying to get rid of them as quickly as possible. There is no way that she couldn't think that the issues Lucy was raising were important. It was crucial, and he was amazed that none of the police who had attended the scene had followed it up. But then the police had been very quick to decide that Nathan McVie's death had been suicide. He wasn't aware that any other possibility had been considered. Was Corinna part of a cover-up, or scared for her safety? Either way, he'd suggest to Mona that they paid her another visit, first thing tomorrow morning.

'Do you have any thoughts at all about how he might have got in, Lucy?'

'Well, it seems to me the only remaining possibility is that someone got in via a window on the third floor. They are all skylights, though, so it wouldn't be easy.'

'But the burglar alarm? And the CCTV?'

'There isn't any CCTV up there. There's nothing of value, just a meeting room and some storage. But whichever way I look at it, I don't understand why the burglar alarm didn't go off.'

'Could Corinna . . .?'

The waiter chose that moment to reappear. 'Everything all right with your meal?' he asked, sweeping up the empty dishes.

'Lovely. Can we have the bill, please?' As soon as the waiter was out of earshot, Bernard put the question again. 'Could it have been Corinna that Nathan was meeting with? She could have left the alarm off when she left for the night, then they both could have got back in?'

'I suppose so. But why?'

'I don't know. But I think we've overlooked a possibility about Nathan's death. Everyone assumed suicide, in fact I think some of my colleagues were very keen on that being what happened. But we never considered whether he might actually have fallen. Could he have been trying to get out?'

'There's a huge skylight that lights up the stairwell. He could have been reaching for that, but why would he not just have gone back the way he came?'

Bernard closed his eyes for a second, trying to picture the scene. He recognised the description of the large skylight at the very top of the building, but as a mere Museum visitor he'd never been above the second floor.

'Lucy, please say if this puts you in an awkward position, but I'd really like to have a look at the third floor.'

'Do you want to come in first thing tomorrow?'

'Tell me if this is crazy, but is there any chance we could go now?'

She looked at him a little uncertainly. 'Corinna might be annoyed.'

'I'll take full responsibility. It could really help our case.'

She reached into her bag and pulled out a cluster of keys on a chain. 'Well then, let's go.'

'Wait.' Bernard reached for the keys. They were attached to a key ring, which featured a small replica of a black-and-white face mask, its mouth distorted to the side. 'Your key ring.'

'Oh, yes, that is interesting. It's a copy of a Mbangu mask. It represents a hunter who has been stricken with disease. It's very rare to see an African mask that actually depicts illness. Usually they are . . .'

'African?' Bernard interrupted her. 'Not Native American?'

'No.' She looked surprised. 'We're working on an exhibition next year about African responses to pandemic. Ebola, of course, was devastating for several African countries. Corinna has been back and forth there over the past few months.'

He stared into space, wondering where Africa fitted into Helen Sopel's disappearance. Had she been drawing their attention to the Museum's exhibition? It was too much of a coincidence that the civil servants were meeting there, but he couldn't piece it all together. Maybe Mona would . . .

'Bernard?' Lucy's voice interrupted his thoughts. 'Do you still want to go to the Museum?'

'Yes, sorry.' He got to his feet. 'We should hurry.'

10

Mona put her key into the lock and gently turned it. Pushing it open slowly, she peered into the dark of the hallway, trying to establish if there were any signs of life. Her initial assessment was that the coast was clear, and with her back against the wall, she slowly and silently made her way up the stairs.

'Mona! You're home. I didn't hear you come in.'

So close. 'Hi, Mum.'

'I'm making steak and kidney pie for tea, but it won't be ready for an hour or so. Would you like a cup of tea to keep you going?'

'No, I'm fine. I just need to get a bit of work done before I eat.'

'Oh, well, I'll see you then.'

She sensed her mother's disappointment. It couldn't be easy, stuck in the house by herself all day. Mona was probably the first person she'd spoken to today. She hesitated. It wouldn't kill her to go and get that cup of tea, have a quick chat before she looked at Helen Sopel's text messages. On the other hand, she could just have a quick look at the mobile, check out if there was anything urgent on it, then head downstairs. She ran up the remaining stairs.

Sitting cross-legged on the single divan in her childhood bedroom, she turned on the phone, and waited as a number of texts downloaded. She scrolled through the list of recent calls. As Simon had indicated, there was one number that had suddenly started appearing over the weekend, and had been calling, and been called, repeatedly over the past few days.

She jotted down the number then flicked over to the text messages. There were very few from the number she was looking for, but then Simon had talked about numerous furtive phone calls. Perhaps Helen and Anneka preferred to talk rather than text.

The six messages she could see revealed very little. In fact, unless they were in code, she was pretty sure that they were shopping lists. *Cheese, bread, deodorant. Diet Coke (2 bottles).* You wouldn't have to be a master of deduction to take from this that Helen was hiding out, probably somewhere not very far away, and Anneka was keeping her supplied.

She picked up her own phone and dialled Paterson's number. It went straight to voicemail. She checked the time, and realised that she was in the middle of the couple of hours during which Paterson's wife insisted that he didn't answer his phone. The second Mrs Paterson had very particular ideas about how engaged the Guv should be in the nightly ritual of tea, bath and tooth-brushing for his young kids. As often as not the Guv broke this particular rule, but it would appear that tonight he was behaving himself.

'*Guv, we need to bring Anneka Tomas, Helen Sopel's assistant, in for questioning, ideally tonight. I think she knows where Helen is. Call me when you get this.*'

Mona rearranged the pillows on her bed, trying to make herself comfortable while she went over the options in her head. Anneka would have realised it was missing by now, but they had no way of knowing whether she would have managed to alert Helen to that fact. If she had, there wouldn't be any further calls to it, and knowing that they had been found out, there was every chance that Helen might decide it wasn't safe for her to stay where she was. If she didn't yet know, they had a tiny window for action before Helen realised she hadn't heard from Anneka for a while. Usually, in this situation, she'd have given Marcus the number in the hope that Helen would continue to use it and they would be able to trace her location. But Marcus – and Bryce – were out of the picture, and she didn't know who else to ask.

All this would be so much easier if she could actually speak to Paterson. She scrolled through her phone's address book, and looked for his home phone number. When she'd added this to the address book, against the entry she'd typed 'Home Number ONLY FOR EMERGENCIES,' to make sure that she didn't acci- dentally ring it and get a bollocking. She might well still get into trouble, but nobody could deny she needed his help immediately. Paterson would know what to do. She dialled the number, steeled herself to explain to Mrs Paterson that she was phoning from work and felt an increasing sense of anti-climax as the phone rang and rang.

She groaned in frustration. Laying the two phones side by side on the bed, she wondered what to do. Not only was she losing valuable time in catching Helen, in the meantime, she had the thorny problem of what to do with the phone. It *should* be securely held under lock and key, but where exactly was safe these days? Somewhere in Fettes, where Ian would know about it? Hand it over to Stuttle for safekeeping? Neither option appealed.

There was also the issue that if Anneka had enabled her *Track My Phone* option, she might even now be sitting looking at details of where her phone had last been switched on. Given what she'd been using the phone for, she'd need a brass neck of no mean order to actually turn up and demand it back, but considering Simon's description of working with her, and her own experience of meeting her, it couldn't be ruled out. There was also the possibility she might not come alone. She could be sitting outside her house at this very minute, in a car with the lights off and someone large and menacing in the passenger seat.

She looked over at her window. *This was Bernard-level paranoia.*

Or was it? The high death count to date on the investigation suggested that some degree of caution should be followed. She leapt off the bed and switched off her light. Peering cautiously from behind her curtain, she scanned up and down the road, and could see nothing out of the ordinary. She heaved a sigh of relief, and feeling slightly sheepish, let the curtain fall into place. Her safest bet was to switch off the phone, and keep it on her person, at least until the Guv came up with a better idea.

At that very moment, her phone started ringing. The Guv must finally have wriggled free of his domestic duties. She snatched up her phone but it wasn't making a sound. On her bed, Helen's phone was lit up. She leaned over, trying not to touch it in case she accidentally answered it. The number was the one that she'd hoped to see. It looked like Helen didn't know that the phone had been stolen, which was interesting. Anneka should have been round there as soon as she noticed it was missing. Was there some reason Anneka had been detained?

She was tempted to answer it, but had no clear plan of what she would say. This was so frustrating! Marcus would have had the whole thing sorted by now. The ringing stopped, and a few seconds later the phone binged, to indicate a text message had arrived. Very, very carefully, Mona pressed the button to read it.

Setting off now. Museum meeting at 8 and if not in touch by 9.30 you know what to do

She considered this message for a moment, her mind working overtime. She reached for her own mobile, and pressed Bernard's number.

'Bernard, are you still with that woman from the Museum?'

'Er, yes? Hang on.' She heard him murmuring apologies, no doubt to the woman in question. He was probably moving himself to a discreet distance before continuing the conversation.

'Great. I need you to ask her if she can let me in there tonight.'

'Ah, right, funny you should say that. I've just asked her the same thing.'

'You want access to the Museum? Why? Actually, tell me when I see you. Where are you?'

She noted the name of the restaurant, and ran down the stairs, pulling her coat on as she went. 'Mum!'

Her mother limped slowly out of the kitchen. 'What is it?'

'I'm so sorry to do this, but I need to go out.'

She looked horrified. 'But what about your tea?'

'I'm sorry, but it's an emergency.' Any guilt she felt was being entirely swamped by adrenaline.

Her mother turned back to her cooking. 'It always is.'

11

Bernard hoped that Mona would find the café OK. He had discussed its merits with her once before, while stuck in a car waiting for a Health Defaulter to show. He'd sung its praises, noting the many awards it had won, but she'd claimed never to have heard of it, because *all-vegetarian menus never appealed to her*. He could believe that. As a former health promotion specialist he'd been able to point out to her the many shortcomings of her diet, which from what he could see consisted largely of coffee, Diet Coke, packets of crisps and the occasional takeaway curry when she finally remembered to eat. Maybe, when all this was over, they could both come here to celebrate. Assuming they were both still alive.

Here she was now, standing in the middle of the room, scanning the tables. He waved. 'That's my colleague here now.'

Lucy swivelled round. 'Oh, she looks nice.'

Mona gestured him over, with a manner that was less suggestive of niceness than of extreme impatience.

'Back in a mo.'

He hurried over. Mona looked at the tables surrounding them and appeared to decide that it wasn't private enough, shoving him less than gently toward a quieter area near the door. 'Right, don't talk, just listen. I spoke to Professor Bircham-Fowler, and he told me what Helen and the other civil servants were up to . . .'

'How did he . . .?'

'No talking, just listening.'

He nodded.

'They were running an illegal drugs trial in Africa, using street children. Several of them died after taking the drugs, and Jasper Connington had a fit of conscience and told the Professor. He was preparing to denounce the trials in Parliament when he had his heart attack.'

He stared at her.

'I'm finished now, Bernard, you can say, "that's terrible."'

'That *is* terrible. And Helen was caught up in all this?'

'It appears so. And I got a message on her mobile saying she's coming to a meeting at the Museum at 8pm tonight.' She pointed in Lucy's direction. 'Your friend from the Museum, can we trust her?'

'She's not my friend, I only met her as part of the investigation.' He followed Mona's gaze. Lucy was shrouded in candlelight again. 'I don't know if we can trust her. Given that one of our IT support workers seems to have been an undercover terrorist, I'm struggling with trying to trust anyone.' Lucy reached up and curled a stray lock of hair behind her ear. She'd never looked prettier. He sighed. 'But I really hope we can.'

Mona elbowed him gently. 'Bernard, is this a date?'

'No!' He did his best to sound annoyed, before his natural honesty reasserted itself. 'Well, maybe.'

'Bernard, you . . .'

'If you are about to say the word "badass" I will not be responsible for my actions!'

'OK.' She smiled. 'Let's get to the museum.'

'What are all these plants doing here?' Mona pushed angrily past the row of tubs in her way.

'They're . . . oh never mind.' Bernard suspected that she wouldn't welcome a full explanation of the medicinal properties of the foliage. Maybe later when she wasn't looking quite so, what was the word, focused?

'Lucy,' Mona suddenly spun round to talk to her, making her jump a little bit, 'once we're in the building will it be obvious to anyone else that we're there? I mean, if they were also to come here tonight?'

'Well, I suppose they would know if the alarm wasn't on. But why would anyone else be here tonight? Do you mean Corinna?' She turned her key, pushed open the door, then paused with the key still in the lock. 'Oh, the alarm isn't on.'

'Does that mean someone is already here?' asked Bernard.

'I don't think so. The lights aren't on. I don't understand. Maybe Corinna forgot to put it on when she left?'

'Or maybe she's planning to come back later tonight via another route.' Bernard explained to Mona about his earlier discussions with Lucy.

'I don't really understand what's going on here.' Lucy was starting to look worried. 'I don't want to get into any trouble.'

'You're assisting with a Health Defaulter enquiry. You can blame us for any actions we've requested that you take,' said Mona.

She didn't look convinced by this. Bernard thought she

was right to be concerned. He tried another angle. 'Your assistance tonight might help us find out what actually happened to Nathan McVie.'

This seemed to do the trick. 'Poor Nathan.'

'So, Lucy, we think there is going to be a meeting here tonight between Helen Sopel . . .' said Mona.

'The missing civil servant?'

'Yes,' said Mona, 'and someone else.'

'Possibly Corinna,' added Bernard. 'It seems likely seeing as she's left the alarm off.'

'I don't understand where she fits into all this, but yes, possibly.' Mona looked thoughtful. 'I suspect someone else as well.'

'Carlotta Carmichael?'

'My money would be on Jonathon.' She turned her attention back to Lucy. 'If they are coming in via the roof, which meeting room do you think they would use?'

'If they were wanting to avoid the CCTV, they'd probably stick to the third floor. There's a meeting room there,' she pulled a face, 'although it's not very comfortable.'

'If I wanted to listen to the conversation in the meeting room, is there somewhere I could hide?' asked Mona.

'I'm not sure. Shall we go and look?' She started up the stairs.

'Ehm, hang on just a minute, Lucy.' He pulled Mona to one side, speaking quietly in the hope that Lucy wouldn't hear them. 'What are you doing? All we need to do is find Helen and take her to her Health Check. We don't need to know about what's happening at the meeting.'

'You don't want to know what's actually going on?'

'Of course I do, but it's nothing to do with us. It's the responsibility of . . .well, I don't know exactly, but it's not our remit.'

She had the particular look of irritation on her face that he recognised from previous arguments. It was the expression she always wore when she was very annoyed with him, but didn't actually have an answer to his question. He could see her thought processes at work, and after a second a look of triumph came over her face. 'I need to scope the situation out, Bernard. She may not come willingly, and we don't know how many of them will be at the meeting. It makes sense to check out what we're dealing with. I can be in there and let you know how many of them there are, and if you need to call for backup.'

'Yes, but–' He suspected any such call would be made after Mona had satisfied her curiosity about the content of the meeting.

'Bernard, we don't even know if people at the meeting will be armed.'

'Armed? It's a meeting between a civil servant and a museum curator. There's as much chance they're packing heat as I am!'

'"Packing heat", Bernard? You watch too many films.' She started up the stairs.

'Mona, don't get yourself killed or sacked trying to help the Professor.'

'That's not what this is about, Bernard.'

'Really? This isn't about you having misplaced feelings of guilt about his heart attack? And you wanting to finish the work that he started?'

'No, it's not.' Her look of irritation was back. 'Anyway, they can't sack us. Recruitment being what it is they'd never replace us. Let's pick up the pace.'

As instructed, Bernard ran up the stairs behind Mona, taking them two at a time in his haste. As he reached the second floor he realised that Lucy was no longer with them, and peered over the banister. She was walking up quite slowly, her hand on her side as if she had a stitch. He stopped to let her catch up.

'I'm not as fit as you and your colleague are, Bernard. All that food then rushing around – I think I need to sit down for a minute.'

'Come on, we're nearly there.' He hesitated for a second then took her arm. 'You can lean on me.'

'Thank you.'

Mona's head appeared above them. 'Come on. We're running out of time!'

Lucy groaned, but let Bernard hurry her along. Once they reached the third-floor landing she stopped suddenly. 'There.' She pulled away from him and patted something on the wall.

'What?'

'It's not there,' she panted.

She hit the wall again, and he saw that she was actually tapping a metal bracket. It had a couple of curved arms sticking out from it, which looked as if they should be holding something in place.

'There should be a wooden pole there, with a hook on the end of it. We use it to open the skylight if it gets too hot in the entrance hall. If poor Nathan was trying to use that to get out of the building . . .'

Bernard looked at the skylight. To access it Nathan would have to have hooked it open, then climbed over the banister and somehow levered himself out of the window. It was possible but, he looked down to the ground floor below, a pretty terrifying route to take. What would Nathan have been so worried about that he would have risked his life to escape in this way? 'It still doesn't explain why he didn't go back out the way he came in.'

Mona joined them. 'Come *on*, guys. These discussions will have to wait.' She looked at the window above them. 'Please tell me that's not the way into the building you were thinking about.'

'No.' Lucy shook her head. 'There are a couple of skylights in our storage areas, I think. To be honest, I'm not up here all that much.'

'What's the nearest one to the meeting room?'

'Over there.'

Bernard walked to the door Lucy was pointing at and opened it. There was a small set of wooden steps just below the skylight. He went in, leaving the light off, and climbed up to the window. He pushed it gently, and found it wasn't locked. Cautiously, he stuck his head out, and saw that there was a flat roof only a few feet below them. 'Mona, this looks like their way in.'

She looked into the room. 'Looks like it. Now can you get Lucy somewhere safe, then give Paterson a ring. See if he can get us any backup.' She turned to go, then stopped. 'But just tell him that we think we've found Helen Sopel. Don't mention . . .' she caught sight of Lucy listening in, 'the other stuff I told you at the restaurant.'

He thought about asking why, but decided there wasn't time. 'OK. Mona – are you sure about this?'

She shooed them in the direction of the door. 'Totally.'

12

Lucy was right about the third-floor meeting room. It was not in any way, shape, or form comfortable. The climate control of the Museum obviously didn't extend this far, unless the climate they were aiming for was polar ice cap. The meeting room had a small adjoining space, a large cupboard, really, which seemed to be used to store paper records back to the day the Museum was founded. Or possibly back to the day paper was invented, judging by the age of some of it. Mona could not have hoped for a more perfect spot for eavesdropping. She crouched in the dark, and hoped that her shivering didn't give her away.

How should they to play this? Helen probably wasn't going to be cooperative. Between Bernard and herself they could strong-arm her into a taxi and to the nearest emergency Health Check. They'd done it a stack of times before, usually with a Health Defaulter under the influence. She'd managed to get Bernard trained to the point where he didn't take several large steps backwards whenever the punches started flying, and he could usually be relied upon to hold someone's arms effectively behind their back. And duck at the appropriate moment.

But that worked when they had a single person to deal with, and who knew how this Corinna woman going to react? Maybe she'd leap to Helen's defence. Maybe there were other people attending the meeting, who wouldn't be keen to see Helen carted off to a Health Check. And there was the question of how Helen herself would react. Most of the reluctant Defaulters she hauled in were unwilling to co-operate because they were drunk, or worried about missing their next fix. Judging by Nathan McVie's willingness to risk his life to get out of the building, Helen was potentially highly motivated to stay out of the reach of the authorities.

She heard a crash, followed by several bangs. It looked like the party was about to begin. Adrenaline surged through her, and without consciously thinking about it her hands formed into fists. The sound of female voices drifted through to her.

'So, how are you?'

'How am I? How do you think I am? I'm in hiding, my job is on the line and I'm in danger of taking the blame for this whole fiasco. I'm just dandy, I really am.'

'Just trying to keep this civilised, Helen.'

Helen. Tick.

'Civilised? It's a bit late for that. Anyway, what time is Jonathon getting here?'

Jonathon. Tick.

'Soon. Although he's not happy with that stunt that you pulled passing the bills on to the HET officers with his phone number on it. It put him and Carlotta in a very difficult position.'

'My heart is breaking for them, Corinna.'

Corinna. Final tick.

'Still, I'm sure Jonathon will have a plan. After all, that's what he does, isn't it? Sorts out the messes that his wife has created.' There was the sound of a chair being scraped back. 'I really don't care about Jonathon

Carmichael's problems. All I want is my passport back, then I'm out of his hair.'

'He's going to want to know what other little self-protection measures you've put in place. Who else will be running to the authorities? Your pal got some more information? What about your sister? Or that assistant of yours?'

Anneka. All the suspects present and correct.

'Leave them out of this,' Helen said. 'Nobody will say anything – assuming nothing happens to me. I'm going to take six months' unpaid leave, somewhere far away from here, until all this heat from Nathan and Jasper's deaths dies down.'

'And what then? You're just going to turn up and reclaim your job?'

'Why not? I haven't done anything wrong. We were participating in a legitimate project.'

'One which Carlotta Carmichael knew nothing about.'

'Knew nothing about? Her husband was . . .oh, never mind. I keep forgetting that the only thing you care about in life is this museum. After all, you got your friend killed because of it.'

'Nathan's death was nothing to do with me!' Corinna's voice rose sharply.

'Really? Let's just remind ourselves of your role in all this. You provide us with a meeting space here in your lovely museum, at the request of Nathan. Your friend, remember him? In return you get a nice fat bung to organise an exhibition about Ebola and all the other infectious diseases you can get in Africa. And we get a cover story, if anyone asks, about this fantastic inter-continental cooperative show that we are putting on.'

'That's not how I . . .'

Helen talked right over her. 'But nobody does ask, do they? And our little experiment continues on, killing children as it goes, not that anyone is going to miss them, except maybe their pals on the street or in the orphanage . . .'

'Shut up.'

'Nobody notices and nobody cares. And that's just the way it would have stayed if the research hadn't started looking just a little bit promising.'

This was news. In her excitement, Mona brushed against a tower of papers. She bit her lip, but fortunately nothing moved. She concentrated on staying as still as possible.

'Enough progress for the trials to continue, as a legitimate partnership between the Scottish Government, a couple of our research institutes and the University of Liwawe. I hear it's got Ethics Committee approval and everything. Apparently the anti-virals are looking really promising. Could be big money in it.'

Mona was beginning to understand Helen's sudden disappearance. The Government might have been willing to take the heat if the existence of an unsuccessful and morally reprehensible drugs trial had leaked into the public domain. Heads would have had to roll – Carlotta's probably amongst them. Helen would be facing criminal charges. There would have been some public soul searching about the limits of what should be done to fight the Virus. And in six months the whole scandal would be forgotten. But an actually promising anti-viral drug trial? No one would want to risk a proper study being undermined by its unethical start. Helen Sopel, as the remaining person able to let the cat out of the bag, was in a delicate position.

'So, Friday morning you give us the use of your beautiful building once more, don't you? So that Carlotta Carmichael can update us with the good news about the future of the project. And, of course, the bad news for any of us people who know the real truth about how the research really got started. We're immediately dropped from the project, and banned from discussing it, even with each other.'

'Well, I wouldn't know, would I?' Corinna sounded defensive. 'I wasn't at the meeting.'

'Yeah, Corinna, but by then your involvement in this had stopped being a favour that you were doing for Nathan. It took me a while, but I figured it out. By the time of that last meeting you were totally in the pocket of that awful man.'

Mona's ears pricked up even further.

'Yes, that delightful man. I'd describe him as our minder, but you probably see him more as a benefactor of the arts.'

'Fuck you.'

'What did he offer you, Corinna? A fully funded exhibition every year for the next ten years? And all you had to do in return was offer up Nathan.'

Mona waited for a rebuttal, but there was silence.

'Because Carlotta was nervous, wasn't she? Could she rely on us all not to run to the press, or even worse, that mad old professor? She was really paranoid about him. So we all get a text message, mine supposedly came from Jasper, although I dare say his supposedly came from me, suggesting a meeting here Friday evening, so we can discuss what happened. Top secret, of course. Enter via the tradesman's entrance so that no one knows we've been here.'

'You are so full of . . .'

'Except only poor Nathan turned up. You must have known what would happen when you handed him over to that man.'

'I didn't hand—'

'What were your instructions? Welcome them in, give them a nice cup of that special tea that will make them all nice and sleepy and malleable, and let that man,' she spat out the words, 'take care of it.'

Again silence filled the pause.

'And my guess is that Nathan twigged what was happening. Did he beg you for help, Corinna? Because he must have been pretty bloody desperate to try to climb out of that window.'

There was a large sniff, followed by the sound of tears, which led Mona to believe that Helen's version of events had been pretty close to the truth.

'Where is Jonathon?'

'Jonathon's not coming. He's not bringing you your passport.' Corinna's tears had turned to anger. 'Did you really think that he wanted it so he could get you a visa for that visit to Africa? Didn't you wonder why it never quite happened? He's been sitting on it all this time, just in case things got awkward.'

There was a banging sound, which Mona recognised as the sound of window opening.

'I wouldn't run off if I were you. There's someone else here to see you.'

Further thumps followed as the unknown person joined the fray.

'Hello, Helen. What an interesting discussion you ladies have been having. Anyway, I thought it was time for the "awful man" himself to join the conversation.'

Mona heard the familiar tones of Ian Jacobsen.

13

'Where should we wait?' asked Lucy.

'Somewhere out of the way where we can't be seen, but near enough that I can hear Mona if she shouts for help.' He looked back at the door behind which his colleague was hidden. He didn't like this. He'd have been happier if all they were doing was waiting for Helen Sopel to appear through the window, then requesting her immediate appearance at a Health Check. Though he had to admit she had a point that they didn't actually know who else might be there. He'd be even happier once he'd phoned Paterson and made all this his problem.

'My office is one floor down – would that do?'

'Sounds good.' He took her arm again. 'We'd better hurry.'

Lucy's office was small, with most of the floor space taken up by a large wooden antique desk. It was impossible to open the door fully. Bernard squeezed through the space and surveyed the room. Every available surface seemed to be covered either by papers or by books. She fussed around, rearranging enough stuff to allow him to sit down. He pulled out his mobile and pressed his boss's number.

'Paterson.'

'It's Bernard.'

'I know. The phone told me. What's up?'

260

He wondered where to begin. 'Ehm, right, OK, thing is . . .'

Something approaching a growl emanated from the phone. 'Cut to the chase, Bernard.'

'We're at the Museum. We think Helen Sopel will be meeting someone here, but we don't know who.'

'Excellent work! Give me a ring back after she's had her Health Check.'

He panicked that Paterson was about to hang up. 'Wait! The thing is, Mr Paterson, Mona was wondering if you could send some backup.'

There was a loud snort. 'I'd love to, Bernard, but who? Maitland's still in hospital, Carole is worse than useless, and unless you are both staring down the business end of a sub-machine gun, there's a limited chance of me being able to get any local plod round to you. The only chance would be going back to Stuttle, and I can't do that unless you are telling me it's either a matter of life and death or a matter of national security. Is it either of those things?'

Was it a matter of national security? He wasn't sure, and Mona had been pretty adamant that he didn't share too much with Paterson.

'Bernard!' The phone shouted at him. 'Are you OK?'

'Yes, fine, just thinking.'

'So, do I need to call Stuttle?'

'No . . .probably not.'

'Are you sure? Because I'm getting the impression that you and Mona aren't sending all the information you should be up the chain.'

In contrast to earlier, he now had a sudden urge to get Paterson off the phone. 'It's fine, Mr Paterson, we'll cope.'

'Tell you what, Bernard, I'll come. I've had a couple of

beers so I'll need to get a taxi, but I'll be there as soon as.'

'OK, good,' he said, but the phone was already dead. He hoped Mona would be OK with this.

Lucy smiled at him. 'Reinforcements on the way?'

'Something like that.' He gave a slightly queasy smile. The cavalry were some way off mounting their steeds and riding to the rescue. 'How far away is Corinna's office? I seem to remember it's on this floor.'

'It's a couple of doors down.'

'Is there any chance of a look at it?'

She wrinkled her nose. Bernard sensed they were reaching the limits of Lucy's willingness to co-operate.

'I don't know – don't you need a warrant or something like that?'

'How about I promise just to look and not take anything away? She won't even know I've been there.'

'Well, OK, I suppose.' A look of doubt still clouded her face. 'But if she walks in on us I hope you can say something that stops me getting sacked.'

'I'll think of something.' He sincerely hoped Paterson would have arrived by then. He didn't care whether his boss praised his efforts, or yelled at him for his approach, he just wanted someone else to come along and take charge.

Bernard stuck his head out of the door, and gave a cautious look around. The sound of muffled voices could be heard upstairs.

'Quick, and be very quiet.'

They scurried along the corridor. Lucy gently eased the door open and they went in.

'What are you looking for?' she asked.

'Accounts.'

'Try the filing cabinet.'

'It's locked.'

'I think the key is in her top drawer. I'll get it. Oh.' She looked over to him. 'What was the name of the civil servant you were looking for? Is it Helen Sopel?'

'Yes.'

She pointed to the desk. 'There's a document here with her name on it. It seems to be some kind of resignation letter.'

He walked round to her side of the desk and started to read the typewritten document.

Dear
    I wish to tender my resignation with immediate effect, for personal reasons.

Yours sincerely,
Helen Sopel
Head of the Virus Operational Response Team at the Scottish Government

There was a second sheet of paper sticking out under the top layer. He pulled his jumper down over his fingers and gently eased it out.

Dear Joanne
    I can't do this any longer. I'm so sorry that I've caused you any worry. I'm taking some time away to think about things. I'll ring you when I'm settled. Love you,

'Why are these here?' asked Lucy. 'I don't understand why this lady would come here to write these letters. And when was she here?'

'I don't know. But I have a horrible feeling that she didn't write them, Lucy. I think perhaps that someone else wrote them and they're hoping she signs them tonight.'

'No.' She looked nervously over her shoulder. 'Can we go, Bernard? I don't like this.'

'OK.' He had to admit his stomach was starting to churn a bit too. He pulled open the nearest door.

'That's a cupboard, not the way out,' said Lucy.

He didn't move, just stood staring at what he'd found.

'Bernard, what is it?' She came over to see what he was looking at.

'Lucy, is that what I think it is?' He pointed at a long wooden pole with a brass hook at the end of it.

'Oh dear.' Her hand flew to her lip. 'Yes. That's the pole for opening the skylight. It shouldn't be here. It should be . . .'

'On the third floor. Next to where Nathan fell, if he did fall, to his death.'

14

'What are you doing here?' Helen's voice was high-pitched and squeaking with fear.

What *was* Ian doing there? Whatever his interest was in Helen, it didn't relate to her being late for a Health Check. She suspected that his interest wasn't official Police Scotland business either. She didn't know why he was here, or what he was up to but she suspected that Helen was right about one thing. He really was an awful man.

Should she reveal herself? Deep within the HET handbook there was a protocol for how the HET and Police Scotland should work together. In an emergency situation the procedure made it clear that HET staff were compelled to defer to their police colleagues. She couldn't help but feel that the nuances of this particular situation were not adequately covered by the handbook's rules. And she'd be damned if she was revealing herself before she'd found out what Ian was up to. It wasn't just idle curiosity; the more she heard of the conversation, the better she would be able to protect Helen from whatever Ian had in mind.

'I had a little chat with the Carmichaels, and we agreed that I would take it from here. That little stunt with the phone bills didn't go down at all well.'

'I'm sorry.' There was a squeaky tone to her voice,

betraying her nerves. 'It wasn't supposed to happen. I didn't ask anyone to do it – my friend panicked when your lot turned up and started questioning her.'

'Yeah, mistake or whatever doesn't make up for the fact that it did happen. And by the way, if you are relying on Anneka Tomas to raise the alarm for you, guess again. We've had her in custody since this morning.'

'Well, fuck you.' She seemed to be rallying. 'What was I supposed to do? Jasper had sold us out to that Professor, Nathan was dead, and Carlotta wouldn't give me any reassurance that I wouldn't end up taking responsibility for the whole thing. She was talking about me being extradited to the Democratic Republic of Africa on manslaughter charges. I could end up in an African jail!'

'Believe me, that won't happen.' Ian's tone was soothing. Mona recognised the fake sincerity from her previous conversations with Ian. She knew exactly how quickly it tipped over into threats. 'Now, Helen, I need you to sign a couple of things for me, then we're going for a drive.'

'I'm not going anywhere with you. You can't make me.'

'Oh, Helen.' He gave a little, sarcastic laugh. 'You cause us so much trouble. Put it this way, you can sign the things we need, and walk to the car, or I can shoot you in one of your legs and drag you there.'

Helen let out a small scream.

Mona texted Bernard. *Dial 999. Man with gun.*

'Is this really necessary?' asked Corinna. 'We could . . .'

'Shut up. So, what's it going to be, Helen?'

The time had come. Mona carefully got to her feet, and in one smooth motion yanked open the cupboard door and stepped out into the meeting room. 'I suggest you don't do anything.'

'What the . . .' Ian gawped at her, astonished. She was disappointed to see that he *was* actually holding a gun. She'd been hoping it was a bluff, but, hell, she'd work with what she'd got. Ian's expression hardened. 'What are you doing here?'

'Looking for a missing Health Defaulter.' She smiled. 'Hey, Helen, good to meet you.'

'For Christ's sake, Mona.' He started to laugh. 'You are totally wasted in Health Enforcement. Why couldn't you make the same half-arsed attempt to track down Defaulters as the rest of the HET staff?'

'Just like to see things through.'

She started calculating her odds. Ian had a gun and an apparent ruthless streak on his side, and she had her bare hands, Bernard one floor down, a 999 response that could take God knows how long, and two civilians with very questionable loyalties. There was the potential for someone to end up very dead in this scenario.

Without moving his aim an inch, Ian reached into his pocket with his free hand and pulled out his mobile.

She took a step in his direction and he motioned her back with the gun.

'Bob?' He spoke into his phone. 'Guess which lovely lady has joined the party?'

Bob. It must be Bob Ellis, Ian's partner in crime, whom she'd last seen driving off with the Professor, allegedly taking him to a safe house. She wasn't privy to Bob's response, but she guessed it would be something sarcastic, sweary and with an unpleasant undercurrent of sexism.

'Mona Whyte.'

This time, even from where she was standing, she could hear Bob's response loud and clear.

'Yeah, that bitch. Going to need some backup in case

she tries to scratch me with her fingernails. You know what girls are like.'

Shooting her a fake smile, he popped the phone back into his pocket. 'Bob says hi.'

'Ian, what's going on?' Corinna stepped around the table to stand behind him. 'Who is she?'

'She's a minor irritation.' Ian's eyes never moved from her face. 'Which I'll deal with. Do you have the paperwork?'

Corinna still looked anxious. 'It's in my office.'

'Go and get it.'

Mona wondered if Bernard was up to this. He wouldn't have been her first choice as back up, but he was getting better. He was better in a crisis situation than he was when he had time to stop and think about all the things that could go wrong. If he'd any sense, once he'd got her text he'd have got himself and Lucy out of the building.

With a last glance in Mona's direction, Corinna disappeared from the room.

'Don't let him take me.' Helen's breath was coming in short bursts.

'I won't.' She kept eye contact with Ian, who snorted.

'If she's your only hope, Helen, you're doomed.'

Mona continued her calculations. How far away was Bob? Once he arrived, presumably armed, there was no chance of her stopping Helen coming to harm. She caught Ian's eye and guessed similar scheming was going through his mind.

'We're not there yet, you know,' said Mona.

'What?' asked Ian.

'We're not yet in a world where police, or whatever you actually are, can go around shooting innocent people and justify it because of Virus control.'

'Innocent?' He shook his head, a small smile on his face. 'I could find many words to describe Ms Sopel here, but innocent wouldn't be one of them.'

They were interrupted by Corinna returning.

'There's someone down there. I can hear them talking.'

'Yours, I presume?' Ian turned to Mona. 'Is it Maitland or Bernard?'

She said nothing.

'It's Bernard, isn't it?' He threw his head back and laughed. 'I was almost worried for a minute there. Corinna, does this room lock?'

'Yes.' She walked over to the door and pulled a large, old-fashioned key out of the keyhole.

'OK. Get her locked in. The rest of us are going downstairs.'

'I could stay here . . .' said Corinna.

'No. I'll need your help.' He turned and pointed the gun directly at Mona's face. 'And, bitch, don't try anything. I really will shoot you.'

She believed him.

'Don't leave me here, Mona.' Helen grabbed her arm. 'Please.'

She gently prised her fingers off. 'I'll be back. Don't worry.'

'Don't bank on that, Helen. You,' he pointed the gun at her, 'move.'

They walked down the stairs in single file. Above them they could hear Helen Sopel hammering on the door and screaming Mona's name.

'Corinna, which room are they likely to be in?'

She wasn't listening, too busy looking back up the stairs, in the direction of the noise. Mona guessed that the evening was not working out the way that she had hoped. Ever since Ian had started threatening to shoot people, Corinna had been looking increasingly pale. She was a walking definition of 'out of one's depth'.

'Corinna, focus!'

She jumped.

'Which room will they be in?'

'Oh, right. Probably my assistant's. That door there.' She pointed.

'Bernard!' he shouted. 'Come out before I shoot your boss!'

There was a second's delay, then Bernard appeared, with Lucy's head peering over his shoulder.

'Corinna,' said Lucy, 'What's going on?'

'Just . . .' She looked on the point of tears. 'Just do as he says. Please, Lucy.'

'Wise words.' Ian turned to Corinna. 'Does your room lock?'

'Yes, but . . .'

'Everyone in there, please, quick as you can.'

Mona was embarrassed to see Bernard leading the way, disappearing into the room as fast as he could go, with little thought or concern for the others. If he had been hoping for a relationship with that woman from the Museum, he could forget about it now, after this lack of chivalry. She'd spent months trying to build up his confidence so that he wasn't an embarrassment in these types of situations. Couldn't he at least have put up a token show of resistance?

'Great backup you've got there, Mona.' Ian sniggered. 'First rate.'

'The Police will be here any minute, you know. We've dialled 999.'

'I'd be delighted to see them.' He looked unconcerned.

'One phone call from me and it's you lot that would end up under arrest.'

She tutted, her annoyance compounded by the fact that Ian was probably telling the truth. She walked as slowly as she dared in the direction of the office, desperately trying to formulate a plan of action with the limited resources she had at her disposal. With a half-willing accomplice, a Maitland, for example, the two of them could surely have overpowered Ian, gun or no gun. But she didn't have a partner on this one. She had Bernard. She might as well have been on her own.

'Speed it up, Mona.'

With a final glare at him, she stepped into the office. Immediately she was grabbed by Lucy and pulled in to a corner. Wrong-footed, she tried to work out what was happening. Bernard stepped forward, and as soon as Ian walked through the door hit him in the face with what looked like a large wooden pole.

'Ow, my nose.'

Bernard brought the pole down again, this time on his arm.

'Careful, Bernard!'

Glad as she was to see Ian getting beaten up, she didn't want anyone killed by the gun going off by accident. Ian cried out in pain, and the gun fell to the ground. Mona made a grab for it, and her fingers closed round it seconds before Ian crashed into her. Bernard gave Ian a further blow with the pole, this time on the back of the head. He fell to the ground, moaning.

'Fuck's sake, Bernard! Stop hitting me!'

Mona pointed her newly acquired gun at Ian.

'Lucy,' she said, 'get the keys to the meeting room and let Helen out.'

'Don't do this, Mona.' Ian levered himself up on his good arm. 'You've no idea what is going on here.'

'Stay there!' She pointed the gun at his head. Bernard, and the wooden pole, stood guard over Ian to stop him making a grab for her.

'Can I have the keys, please?' Lucy held out her hand, and Corinna passed them over without a murmur.

'Mona, give me my gun back.' Ian had propped himself up against Corinna's desk. From the way he was nursing his arm, she doubted he would actually be able to fire it. 'If you give me it now, we can minimise any comeback on you or Bernard for your behaviour today.'

'I don't think so.'

'You know I outrank you!'

'No, actually, I don't. I don't know who the hell you are or who you work for these days. I only know that bad things happen around you.'

'You don't understand what is happening here. You don't . . .' Ian's voice tailed off. His skin had turned a strange shade of grey. After staring at them blankly for a second, he slumped forward, his head crunching off the floor as he fell.

They looked at him in a silence broken only by the sound of Corinna's heels clicking as she took off down the stairs.

'Should we . . .?' asked Bernard.

'No. Let her go.' She pointed at Ian. 'Do you think he's faking it?'

'I don't know. I did hit him quite hard.'

'Check his pulse.'

'He's still breathing.'

'That was a fucking high-risk strategy there, Bernard. What if the gun had gone off when you hit him?'

272

He frowned. 'I thought he was planning to shoot us all. It seemed like a risk worth taking. Has he gone mad, or something?'

'No, he's sane. Beyond that, I have no idea of what's happening. Look, we need to hurry – Ian's already called for backup. I'll call an ambulance and stay with him. You need to get Helen and Lucy out of here. Go out through the skylight and let's hope they're not watching the back of the Museum. Here – take the gun.'

'No way.' He shook his head vigorously. 'Sorry, Mona, but I'm not touching that thing.'

'OK.' It was probably for the best. The last thing they wanted was Bernard unintentionally shooting someone, probably himself. He gave her a worried little nod, then turned to leave.

'Bernard?'

'Yeah?'

'Well done.'

He nodded solemnly. 'I'll probably be in loads of trouble for this.' He ran up the stairs, and she heard him calling out to Lucy.

She pulled out her mobile and dialled 999. 'Ambulance, please. HET code 924.'

After securing the emergency response, she turned back to Ian. His breathing seemed regular. She debated putting him into the recovery position, but didn't want to get too close.

What was she going to say when the Police and ambulance finally arrived? And what story would Ian and Bob spin them? If Ian had been telling the truth when he said he could get her arrested, Bob would have similar powers, and seeing the state that his colleague was in, might well feel moved to use them.

'Mona?'

The Guv's voice echoed up the stairs. Corinna must have fled without taking the time to lock up behind her. She stuck her head over the banister and was horrified to see Bob right behind him.

'Are you OK? Bob said there'd been a bit of trouble?' *And the lies and damage limitation had begun.*

She watched them walk up the stairs. A movement caught her eye and she turned back just in time to see Ian lunging full tilt toward her. She stepped back and her feet went from under her. She grabbed the banister to pull herself upright, but before she could fully right herself, he was on her, grabbing her arm. To her horror she realised he was pushing her backwards over the banister, intend on reclaiming his gun. If he kept up this pressure another minute she would tip over and fall, but at this distance if she fired the gun it would be fatal.

'You stupid, stupid bitch.' Blood was dripping onto her from Ian's ruined face. His eyes were wide and staring, and his teeth were bared. He looked like an animal moving in for the kill.

'For God's sake, Ian!'

The sound of her voice seemed to bring him back, and he released his grip slightly. He was holding her with his left hand; Bernard had obviously done some serious damage to his other arm. She tried to move but his grip on her tightened. She had one option left. Opening her hand, she dropped the gun. After a second she heard it crash to the ground; she hoped it had hit the floor and not some irreplaceable artefact.

'What the bloody hell is going on up there?' the Guv's voice rang out. 'Jesus Christ, is that a gun?'

Ian released his grip, as if he was suddenly weary. She

stared at him. His nose looked like it might be broken. Blood was smeared across his face, and most of his clothing. His right arm was hanging limply at his side. She really was going to have to buy Bernard a vegetarian meal, and toast him with the non-alcoholic beverage of his choice. He'd given Ian a total doing.

'Why do you have to make things so difficult?' he asked her. He started sliding slowly down the wall. 'You could have worked for us, you know. We had you marked out as having potential. But now you've fucked up a major police operation. Well done. But we'll get Helen Sopel. She's going nowhere.'

'Mona? Mona, are you OK?' The Guv was sounding frantic.

'I'm fine,' she shouted, then turned and ran as fast as she could up the stairs. The skylight was still open and she stepped out into the darkness.

The roof was deserted.

15

'Where to?' The taxi driver sat with one hand on the wheel, awaiting instructions.

Bernard looked at Lucy and Helen, who both looked back at him. He had literally no idea where he should be taking them. He should probably have asked Mona where he was supposed to go. He should probably have asked Mona a lot of things about what she was expecting him to do, but there hadn't been time.

Helen took charge. 'Centre of town. Quick as you can.'

'Where are we going?' asked Bernard.

'I don't know, but I thought getting away from here as fast as possible would be a really good idea.'

'Yes, of course. Have you any idea what was going on back there, Ms Sopel? Ian wasn't really planning to shoot us, surely?'

Helen snorted. 'Yes, he was. He'd have shot me without a second thought. The man has no conscience.'

Now that the adrenaline was leaving his body, Bernard could feel his usual state of apprehension flooding back. This time his anxiety was particularly focused on the fact that he had just broken the nose of someone who was apparently a cold-blooded killer. 'Oh dear.'

He wondered how Lucy was bearing up to the evening's events. He was pretty shaken, and he was used to the ups and downs of life at the HET. Lucy was used to the ups and downs of life at a Museum. He looked past Helen to the far side of the taxi, where Lucy was staring out of the window.

'Lucy?'

'Yes?'

'Are you OK?'

'I think so. Just trying to take it all in.'

He leaned forward. 'You were so clever suggesting that we climb over the roof and use a different fire escape. I'm sure that's what let us get away.'

She smiled at him, then reached past Helen and lightly touched his hand. 'And you were magnificent back there. I've never seen anyone be so brave.'

He felt himself blush.

'Oh, for God's sake,' said Helen, returning Lucy's hand to her own side of the taxi, 'it's his job. Can we focus here?'

Bernard opened his mouth to say that nowhere in his job description did it say anything about facing down supposed colleagues armed with a gun, then thought better of it. Helen didn't seem that much less scary than Ian.

'I want to speak to a journalist.'

'I thought you weren't allowed to talk to the press?' he asked. 'Haven't you signed the Official Secrets Act?'

She looked irritated. 'Yes, but if it's a choice between being dead or being in prison I know which option I'll choose.'

'Dead?' Bernard was still struggling with this formulation of events. 'Are you sure Ian wasn't just trying to . . .'

'Trying to what? Scare me? Give me a good talking-to? I'm an embarrassment to the government.'

'We could go to the Scotsman's offices?' said Lucy, helpfully.

This brought a curt shake of the head. 'No. I don't know who I can trust there. Can we go somewhere quiet where I can think?'

'We can't go to my house – Ian might know where I live,' said Bernard. Did Ian know where he lived? He was definitely going to have a few sleepless nights.

'And Corinna knows where I live,' said Lucy. 'Oh, I know! My parents are on holiday. We could borrow their house for a couple of hours? Assuming there won't be any more men with guns. Mum and Dad really wouldn't like that.'

'I certainly hope not.' Bernard wasn't sure he could face down any more guns. Particularly any held by Ian Jacobsen who would surely be nursing a very big grudge against him.

'Just tell the driver the address, please,' said Helen, impatiently.

Bernard was taking quite a dislike to this woman.

Lucy's parents lived in a detached house in Cramond, with a side garage and a neat garden out front. The taxi had driven past street after street of other similar houses before pulling up. Bernard felt reassured by the anonymity of the surroundings. *Safe in suburbia.*

'Take a seat,' said Lucy, ushering them into the living room. There was an upright piano against one wall. Bernard wondered if Lucy played. He'd put money on her being able to roll out a sonata or two. A little Chopin, or Bach perhaps. She was probably extremely musically gifted. As well as intelligent. And brave.

Helen threw herself onto the sofa.

'Shall I pop the kettle on?' asked Lucy. 'Although there might not be any milk in the fridge.'

'I need a journalist I can trust,' said Helen to the room in general. 'One who will put my side of the story.'

'Your side?' said Bernard. He was about to challenge what her side might actually be when he remembered that Lucy was still in the room, and probably shouldn't hear any more. 'Any chance of that cup of tea?'

'Oh, yes. I'll see what I can do.'

He waited until the door closed behind her, then returned to Helen Sopel. 'I really can't see any way a journalist could make this a sympathetic story. What you were doing to children in the Developing World was awful. People will be appalled whatever spin you put on it.'

'Oh grow up!' She raised a couple of exasperated eyebrows in his direction. 'We already see these countries as a source of spare parts.'

'We do not!' Bernard was outraged.

'What about all the tourists who head to India to get a kidney bought from a local, or who use a surrogate mother from one of the poorer corners of South America? Everyone is opposed to these kinds of things until they are going through a medical crisis of their own, and they find out how long they have to wait on the NHS, or how much it'll cost them to jump the queue. Then suddenly they find themselves able to think the unthinkable, and before you know it they're whipping out their credit card and getting themselves on the next flight to some godforsaken hole or other. And now that the entire country is in the middle of a crisis, people are ready for this kind of thinking.'

'I'm sorry, but I don't believe that.'

'If the project succeeds there's not a parent in the land who wouldn't be giving thanks and stocking up on our pills.'

Bernard's mobile rang, flashing up an unfamiliar number. He regarded it with some trepidation but pressed the button to accept the call. 'Hello?'

'Bernard, it's me.'

'Mona! Are you . . .'

'Yes, I'm fine. Phone me back from a landline on this number.'

He popped his head into the kitchen, where Lucy was busy putting cups on to a tray. 'OK if I use your phone?'

'Of course – it's in the hall.'

He dialled, and Mona answered on the first ring.

'Where are you?'

He gave her the address. 'It's Lucy's parents' house. They're not here.'

'Excellent. I'm on my way. Is everything OK at your end?'

'Yes, I think so.' He lowered his voice. 'Although I have to say I don't much like Helen Sopel.'

He peered through the crack in the door into the living room. Lucy seemed to be showing Helen the contents of her parents' drinks cabinet.

'We don't have to like her. We just have to get her into a Health Check, somehow.'

'She thinks Ian wants to kill her.'

There was a silence. 'She might be right.'

'What about us, Mona? Are we in danger?'

She ducked the question. 'I'm on my way.'

'Before you hang up, she's saying she wants to talk to a journalist. She wants this in the public domain, thinks it will save her life.'

'She's probably right.'

'But she doesn't know who she can trust, and then I thought, you, ehm, know a journalist. Not the kind of journalist I like, but I'm sure she'd love this story.'

The phone was silent.

'Mona, are you still there?'

'I'm not sure I want to go there, Bernard.'

'Really? Because I'm thinking that it might not just be Helen Sopel that's safer with all this out in the open. Where do we fit into all this?'

There was a long sigh. 'I'll pick her up en route.'

16

'So I was right about Helen Sopel.' Elaine grinned at her.

She'd explained the situation in a phone call, which had been surprisingly short given the complexity of the issues involved. She suspected Elaine could tell a good story from bad in the first two sentences. Now they were in Elaine's car, driving through quiet back streets, heading for Cramond.

'Stop gloating.'

'I'm not. I'm just delighted that when you wanted to give a journalist such a fabulous scoop your first thought was little old me.'

'You were the only journalist I had a phone number for. I tend to avoid them, especially the muck-raking type.'

'Well, I'm glad you held your nose and called me anyway. God, it's good to see you, Mona.'

'Can you move your hand back to the steering wheel, please?' Elaine's fingers were gently massaging the top of Mona's leg. It was very distracting. 'We need to focus.' She looked as they passed yet another street of detached houses. 'Number 37! I think we're here.'

'So, are you sure this Sopel woman will talk to me?'

'She requested a journalist, so I guess so. Let's find out.'

Mona spotted a pair of nervous eyes and a slightly balding head sticking out from behind the curtain in the front room of the house. She waved to Bernard who disappeared from view, appearing again a second later at the front door.

'Come in.' He still looked worried. 'Helen's had a couple of whiskies.'

'Not sure that's a great idea, Bernard.'

'That's what I said! But she's not an easy woman to reason with. They're in here.' He pushed open a door, revealing a large and airy living room. Helen and Lucy eyed her from their seat on a cream leather sofa. Helen was nursing what looked like a double, and Lucy was nursing a worried expression. She'd get Bernard to replace whatever bottle it was that Helen was currently destroying.

'Is she a journalist?' Helen pointed at Elaine.

'Elaine McGillvary, delighted to meet you.' She extended a hand. Helen didn't take it, and after an awkward moment, she pulled her arm back.

'McGillvary, I know that name.' Helen brow wrinkled as she tried to join the dots, then smoothed out as realisation hit. 'You're Cassandra Doom!'

'Guilty as charged.'

'Your column is appalling.' Helen threw back the last of her drink. 'The kind of gutter journalism that you indulged in made our job tackling the Virus ten times harder. Your lowest denominator populism led to us abandoning good ideas because we know that spin that Cassandra Bloody Doom would put on them.'

Elaine smiled. 'All that may or may not be true, but the most important thing is that people do actually read my column in huge numbers. So you can talk to me, and the whole of Scotland will be talking about it tomorrow, or we can wait and see if the *Guardian* can fit you in for a profile some time next week.'

'If you can guarantee this goes out tomorrow, the interview's yours.'

Bernard's face was contorting through a variety of expressions of disgust. Mona had some sympathy with his feelings.

'OK, Helen, let's head over to my office then, just in case anyone has worked out where you are.'

'Hang on.' Mona stepped swiftly into the doorway, to stop anyone from leaving. 'Ms Sopel needs to attend a Health Check in the very near future . . .'

'Oh, for God's sake!' Helen looked furious.

'Ms Sopel, my colleagues and I have risked life and limb to track you down for this Health Check, and it's just as well that we caught up with you when we did, or who knows what would have happened to you. I know that you are very keen to speak to the press, but . . .'

'Mona . . .' began Elaine.

'And, yes, I know that you are also keen to get the interview, but . . .'

'Mona, stop!' She put a hand on her arm. 'It's really not a problem.'

'Isn't it?'

'We have a sympathetic doctor, darling. Helen's not the first interviewee we've had who's been a bit naughty with their health care.' She winked, and in spite of herself Mona smiled.

'Well, I'll need to come and oversee it.'

'Fine, fine.' There was a breezy wave of the hand. 'Shall we?'

17

'So, what now?' asked Lucy. The house felt very quiet now that the others had left.

'I don't know,' said Bernard. 'Were you planning to stay here, or did you want to go back to your own home?'

'Home, I suppose.' She thought for a moment. 'I'm not really supposed to be here. They only left me the key in case there was an emergency.'

'I'll see you back to your house.'

'Oh, I couldn't put you to any trouble,' said Lucy.

He smiled. 'Believe me, it's the least we can do after what you've been put through.'

'It has been quite an evening,' she admitted. 'I'm still getting my head round everything that happened.' She stood up, collecting her mug and Helen's empty glass as she went. 'I'll just get these.'

'Ehm, OK.' He watched as she left. Would this be a good time to suggest meeting up again? He could frame it in the context of concern about her – wanting to check she was OK, maybe tomorrow over coffee?

His thinking was interrupted by the sound of his ringtone. He dug out his phone, and saw Paterson's name on the screen. His hand lingered reluctantly over the small green telephone icon. Someone needed to update Paterson on everything that had happened since he'd summoned him earlier, but he really hoped that Mona had already done it. She hadn't updated him on what the official version of events was.

'Bernard, have you heard from Mona? I'm trying to ring her but she's not answering.'

Damn. 'She's fine. There's really nothing to worry about.' That might not be entirely true.

'Thank God. Last time I saw her Ian Jacobsen was holding her over a banister. And Jacobsen was in a terrible state. His face was all smashed in and I think he had a broken arm. Someone had given him a right doing, but I couldn't get any sense out of him or Bob Ellis.'

'Oh yes, actually that was me.'

'What was you?'

'The, ehm, "doing".'

'That was *you*? What the— Why did—' The ramblings at the other end of the phone were getting increasingly incoherent. 'What the hell is going on here, Bernard? Why are my colleagues suddenly trying to kill each other?'

He didn't answer.

'Right. I'm coming over. Where are you?'

Bernard started to panic. He didn't know what was going on, he couldn't explain it, he'd broken probably every rule in the HET handbook (and possibly some criminal laws as well), and worst of all he was still at Lucy's parents' house. His potential relationship stood no chance of blossoming if Lucy watched him being savaged by Paterson.

'Actually, Mr Paterson, I'm not at work any longer I am now on my, ehm, own time.'

'Your own time?' Paterson's voice was probably audible in Glasgow. He held the mobile a little further away from his ear. 'Do you not think that this is exactly the wrong time to be clocking off?'

Bernard didn't have an answer for this, so did the only thing that he could do and hung up. He turned the phone to silent; there would be consequences but he'd deal with them later, when he was far, far away from Lucy. And given the amount of trouble he was in, he decided he might as well be hung for a sheep as for a lamb.

'Let's call a taxi, Lucy. The HET office will pay.'

'Oh, if you're sure . . .' She started gathering up her possessions.

'And—' It was now or never. 'Would it be all right if I gave you a ring tomorrow, just to, you know, check if you are OK?'

She smiled. 'That's so thoughtful. Yes, of course.'

Lying in bed that night, Bernard smiled to himself. Despite the horrors of the day, he felt a certain sense of achievement. Although he had done nothing that Maitland could describe as a 'move', Lucy certainly hadn't discouraged him from getting in touch. And she had commented on his bravery. And she'd touched his hand in the taxi. He could definitely be in a worse position.

He rolled over, wrapping himself up in the duvet in an attempt to get warm. His eyes were closing when the thought occurred to him that in the morning not only was he going to have to explain himself to Paterson, he was also going to have to deal with Ian Jacobsen. And Stuttle. And possibly Police Scotland if they wanted to charge him for assaulting a policeman.

He rolled over on to his back. In spite of his tiredness, he suspected this was going to be a sleepless night.

287

18

The streets were deserted. She'd given up trying to find a cab and had set off on foot from Elaine's office back to her mother's house. Her feet were weary, but she was glad of the opportunity to think over the evening's events. She'd need all her thoughts in order before she went into work tomorrow. If she had to face the music she wanted it to be with a conductor's baton. Stifling a yawn, she had a quick look over her shoulder to check that the streets remained deserted. She half-expected to see Bob Ellis standing behind her, ready to finish what Ian had started.

Stopping at the end of her mother's street she had a final look around. To her dismay, there was a car parked across the driveway of her mother's house. She reviewed her choices. Turn tail and flee? But then she would be leaving her mother to the mercy of whoever the visitor was. Not an option. Call for backup? Difficult to think who exactly would come to the rescue. She sidled closer to the house, and as she did the passenger door was flung open.

'Get in.'

She hesitated.

'Get in, Mona. I'm fed up of being messed about.'

'Sorry, Guv.' She got into the car, pulling the door shut gently behind her. 'How did you know I was here?'

'Credit me with some detecting ability, Mona, seeing

as you credit me with nothing else. Any chance of you telling me what the hell is actually going on?'

Turning away from him toward the window, she noticed that the hall light was still on in her mother's house. 'I'm not sure I know what's going on, Guv, but I can certainly tell you what happened this evening.'

She went through the events of the evening as quickly as she could, trying to keep any emotion out of her voice. If she stopped to think about what had happened she wasn't sure she could control herself. Paterson listened in silence.

'Bernard faced down a man with a gun?'

'He did indeed. He's actually pretty good under pressure, just really bad when he has time to think about things.'

'Pretty high-risk strategy hitting a man with a gun in his hand.' He shook his head in disbelief. 'He could have ended up getting one of you killed.'

'I know, I told him that, and I'll have a chat with him about gun safety when all this is over. But it wasn't entirely irrational, Guv. He thought Jacobsen was shepherding us all into the room so he could kill us. He'd already threatened to shoot me if Bernard didn't appear.'

'Well, he's got more balls than I credited him with, I'll say that.'

'And the thing is, Guv, I don't know if he was right or wrong about it. Maybe Jacobsen was going to shoot us. What do you reckon his game is? Whose side is he on?'

'No idea. And I can't believe I'm going to say this but do you need to lie low for a while? Just until we can figure out what the story is?'

She shook her head. 'Oh no, I'll be at work tomorrow. I've done nothing wrong. We were looking for a Health

Defaulter and we found her. Every single thing that Bernard and I did tonight was a legitimate reaction to the situation we found ourselves in.'

'Do you think Stuttle will see it that way?'

'It's not Stuttle I'm worried about. Unfortunately, I don't know who it is that I *should* be worried about.'

'Anything you need, Mona, anything at all, you just have to ask. And bloody Bernard – what a star, eh?' In spite of himself, Paterson cracked a small smile.

She smiled back. 'Good night, Guv.'

The key scraped the metal as she put it into the lock. She winced, and edged the door open as quietly as she could.

'You're back late.'

Her mother materialised in the hallway, her dressing gown on.

'Mum! It's,' she looked at her watch, 'two in the morning!'

'I was worried, Mona. You didn't say you were going to be late. What have you been doing?'

What had she been doing? Her job, obviously, and on paper the result was a good one. A difficult to find Health Defaulter had been tracked down and delivered to a Health Check. There was a big tick for that. But the other stuff? She wasn't entirely sure what exactly she'd been thinking. Bravely doing her public-spirited duty to highlight wrongdoing? Or foolhardy meddling in something that was none of her business?

She opted for the one word that was definitely true. 'Working.'

'I'll make you a cocoa.'

'You don't need to bother, Mum . . .' but she was gone.

She stumbled through to the living room, and sat on the

sofa. And Bernard, God bless him, had shown levels of bravery and ingenuity she would not have known he had in him. And she'd left him to make sure his new friend was OK. She was glad he had a girlfriend. He deserved it. A yawn swallowed her.

Tomorrow was another day. Whatever the fallout was, she'd deal with it.

She closed her eyes. By the time her mother came back into the room she was snoring.

FRIDAY

MAKING THE PAPERS

I

For the third time that week Bernard was in early. After a fairly sleepless night he'd decided the best thing was to get up, head to the office and find out if he was either sacked or under arrest. The week's events had left him well aware that the HET was a difficult organisation to leave voluntarily, so he assumed that they wouldn't be in any hurry to sack him if they could avoid it. However, breaking the arm of a co-worker, whatever the circumstances, might be pushing organisational tolerance to its limits. So here he was, bright and early, ready to learn his fate. Except, to his surprise, he was the only person there. He'd been sure Mona would have shared his 'let's get this over with' mentality.

Unless something had happened to her? He pulled out his phone to make contact, and quickly shoved it back into his pocket when Paterson flung the door open. His head moved swiftly back and forth as he surveyed the room. 'Where is everybody?'

'I don't know,' said Bernard. 'Ehm, have you spoken to Mona?'

'Yes, you can relax. Your designated spokeswoman has brought me up to speed on what's been happening. And when all this is over, you and I are going to have a serious conversation about who you answer to. I'm your line manager, not Mona Whyte, whatever she may think. You need to keep me informed.'

'When will this be?'

'What?'

'Our serious conversation?'

'Well, I don't know. Does it matter?'

'If you are going to be shouting at me, Mr Paterson, I'd just like a timeframe for when it's likely to be.'

'Bernard, you're an idiot.'

He wondered if that was the extent of the 'serious conversation' that they were going to have. He thought about attempting to clarify the situation, but his boss's expression didn't really invite follow-up questions.

'Anyway,' began Paterson, then stopped, catching sight of something over Bernard's shoulder. Bernard turned to see Carole hovering in the doorway.

Paterson flung his arms up in the air. 'Fantastic. As if I don't already have enough to contend with, now *you've* decided to show up. Well, whatever attitude you've brought to work today you can stuff it. I'm not in the mood.'

'No attitude,' said Carole, holding her hands up in a gesture that resembled a POW surrendering. She pulled the door closed behind her, sat on the nearest chair and started taking her coat off.

'Oh?' Paterson eyed her suspiciously.

'Really.' She nodded. 'I feel terrible about what happened to Maitland. It was the worst moment of my life thinking that something had happened to him and that I was partly to blame.'

'So, you're back at work and planning to behave yourself?'

'If by that you mean am I willing to work hard, and not cause trouble, yes.'

'Are you dropping the lawsuit then?' asked Bernard.

She shook her head. 'No, I'm afraid not. I don't want to work at the HET any more, but I am going to try and do a good job until my lawyers get me out of here.'

'Well, what a fabulously motivated team I have.' Paterson grunted. 'And I'd keep the hell out of Stuttle's way, if I were you.'

There was a gentle tap at the door.

'That'll be Maitland, saying he's willing to come back to work but his lawyers say he needs forty minutes' siesta every afternoon.' Paterson pulled open the door. 'Marcus!'

Marcus was a vision of despair. His hair was half-hanging out of its ponytail, and his T-shirt showed all the signs of being slept in. There was a large stain on the leg of his jeans, which Bernard hoped was spilt coffee. And judging by the bags under his eyes, Bernard wasn't the only one who'd had a sleepless night.

'You were the last person I expected to see today,' said Paterson. 'Are you OK?' He pulled out a chair, and Marcus half-sat, half-fell into it.

'It was awful,' said Marcus. For a horrible minute Bernard thought his friend was about to cry. He looked over at Paterson, who shot him a slightly helpless look in return. Fortunately, Carole stepped up to the plate. She moved into the chair next to Marcus, slid her arms round him and gave him a hearty, maternal hug. He rested his head on her shoulder and sniffed loudly.

'Have you had any breakfast?' she asked. 'Would you like me to fetch you something?'

'A cup of tea would be nice.' He sat back upright, and wiped his eyes. 'Milk, no sugar.'

'Milk, no sugar,' she repeated and headed out the door.

'But they let you go?' said Paterson.

'Yes, Mr Paterson,' said Marcus. 'I've spent the night in a meeting room on the second floor. They were going to transfer me to a station with cells but decided against it. The police officer's exact words were "consider your-self lucky that you are a friend of Ian Jacobsen", which is strange because I don't think I've said more than two sentences to him in my life.'

Bernard looked over at Paterson, who was staring thoughtfully into space.

'Anyway,' Marcus continued, 'about midnight last night they worked out that I was in the middle of a very long phone call to a HET officer in West Lothian who had accidentally deleted a registry file when the bomb hoax call was made.'

'At midnight? Why didn't they let you go then?'

'They said I was free to go, but the PC who locked me in the interview room took away my belt, my money and my shoes. By the time they released me she'd gone home and nobody knew what she'd done with them. I still haven't had them back.'

Bernard looked down at Marcus's feet, which were clad only in a pair of bright blue socks with an S for Superman logo on them. It struck him that no one had ever looked less like a superhero than Marcus did at the moment.

'Well, that explains what the fragrant smell in here is,' said Paterson. 'Bernard, nip down to the front desk and see if you can reunite the man with his shoes, so we can all breathe easily again.'

'Sorry,' said Marcus. 'If I'd known the turn that events were going to take yesterday, I'd have worn clean socks. And underwear.'

Bernard sincerely hoped that he meant *clean* underwear. 'I'll see what I can do.'

It took three phone calls, and trips to two different offices to finally locate all of Marcus's belongings. Bernard hurried back toward his temporary office, with the plastic bag of goods tucked under his arm. En route he caught sight of a newspaper stand and was reminded about Helen Sopel's interview. He grabbed a *Daily Citizen* and paid his money at the Kiosk. He was keen to read the article before drawing Paterson's attention to its existence; Mona's debrief may not have included updating Paterson about the interview between Helen Sopel and her girlfriend. Or whatever Cassandra Doom actually was to Mona.

He spread the paper out on a table but before he had time to locate the Cassandra Doom column, he heard his name being called. He turned in the direction of the voice and saw an apparition that was probably Ian Jacobsen. He wasn't instantly recognisable under the facial bandages, purple bruising and the sling, although the dressings did correlate to where he'd hit him last night. If Marcus had looked bad, Ian looked a million times worse. And the most awful thing about his appearance was the expression with which he was regarding Bernard. If looks could kill he was going to be very, very, dead indeed.

'Bernard,' he snarled.

'Wh . . .wh . . .what are you doing here?' He scrunched up the newspaper and started looking round for a way out.

'I work here. I'm a police officer, remember.'

The kind of police officer that tries to shoot unarmed civilians, he remembered that much only too well. Bernard

299

wondered if he should say something. Should he shout, tell the other officers at Fettes that there was an armed criminal in the building? He decided his safest option was to get back to the meeting room where his colleagues were and try to tell Paterson what he thought was going on. He would know what to do. Unfortunately, Jacobsen was in between him and the safety of his line manager.

'You don't look well, Ian,' he tried.

'Are you taking the piss? It's not surprising I look like shit, given what you did to me last night.'

'But I . . .'

'Six to eight weeks, Bernard, and this thing comes off.' With his good hand, he pointed at his sling. 'Six to eight weeks, then you better start watching out for yourself. You better start looking over your shoulder.'

'OK.' Bernard was happy to accept Ian's suggestion. He was very much planning to keep looking over both shoulders for the foreseeable future.

Ian's only visible eye stared at him. 'Is Mona in yet?'

'I don't think so.'

'Well, as soon as she gets here, tell her she's wanted at Stuttle's office.'

His stomach lurched. Was this the beginning of the process of sacking/jailing/possible executions? 'Just Mona?'

'For now. But I can find you anytime I need to.' For emphasis, he poked Bernard with his remaining good hand. Bernard noted that it still packed quite a punch. He side-stepped around Ian and hurried back to their temporary office.

'Mr Paterson, Ian Jacobsen is downstairs and I think he wants to kill me.'

'From what I heard he's got reason to.' Paterson looked

up from the laptop. 'Ignore him. He's not going to come anywhere near you under the circumstances.'

Bernard did not feel particularly comforted by this. 'But maybe I'll have an accident some dark night in a few months' time.'

'Morning all.' Maitland appeared in the office, followed by Carole, holding a plastic cup.

'Oh, look who it is. We were about to start looking underneath desks to see if you were asleep somewhere.'

'Yeah, sorry about that, Guv.'

'Stuttle wants to see you when you're feeling better.'

'OK.' He grinned.

'Why are you looking so cheerful? Stuttle's not inviting you round for tea and cake, you know.'

'I get that, but I've just escaped a near death experience, so of course I'm cheerful. And having just cheated death makes you think about things. So, as soon as I got out of hospital I decided to seize the day. Long and short of it is, I've, ehm, asked Kate to marry me, and I'm delighted to say she said yes.'

'That is wonderful news,' said Carole. She leapt up to hug him.

Maitland was still beaming from ear to ear. 'She wants to finish her degree and everything first but I think we're looking at a summer wedding next year.'

'Congratulations,' said Paterson. 'Have you been thinking about this for a while?'

'Yes,' muttered Bernard. 'Ever since he found out she wouldn't sleep with him until they were married.'

Maitland winked at him. 'It's going to be the best wedding night ever.'

Bernard wondered if there was any way at all he could talk Kate out of making the biggest mistake of her life.

Paterson slapped a £20 note on the table. 'In light of the happy event, it's bacon rolls all round and I'm buying. You two,' he pointed at Maitland and Carole, 'shift your arses down to the canteen.'

Bernard waited until they left, then turned to Paterson. 'Mona has to go and see Mr Stuttle.'

'I know. Stuttle phoned here as well. She's on her way.'

'What do you think Mr Stuttle's going to say to her?' he asked.

'I have no idea, Bernard, nobody ever tells me anything.' Paterson sighed. 'I suspect it's not a tea and cake invite for her either, but if it's an out-and-out bollocking about yesterday's fiasco I would have thought you'd be in the firing line too. Hopefully she will come back to us with some answers to whatever the hell has been going on. But until someone tells us otherwise I suggest we get on with doing the day job. Has anyone tried to see if the computer systems are working yet?'

'I'll have a look,' said Marcus. 'Does anyone have a laptop?'

'Here, take mine,' said Paterson.

'I bought a newspaper,' said Bernard. 'I think there's going to be an interview with Helen Sopel in it today.'

'In the *Citizen*? Why's she talking to that pile of . . .?' Realisation hit him. 'It's Cassandra Doom, isn't it?'

'Actually, yes, Mr Paterson, I'm afraid so. Ms Sopel wanted everything out in the open, you know, she wanted everyone to know what the Carmichaels had been up to.'

'Is this Mona's doing?'

'Ehm . . .'

Paterson snatched the paper out of his hand, and swept through the pages, muttering as he went. He found the column, smoothed out the by now rather battered page and started reading.

'*Hamfisted HET officers do it again.*'

'That's an odd headline,' said Bernard. He moved to the other side of the table so he could read it for himself. 'Mona saved Helen Sopel's life – I thought this would be a positive article about us.'

'It gets better. *The Stormtroopers of the HET have really surpassed themselves this time. Not content to stick to harassing the general public, they have now endangered a brand new multi-million pound Virus research partnership with the University of Liwawe by holding the civil servant leading on it hostage until she participated in one of their pointless Health Checks.*

Helen Sopel said, "This really was ridiculous. I missed my flight and some crucial meetings. We are fully supportive of the Health Check regime, but I am needed urgently in Democratic Republic of Africa to begin the research project. I had to call on Carlotta Carmichael to resolve the situation. She will be having a very serious conversation with the Scottish Health Enforcement Partnership about the HET's heavy-handed approach."

Another triumph of jackboots over common sense for the HET.'

Paterson screwed the paper up into a ball, and flung it at the wall.

'I don't understand – none of that is true,' said Bernard. 'In fact, it's the exact opposite of the truth! And why is she suddenly best friends with Carlotta Carmichael?'

'Because she's struck a deal, Bernard. She's obviously made one last call to Carlotta and they've agreed some arrangement where Sopel keeps her mouth shut about what's been happening, and by the sounds of things, gets the job as project director of this new research project. She's probably on a plane to Africa even as we speak.'

'But why would Cassandra Doom change the story?'

'Because she's a dirty, low-life, sell her own mother for a story, gutter journalist, Bernard. And, in case we forget, Mona's girlfriend.'

Marcus's clattering on the laptop keyboard stopped. 'She's what?'

'Friend who happens to be a girl,' said Bernard, quickly. Finding out about Mona's sexuality at this precise moment might just tip Marcus over the edge. He'd work up to telling him, maybe in two to three months' time.

'Whatever.' Paterson continued. 'The journalist will have had some kind of bribe as well. Then everyone who knows anything about the previous research trials will have been bought off or silenced. On the one hand we've got a Museum Director with the best funded small museum in Scotland, and on the other, a Professor who's too scared to open his mouth in case his family get hurt. Mona is probably being offered her bribe over at SHEP HQ even as we speak. And the only other people who know anything are right here in this room. I'm not particularly happy with that thought.'

'I'm not entirely sure that I know what's going on, Mr Paterson,' said Marcus.

'So, what do we do?' asked Bernard.

'I don't know, Bernard, I really don't. We hope for the best, and keep doing the day job.'

'That might not be that easy,' said Marcus. 'There's something very, very, strange happening with the computer systems. I've tried logging in as myself, then as the administrator. I've tried to get into the North Edinburgh HET site, then the other Lothian ones, then

I tried Aberdeen just for a change, and the same thing keeps happening.'

'Cut to the chase, Marcus. What thing keeps happening?'

'This.' He spun the laptop round to show them a completely black screen.

'Is it dead?' asked Paterson.

'Give it a minute.'

White words started flashing up on the screen.

WATCH
THIS
SPACE

Paterson flung his hands up. 'What the hell is that supposed to mean?'

Marcus and Bernard looked at each other and shrugged.

'I'm phoning Stuttle.' Paterson starting pressing buttons on his mobile. 'This is ridiculous.'

Bernard reached down to his feet for the balled-up newspaper, and started unfurling it. 'I wonder if Mona has seen this yet?'

2

Mona was not furious.

She spread the newspaper out across her knees and read the article for the second time, confirming to herself that she was definitely, absolutely, not furious. Because fury did not begin to describe the level of rage she was currently feeling. There would have to be a whole new word invented and inserted into the dictionary to adequately describe how she felt at the moment. There just wasn't a pre-existing term to describe the emotion that had resulted from being betrayed both personally and professionally by someone she had misguidedly allowed herself to trust. Someone that she had been considering allowing into her life.

She pressed Elaine's number on her mobile. 'It's Mona.'

There was a brief silence. 'You've seen the paper then, darling.'

'Yes, I've seen the bloody paper! What the hell's going on?'

Elaine sighed. 'I was played. She told me half the story, then disappeared off to the bathroom. While she was there I'm guessing she made one last desperate phone call to the Carmichaels, because ten minutes later Jonathon and a couple of heavies arrived and told me and my editor that there's no story.'

'You're a journalist! You're not supposed to cave in to that kind of pressure!'

'Really, darling? You're a bit of a late convert to freedom of the press. Sometimes you just have to roll with these things.'

'But it was a story you would have *killed* to get.'

'There are better stories.'

The penny dropped. 'And you've been offered one.'

'Several, actually.'

'Well, fuck you.'

'I'm sorry, Mona. This is the world I live in. I didn't want things to work out like this, because I really do like you and if you want to take a bit of time to calm down, maybe we can see each other again, well away from work?'

'That's *so* not going to be happening.'

'Well, that's a shame. But whatever happens, Mona, promise me that you will be careful. We might have got the promise of a couple of good stories, but it was under-pinned by a lot of threats. If we'd insisted on publishing I think things would have got pretty nasty.'

She ended the call, and hurried the last few yards to SHEP's offices. Before she turned into the courtyard in front of the building she stopped.

Theresa.

Paterson.

Elaine.

In the last twenty-four hours, the three of them had all urged her to be careful. All trying to be helpful, of course, and all of them probably right to worry about her. But the one thing that no one had been able to tell her, the crucial missing piece of information, was who exactly it was that she was in danger from. She looked at the magnificent wooden door in front of her. Until the beginning of this week, she'd have regarded the people at SHEP as on her

307

side, but now she wasn't so sure. What if the people in this meeting were the very people she should be careful around? There was a possibility she wouldn't come back out of this meeting a free woman.

She looked back out onto the High Street, indecision staying her feet. She could skip this meeting, but sooner or later they'd catch up with her. At least this way Paterson knew where she was. Before she could change her mind, she strode across the quad and into the building.

The conversation stopped when Mona walked into Stuttle's office. There were three people in the room: Stuttle, Ian Jacobsen and Bob Ellis.

'What are they doing here?' said Mona.

'We need to talk to you,' said Ian, his mouth moving awkwardly in his battered face. He'd been patched up pretty well since yesterday but there was no doctor in the land who would have signed him fit for work. But considering the rules, regulations and criminal laws that Ian had broken the previous night, he probably wasn't too worried about the niceties of HR processes. Again, a new word was called for to describe the emotion relating to seeing someone who was so obviously in pain but had totally brought it on himself. The mixed emotion of feeling sympathy toward someone brought so low, and a very real anxiety that despite all that he could still do her harm. This was not a safe place to be.

'I'm not interested in anything that someone who pointed a gun at me last night has to say.' She turned to leave, only to find the sturdy form of Bob Ellis between her and the door. 'Could you get out of my way, please?' She folded her arms and tried to project a confidence she didn't feel. Bob was a big man, with bulging muscles in all the right places. And one bulge that suggested, as Bernard would have it, that he was packing heat. Bob just smiled and showed no intention of moving.

'Mona, sit down, for God's sake.' Stuttle gestured toward a seat. 'We want to talk to you about Milwood Orders.'

There was no way she was getting out of the room, so she decided to pretend her interest had been piqued by this. 'Milwood Orders? What are they?'

He regarded her for a moment, then laughed. 'You are better at bluffing than your boss, I'll say that much for you, Mona. I'm going to assume from your close personal friendship with Professor Bircham-Fowler that you're well aware of what I'm talking about.'

She shrugged.

'Ian and Bob have both been involved in supporting and protecting the participants in some of our Milwood projects.'

'Minding them, you mean. Checking no one stepped out of line.'

'I prefer my wording. Now, the exceptional nature of a Milwood project requires an exceptional approach to policing, perhaps a little bit more robust than would usually be the case . . .'

'Like threatening to shoot unarmed civilians, for example?'

'I was doing my job!' Even under the bruising, Mona could see irritability written across Ian's face. 'I'm not sure you lot shouldn't be up on some kind of charge for interfering with the investigation. And Bernard should be charged with assault for what he did to me.'

'Now now, Ian,' said Stuttle. 'This comes with the territory. Mona was right – they didn't know what was happening. Everyone was taken by surprise, and, unfortunately, this is where it ended up. All we can do now is try to limit the damage.'

'Bernard won't be charged, will he?' asked Mona.

'That rather depends on you. And Bernard. And, in fact, Marcus.'

'I don't understand.'

There was a long and, she thought, slightly wistful sigh from Stuttle. 'One of our other Milwood operatives has gone rogue. We believe you and your colleagues are in a position to help us track him down.'

'Who?' She racked her brains to think who she could possibly assist with. The realisation hit her. 'Bryce? Bryce was part of Milwood?'

Stuttle gave a small, slow nod.

'What a total cock-up! One of yours was it, Ian?' She grinned at him, and he returned a look of utter hatred in her direction. It was a look filled not just with contempt, but also rage. She'd seen that look before, when he had been pushing her backwards over the banister at the Museum. It was a look that screamed lack of self-control, and she wondered for the second time about Ian's stability. Nathan McVie had fallen to his death rather than meet with him. Helen Sopel had been terrified when he turned up at the Museum. She'd better stop baiting him. And warn Bernard to watch his back.

She looked at Stuttle to see if he'd seen the look, but his head was down over his papers. She looked toward Bob, who was staring thoughtfully at Ian. He'd seen it too. She caught his eye and he quickly looked away.

'Bryce has been embedded with the HET for some months now, keeping an eye out for us on the communications made by staff, to make sure that no one is up to anything that's going to interfere with police enquiries. Usually that interference occurs due to incompetence by the HETs rather that the sterling work of your team. Anyway, he was feeding us a lot of misinformation about Marcus which we think was meant as a distraction,' said Stuttle. 'We think he's begun to identify a bit too much with some of the groups that he has been following.'

'On Milwood Orders?'

'Unfortunately, yes. We have a Milwood operative out there gone rogue, and we need to get him back. We think your skills would be useful in doing that, Mona. What do you think about joining us? Obviously, we would get you Milwood clearance. Marcus and Bernard know Bryce better than anyone else but may be reluctant to assist us without some guidance from you.'

'Do Bernard and Marcus get an apology for how they have been treated?'

'Don't push it, Mona.'

She folded her arms and glared at him.

He stared back. 'There may be a personal interest in this for you, Mona. It was Bryce's shenanigans that led to you almost getting shot.' He smiled, confident that he had her interest.

Dammit. He did. A definitive answer to what had actually been going on the night that she and the Professor had been ambushed was just about the only thing that would persuade her to go anywhere near Ian Jacobsen ever again.

'Can I think about it?'

'Not for long. Sleep on it – give me an answer tomorrow.'

Sensing she was free to go she stood up. Ian followed suit, and Bob held the door open.

'Bob – a word before you go.' Stuttle gestured him back in.

He nodded to Mona and closed the door, leaving her alone with Ian in the deserted office usually occupied by Stuttle's long-suffering secretary.

'Well, that was interesting,' she said. Ian ignored her, staring fixedly at the door. It stuck in her craw to even be civil to him, but she realised it might be best not to antagonise him further. She wanted in on this Milwood stuff, and if that meant working with him, she'd just have to swallow it, even if his recent behaviour suggested he was verging on the unhinged.

'Look, Ian, about what I said back there, I didn't mean anything by it.'

He didn't respond, but walked past her out to the magnificent stairway that led back to the main entrance.

She hurried after him. 'OK, I'm sorry. We could end up working together on this Bryce thing, so we might as well be civil.' With any luck Stuttle would get him signed off for a good long break.

Again Ian said nothing. He was stock still, his eyes on the floor. There was a blankness to his expression, as if all the emotion in him had been emptied out. He looked like a man who had been pushed too far, and that couldn't be good for any of them. She wondered again about Ian and Bob's actual affiliations. She'd guess they both had a military background, but who they were actually working for now she still wasn't sure. Not the kind of person to take kindly to the humiliation he'd suffered yesterday. Cursing herself for winding him up, she gave up on her apologies, and started walking down the stairs.

'I think you need some time off, Ian, to get over this. Give me a ring when—'

A hand hit her hard between her shoulder blades, pushing her up and off the stairs. Shock gave way to fear as she lost her footing and rolled over and over down the stairwell. She flung out an arm to try to grab at something, anything, that could slow her down. The wall loomed up ahead of her, and an image of her mother, frail and alone in her home, came into Mona's mind for the briefest of seconds, before she felt the back of her head connect with the plaster.

The room went dark.

THRIVE AND PROSPER: FINAL SCENE

[The camera pans along a deserted street of derelict shops. In the foreground is MRS HILDA MILWOOD, a young mother in her late twenties. On either side of her are two small children, holding tight to her skirt. In the background of the shot other women, children and frail older people can be seen.]

[The camera moves in closer and focuses on her face. In the background the sound of shouting and children crying can be heard.]

MRS MILWOOD

The times that we have lived through have truly been the worst that our country, and our world, has ever experienced.

Many of our people have died. Our strongest, our fittest, our finest men have been sacrificed. We cannot let their suffering be in vain.

Together we can, and we must, rebuild all that we have lost.

I am only a woman. My life has been my home and my children. I have supported my husband as he went out into the world, and he has provided for us in return.

I have not the physical strength of a man, nor the university education of a leader.

But we women must step up.

314

We must all do tasks that we could not have imagined before this crisis. We must find the strength to risk our health, even our lives.

[Camera pans in even closer.]

Because if we do not take these risks for a better world, there is no one else.

We must suffer the blows that are given to us.

We must rise up stronger, dust ourselves down, and move on with creating our new world, however battered and bruised we are.

We cannot give up.

ACKNOWLEDGEMENTS

Huge thanks are due to everyone at Sandstone Press for their continuing support in producing this book, particularly Moira Forsyth for all the polishing.

Thank you to friends, family, fellow authors and bloggers who make the whole writing process so much less lonely. Love and thanks to Gordon and the kids; if only I was the kind of cool mum who writes computer games...

And finally, thank you to Edinburgh and her many museums, for being so darn inspirational!

Turn the page to read the gripping first chapter of *Murder at the Music Factory*, the fourth book in the *Health of Strangers* series.

I

It was the kind of gun to give you nightmares: black, shiny, approximately three foot long, and far, far, too close for comfort.

The months that he'd spent working for the North Edinburgh Health Enforcement Team should really have prepared Bernard for moments like this, should have given him the negotiation skills required to face down a hostile armed man, and the confidence to stand his ground. There had been an afternoon on guns and other weapons as part of his induction, delivered by an enthusiastic demobilised soldier fresh from a tour of Afghanistan. At the end of three hours he could just about recognise the difference between a rifle and a carbine, but had learned precious little about what to do if you found yourself on the business end of either of them. More time on the subject might have helped, but he was pretty sure that even if he lived to be a hundred he would never, ever, feel at ease dealing with an authorised firearms officer.

The firearms officer who was currently alarming him was stationed in front of the public entrance to the Scottish Parliament, and seemed to be ignoring Bernard's attempts to politely signal that he needed to enter the building. He continued staring straight over his head, his eyes scanning the activity taking place on the street behind him. It was busy, Parliament staff hurrying along in between the tourists stopping to get their pictures taken next to the ornamental pond, and dodging the parkour enthusiasts, who used the steps and landscaping around the Parliament as their own personal gym.

'Ehm, excuse me, I need to get into the building.'

The police officer shook his head. 'No can do. No one is allowed in.'

'But I'm here for the Virus Parliamentary Committee.' He attempted to get his ID into the officer's line of sight.

'Sorry, sir, even so. Nobody's going in here.'

'Why not?'

The question was ignored. 'If you can just step back from the building please, sir.'

He took a few paces backwards, then stood and watched as a number of other people received the same treatment.

'Bernard.'

He turned to see a tall, well-built man with a crew cut striding toward him. *His boss.*

'What's going on here?'

'I don't know, Mr Paterson. They're not letting anyone into the building.'

'Excuse me.'

Something large bumped into his lower leg, and he moved hurriedly out of the way of a large Alsatian dragging a man in black along in his wake. They watched in silence as the armed officer stood to one side to let dog and handler into the building.

'Sniffer dogs? That can't be good.' Paterson shook his head.

'You don't think they're looking for—'

The look on Paterson's face silenced him before he could say the word 'bombs' out loud. He lowered his voice considerably before continuing. 'Do you think this is anything to do with Bryce?'

'Why on earth would you think it was anything to do with our former colleague?'

'Well . . .'

'I mean, just because he proved himself pretty damn handy with an incendiary device when he blew up the HET's offices, are you going to blame him for every unexplained outbreak of chaos?'

This was probably sarcasm, but sometimes it was hard to tell with Paterson. He was staring at him in a manner that suggested he was waiting for a response.

'Well . . .'

'Of course it will be Bryce's work! He's not done with us, is he? Do you think he left a "Watch this Space" sign on our website just for the fun of it? He's probably already updated it with his plans to blow the MSPs to kingdom come.'

'That's a good point.' Bernard pulled out his phone. 'I'll check if it's changed.'

'Let's get a bit further away from the building while you do that . . .'

'John! Bernard!'

One of the glass doors of the Parliament had opened, and the familiar figure of Cameron Stuttle gestured to them to come toward the building.

'Must be a fuss about nothing.' Paterson headed swiftly toward his boss. Bernard hurried after him hoping he was right. Both Paterson and Stuttle had a considerably higher threshold for danger than he did. Their 'nothing' was quite often a substantial 'something' in his opinion.

'Right.' Stuttle stepped out of the building, and an armed police officer immediately positioned himself in front of the door. 'We need to get these people told that the Virus committee is being postponed.'

'Why?' said Bernard and Paterson in unison.

'You take the park side, Bernard, I'll take the area round the pond thingy, and John, you take from here to the Queen's Gallery.'

'And we're telling people . . .?'

Stuttle strode off.

'What are we supposed to say to them?'

'As little as possible. Which shouldn't be too difficult, seeing as we know bugger all.'

Bernard sighed. Ordering people around really wasn't one of his talents. Paterson and Stuttle had had decades of practice at it in their previous lives as police officers. As a Health Promotion Officer, he had extensive experience of supporting people in a non-judgemental manner to realise for themselves that smoking and over-eating were bad for them. Not the ideal skillset for today's task. He approached a couple of young women in business suits, both in an obvious hurry. 'I'm terribly sorry but we've had to cancel today's committee.'

They stopped, frowning at him.

'Oh. Why?'

It wasn't an unreasonable question. Unfortunately, he didn't have an answer. 'Political reasons . . . Unavailability?'

'Yeah right.' One of the women laughed. 'I heard a rumour there was going to be an illegal demo here today. Is that it?'

He shrugged in a way that he hoped was neither confirming nor denying her accusation, and wondered if she was correct.

'So,' began her friend, 'do we just go back to the office then, or what?'

'Yes,' he said, confidently. 'Back to the office.'

The two of them drifted off, occasionally looking over their shoulders at the confusion.

Buoyed by this success he moved on to a group of men. One of them raised his phone as he approached and took a picture of him. Bernard got a flash of a press pass and a strong impression of testosterone. His heart sank. Journalists. *Political* journalists. They weren't about to turn tail and head home without having their questions answered.

'What's the deal here? Why's Cameron Stuttle running round shouting at people?'

Bernard looked over in Stuttle's direction. He did appear to be taking a rather more assertive approach in clearing the area.

'The Parliamentary Committee is cancelled today.'

'Why?'

'Political unavailability.'

There was a round of cat calls at this.

'Who's unavailable? Carlotta? Is she in Africa?'

Bernard attempted some Stuttle-type assertion. 'I can't answer your questions and I have to insist that you vacate the area.'

Nobody moved their feet, although several mobiles were produced.

'You're clearing the area? Can you confirm that there's been another bomb threat?'

'I . . .ehm, look, you just need to get out of here!'

Stuttle appeared at his side, as if he had some sixth sense for a cover story going south. 'Sorry, gentlemen, but I really need to insist you move.'

'Another bomb threat, Cameron?'

'Sorry, gents, time is of the essence. Press conference this afternoon.'

A couple of Police Scotland vans pulled up on the road, to Stuttle's obvious relief. Uniformed officers material-ised, and started moving people away from the building.

Stuttle grabbed both their arms. 'About bloody time this lot got here. I've been calling for immediate backup for about half an hour now. They've all been at some unscheduled demo over at the university.'

Bernard's source had been half right. He couldn't help but notice Stuttle was shepherding him back in the direction of the Parliament building, and this time he was absolutely sure it wasn't a fuss about nothing. He wondered about making a break for it, but Stuttle was holding tight to his arm.

'What's going on, Cam?' Paterson asked.

Stuttle stopped, looking round to make sure he couldn't be overheard. 'We had a phone call forty-five minutes ago telling us to get everyone out of the building or we'd regret it.'

'Bryce?'

'We're certainly entertaining that possibility.'

'Is it another bomb, Mr Stuttle?'

'The caller didn't specify. And as we know from your spate of calls to the HET they are as likely to be hoaxes as real.'

'Well, at least you've got everyone out of the way.' Bernard and Paterson looked round at the dispersing crowds.

'We haven't. The MSPs are still in there.'

'What?' There was a collective dropping of jaws. 'Why?'

'Because if it is Bryce's work, we can't be sure this isn't all part of his plan. Get all the MSPs out in the open so he can take a pop at them. We can't use any of the usual emergency plans, because Bryce is a former . . .' He stopped, suddenly mindful of the level of security clearance of his audience. 'Because Bryce has prior knowledge of them. He knows all the ways we're likely to respond to this kind of threat, and could use that to his advantage.'

'But if he *has* actually planted a bomb in there . . .'

'They get blown sky-high. Whatever we do has the potential to go very wrong.'

'So what are you doing?'

'We're moving them out four at a time, straight into armoured vehicles. The army's overseeing that bit.'

'Sir.' A police officer bounded up to Stuttle. 'Message for you.' He handed over a folded sheet of paper.

'What now?' He read the note and his face contorted. 'Carlotta Carmichael is demanding a meeting with me immediately, on the walkway leading to Dynamic Earth. Is she insane? Does she not realise we are under threat at the moment? She's going to get herself shot.'

'She is insane,' said Paterson, starting to run. 'We all know that. Come on.'

Bernard ran after his colleagues, happy at least that they were moving away from the building. Although he couldn't help feeling that this was not an ideal place to request a meeting. The concrete pathway ran along the side of the Parliament building, and apart from a low wall, was otherwise open on its other side to the park land that led up to Arthur's Seat, Edinburgh's famous extinct volcano. If Bernard wanted to isolate someone and take a potshot at them, this was more or less exactly what he'd look for.

Carlotta appeared, the domed roof of the Dynamic Earth museum looming on her left. She was accompanied by the very tall figure of her secretary, Paul Shore. Bernard had met him a couple of times, and had found him to be one of the more pleasant people working in the world of politics. Or maybe that was just the way he seemed, relative to his boss. Both of them were looking around at their surroundings as they hurried along, Paul with a protective hand on his boss's back.

She stopped directly in front of them.

'Minister . . .' began Stuttle.

'I can't believe this is your idea of a safe area, Cameron.' She pulled her coat collar up to her face, as if it could provide her with some protection.

'Safe area?' Stuttle frowned. 'I never said that.'

'Yes, you did,' said Paul. He waved a sheet of paper. 'We got your note, telling us that this was the designated safe area. You said to get here as quickly as possible.'

'Shit.' Stuttle looked round. 'We need to get you out of here.'

'I don't understand what's happening?' said Carlotta.

'Cameron!' Paterson shouted as a police marksman appeared at the top of the steps leading to Dynamic Earth. 'Over there!'

Both Stuttle and Paterson threw themselves in the direction of Carlotta Carmichael. Bernard looked at Paul, who appeared as confused as he did. A thought went through his head that they should probably get down behind the wall, but he couldn't get his legs to move. His eyes swivelled back to the marksman: his gun was raised and pointing in their direction. A shot rang out, and he heard Carlotta scream out Paul's name.

Bernard found himself sprawling on the ground, as the body of Paul Shore toppled onto him, a stream of blood pooling around them on the concrete.

He lay back, and waited to see if he too was going to die.

www.sandstonepress.com

 facebook.com/SandstonePress/

 @SandstonePress